I was sure someone was trying to kill Marguerite, but why were they trying to kill me too?

The next night I was awakened by Marguerite's voice shouting a question. I couldn't be sure, but it sounded like, "Who's there?"

Her door was open. It had to be or I wouldn't have been able to hear her. Why was her door open? Who was in her room?

I flung the covers off and a chilly draft hit me. The door that led to the balcony stood open.

There was a dark form by my bed.

I opened my mouth to yell, but all I could do was inhale before the shape snatched the extra pillow and crushed it onto my face.

It's been five months since twenty-two-year-old Louisa's cherished grandfather died, and although she's determined to live a life that honors his memory, she's dropped out of college twice, and her refusal to play the corporate game has cost her three jobs. She thinks her new position—a live-in secretary to an elderly author, Marguerite Roberts—is perfect.

But the moment she arrives at the Roberts' house, Louisa senses an undercurrent of menace. The wheelchair-bound Marguerite is confined to her room, and the family members can barely disguise their hostility toward one another. A series of threatening events soon makes Louisa question whether her growing affection for Marguerite is enough to keep her in a house in which she can trust no one—not even Marguerite's grandson, with whom she is falling in love. As the danger escalates, Louisa is trapped. She can't leave Marguerite alone and unprotected. But she may be risking her own life if she stays.

KUDOS for *Don't Fear, My Darling*

"It's been said that money can't buy happiness, but when Louisa Berry finds herself employed by the secretive and elusive children's author, Marguerite Roberts she has her doubts. The family seems to be unfairly blessed with looks, health, and a lot of money. But it doesn't take Louisa long to figure out that something seems definitely off and that even nice families have secrets. And, at the secluded mansion in which they are all living, everyone has something to hide. *Don't Fear, My Darling* is more than a whodunit. It is a psychologically compelling story of love and how, when twisted, it can distort and pervert." ~ Cynthia A. Graham, winner of several writing awards, including a Gold IPPY, two Midwest Book Awards, and named a finalist for the Oklahoma Book Award.

"Chilling, intense, and intriguing, this is a story that will grab and hold your interest from beginning to end. A great read." ~ Taylor Jones, The Review Team of Taylor Jones & Regan Murphy

Don't Fear, My Darling is more than a mystery. It's a story of tragedy, loss, a compelling need for revenge, and the lengths a twisted mind will go to achieve it—a book you will find both poignant and hard to put down." ~ Regan Murphy, The Review Team of Taylor Jones & Regan Murphy

ACKNOWLEDGMENTS

A novel takes a village, and *Don't Fear, My Darling* has an especially large one. My thanks to the following:

The American Indian Society of St. Louis, for welcoming me and allowing me to be a part of their organization and celebrations.

Bill Royce, for the hours of Native American lore and careful explanations of the many artifacts in *Mukwa Canada*, his home.

Rissa Fregeau, Michelle Blechmann, and Tami Fernandez for their help with Hebrew.

My long list of readers, including, but not limited to, Karen Lumpe, Rhonda Johnson, Veraellen Goldie, David Bradley, Rochelle Kress, Juliet Popkin, Becky Keough, Angie Stoecklin, Charlotte Zimmermann, Phyllis Wheeler, and Julia Maranan.

Sandy Schertzl of Issaquah Middle School for her help with my research.

Erin Shanks, for inspiring the story about the painting that wasn't supposed to be Louisa's.

Barbara Peters of The Poisoned Pen, whose excellent feedback took the early novel in a different—and better—direction.

Jill Marr of the Sandra Dijkstra Agency, who critiqued it at the All Write Now! Conference. Many thanks for her encouragement and great suggestions, including replacing my original long and clunky title. Good call!

Debbie Manber Kupfer for her professional editing work. You were a smart choice.

Cynthia Graham for her review.

AUTHOR'S NOTE

Don't Fear, My Darling uses the terms "Indian" or "American Indian" to refer to Native Americans. The novel takes place in 1987. As Louisa tells Tamara, "Indian" was, at that time, the term used by most Native Americans to refer to themselves.

During my membership in the American Indian Society, I became familiar with the phrases "Indian Time" (whenever the individual decides to show up) and "Indian Car" (a vehicle used to transport its owners to powwows, typically festooned with bumper stickers from various locations, and not always in excellent body shape or repair).
These terms and phrases are used to bring authenticity to Louisa's character and not, in any way, to show or indicate disrespect.

Multiple Sclerosis is a disease with many different symptoms and forms, and can be unique to each person diagnosed with it. While some of Marguerite's symptoms are fairly typical, her experience with MS is not meant to represent any experience other than her own.

Don't Fear, My Darling

Laura Stewart Schmidt

A Black Opal Books Publication

GENRE: MYSTERY-DETECTIVE/WOMEN SLEUTHS

DON'T FEAR, MY DARLING
Copyright © 2019 by Laura Stewart Schmidt
Cover Design by Jackson Cover Designs
All cover art copyright © 2019
All Rights Reserved
Print ISBN: 9781644371251

First Publication: MAY 2019

Published by Black Opal Books **http://www.blackopalbooks.com**

DEDICATION

*For my stepdad, Miles Edenburn, who took me to the
corner newsstand when I was thirteen and bought me my
first Writer magazine. I still have it.*

*And my father, Wendell Stewart, who took me to the
bookstore when I was fourteen and bought me my first
Writer's Market. I traded it in for a later edition, but I
still have the cover.*

Chapter 1

Just before my grandfather died, he made me promise to stay in school and stop wrecking my life with what he called my *stubborn impetuousness*.

Five months later, I was doing a great job, if dropping out of community college for the second time and being fired from my third job in seven months could be called *great*.

Now there was a light in the darkness. My new employer had said some strange things during our phone interview, but I doubted she would tell me my hip-length hair and the dressings I loved to wear in it were *unprofessional*—as my most recent ex-boss had made the mistake of doing.

If she did, she would be Job Number 4.

I shook my head and my brush caught in an errant tangle. I couldn't keep getting fired, even if corporate environments made me feel like a falcon shoved into a shoebox. If Grandpa were here, he would be crushed. He'd thought I was capable of a lot more.

This time will be different, I told him silently. *I have an elderly woman to work with. I think we clicked when she interviewed me. I won't let you down this time.*

❦❦❦

Morning rush hour was almost over. It was an easy drive to Issaquah, especially since most of the traffic went the opposite direction into Seattle. I flipped through the radio, pausing on KIRO news. Same stuff as every other day, only worse. President Reagan was admitting responsibility for Iran-Contra after months of investigation and testimony by several of the top people in his administration. Big surprise. Reverend Jerry Falwell thought his fallen comrade, Jim Bakker, who was probably facing some pretty serious prison time, was a scourge on Christianity. Bigger surprise. The Mariners were in second place, the first time they'd done this well in their ten-year history, but the Twins looked unstoppable. I didn't care. I'd never been a big baseball fan.

I shut off the news and switched to a cassette of Tony Rice. Tony's soothing baritone kept me company over the bridge and into Issaquah, and I hit town before seven. Issaquah was a historic mining town, settled into its own little carved-out spot in the mountains, untouched by urban sprawl—so far. I wondered how long it would be before the new arrivals to the area discovered it and jacked the prices up beyond even the stratosphere in which they already existed. Clearly money wasn't an issue for the Roberts family.

Roberts, as in Airtech, one of the biggest companies in Seattle. In the country. As in *Oh, those Roberts*, which was what I'd thought when Marguerite Roberts explained who her family was. Until then I'd thought I was speaking just to a Newbery Medal-winning children's author.

Her newspaper ad had asked for a "competent and discreet" typist to help with her latest novel. I hadn't had a chance to ask her why she wanted discretion. Nor why her family lived with her but *went their own ways*, in her words.

Nor why she had offered me a live-in job within a day after our phone interview—just long enough to check the references I'd given her. If indeed she had.

Clearly there was something Mrs. Roberts wasn't telling me.

But whatever it was, it couldn't be worse than the three jobs I'd been fired from. Nothing could.

And if I kept telling myself that, I'd believe it.

The town was quiet and cool. Morning fog hadn't dissipated yet, and the surrounding mountains were green and silver. It promised to be one of the days when Seattleites say, "The Mountain's out," meaning we can see the white crown of Mount Rainier over the city instead of its usual veil of clouds. Even in mid-August, Seattle mornings are light jacket weather, and I had to run my defroster as I drove down the narrow street past the Historic Society and up the road that wound by the high school.

The side road Mrs. Roberts had told me to look for was about a mile beyond the school. Signs bellowed PRIVATE PROPERTY NO TRESPASSING. The road was so steep I had to shift gears, and then a mansion came into sight, looming before me, a Colonial design with a flat façade.

The gate was open, so I didn't have to bother with the passcode she'd given me. As I drove up the long, curving driveway, I got a better look at the house. *Utilitarian* popped into my mind. The stark, glassy architecture was broken only by a long balcony extending from the front of the house to the right side. The kind of walkway someone was always getting shoved off in old movies.

"You just got here," I told myself. "How about putting your imagination on a leash?" But something about the house didn't give off a welcoming vibe, and I wondered if this had been such a hot idea. I felt like Maria in *The Sound of Music*, arriving at her new job and taking one horrified look before whispering "Oh, help." Like the Von Trapp castle, this house had a personality, and if the inhabitants' matched it, maybe I should turn around and drive like hell in the direction of *out*.

Apparently most of Mrs. Roberts' family had already left for work, as there was only one car in the open garage—a brown Nova, dusty spots from the latest drizzle peppering its trunk, and stickers covering the bumper. *Surf Naked. Party Naked. Study Naked. Let's All Get Naked and Get in a Pile.*

I'd have to find out whose car that was and thank them. I wasn't intimidated anymore.

I knocked on a massive front door with a knocker shaped like an airplane. It was opened by a woman, thirtyish, in khakis and a pink blouse. "Are you Louisa Berry?" she asked.

"Yes."

"I'm Carol, the maid. Follow me, please."

I stepped inside and my scuffed moccasins sank into a cream-colored carpet. I tilted my head back as far as it would go to find the ceiling. When I looked back down, Carol was waiting with a patient twist to her mouth that could have been either a smile or a smirk. "Mrs. Roberts would like you to go to her room." She led me to a staircase and pointed up. "Her door is that first one on your right."

"Thanks."

The staircase was steep as stadium bleachers. No banisters, either. Unless Mrs. Roberts was in exceptionally good health or was younger than I had thought, that probably made it a challenge to get around the house. There was a mosaic of family pictures along the wall. I wanted to take a closer look at them, but it would have to wait until later. I did pause long enough to pick out the people I'd be living with for a while. From what Mrs. Roberts had told me, the impeccable redhead had to be her daughter-in-law, Jenna. A young man with dark hair and eyes and the kind of smile that made you wonder what he was thinking—Mrs. Roberts's grandson. A movie-star blonde, hair worn in stylish chaos and probably dyed, and the kind of suntan most Pacific Northwesterners had to pay for—her granddaughter.

I reached a landing with a bay window that overlooked acreage no one would refer to as a *backyard*. There was a covered swimming pool and a tennis court, surrounded by woods that sloped into the mountains. The fog veil was gone and everything sparkled green.

The next door down from Mrs. Roberts's opened just enough for me to catch a glimpse of tawny hair and hazel eyes narrowed in a frown. I could smell coffee coming from the white cup held in raspberry-tipped and multi-ringed fingers just before her other hand bumped the door closed.

Nice to meet you too.

I took a deep breath, turned right, and knocked at the first door. "Mrs. Roberts?"

"Come in, Louisa."

I opened the door and stopped short.

Marguerite Roberts was not even close to what I expected.

I hadn't realized she would be in a wheelchair. Nor that she would be so attractive.

She smiled at me. "Is something wrong, dear?"

I recognized her voice or I would have wondered if I'd made some mistake. Wordlessly, I shook my head and did some quick mental math. Her son had died six years before, in 1981. He would have been forty-three had he lived, so his mother was at least in her mid-sixties. However, she could have passed for a much younger woman. Her nearly shoulder-length dark hair was only half gray, and her brilliantly blue eyes were clear and unobstructed by glasses. Even in her chair she was tall, and she shared her granddaughter's pert nose and high cheekbones. In her youth, she would have been a very beautiful woman.

Youth, hell. She still was.

"My father had that much gray hair at forty," were the first words out of my mouth.

She laughed.

I did too. "Of course, he had me."

She gestured to the door. "Please close that, then sit down and we'll talk."

I closed the door then sat in the dusty-pink and white wingback chair she'd indicated. She smiled as I draped my hair over one arm of the chair. "What beautiful hair. Do you always wear it so long?"

"I've never cut it." I fingered my hair ties.

"What nationality are you, dear?"

"Yakima. I've been mistaken for a lot of things. One time in college some guy walked up to me and started speaking something like Vietnamese or Thai."

I glanced around the room, which was easily double the size of my apartment's living room. There was enough floor space to allow her motorized wheelchair to move about easily. Her bed was hospital-style, with controls for adjusting the incline. A floor-to-ceiling bookshelf held neatly arranged hardbounds. I could read enough of the titles to tell that Mrs. Roberts's taste ran to classics—both adults' (*To Kill a Mockingbird*, *Jane Eyre*) and children's (*A Wrinkle in Time*, *Julie of the Wolves*). She also had her own books, with several editions of the Newbery winner, *I'll Take the One On Either End*, as well as the expected tools of her trade—a dictionary, thesaurus, and *Writer's Market*. A small television rested on a table in a corner, and a remote lay on top of it. My TV didn't have a remote, but I could see where it would be easier for her.

I studied a five-by-seven photo at my left elbow of a blond young man handsome enough to be a museum piece. Mrs. Roberts saw me looking at it. "That was my son, Carl."

"I thought so." I didn't see a computer of any kind or even an old-fashioned typewriter. "Where's your computer?"

She waved one hand in dismissal. "I hate those things. Jenna bought me a fancy word processor on my last birthday. It was thoughtful of her, but I would have been just as happy with an old Royal standard. I do my first drafts in longhand."

"The computer would probably make things easier, especially if you do a lot of re-writing."

"That's why I wanted a secretary. My handwriting isn't what it used to be, and I'm too old to learn to use a computer."

"Will I have to work with your agent or publisher?"

"I don't have an agent. I was lucky enough that my first manuscript was accepted by a publisher, and I have good business sense, so I've never felt the need for a middleman."

I got the idea Marguerite Roberts didn't feel much of a need for anyone. No wonder I'd bonded to her so fast. "Uhm, do you need help getting in and out of your chair, and can I do that?"

She smiled. "No, dear. As long as the chair is by my bed I can get in and out of it on my own. Remember I have a nurse who comes to check on me twice a week. Your job is the book, period. That's why I didn't tell you

I can't walk. I didn't want you to think you would be expected to do something you're not prepared to do."

"But you can't possibly navigate that staircase."

"There's an elevator," she said. "However, right now it's broken."

"I'm guessing someone's coming out to fix it?"

"Eventually."

She'd said it lightly enough, but I caught the same undercurrent I'd heard on the phone. I wondered how long it had been broken and what the holdup was. However, it probably wasn't something I should be grilling her about when I'd been there less than fifteen minutes.

I changed the subject. "How old are your grandchildren?"

"Joel is twenty-four and Tamara is nineteen." She pronounced the name TAM-uh-ruh.

I was twenty-two, right in the middle. "Do they work at Airtech?"

"No. Joel has a marketing degree from Seattle University and sells stereos. Tamara finished one year at Seattle Pacific University. She had to take this semester off because she had mononucleosis earlier in the summer."

That explained why she was still at home when the others had, presumably, gone to work. The Nova must be her car. "Bad enough to keep her out of school for an entire semester?"

"She also caught pneumonia and had to be hospitalized for two weeks. She's recovering fairly well, but her doctor insists that she not go overboard with physical activity. Jenna's main concern is that Tamara is a competitive swimmer, and nothing in this world can keep her out of a pool. If she's at home, Jenna can keep an eye on her, but once she leaves the house she won't obey anyone's orders." She chuckled. "Tamara inherited her father's stubborn streak, but I don't think you'll—" Slight stress on *you'll.* "—have any trouble getting along with her. You may find her a kindred spirit."

I grinned. It sounded like she loved her granddaughter.

Marguerite gestured to a notepad and pen on her nightstand. "When you come back here, we can get to work."

"How far are you in the book? What's its title?"

"I haven't titled it yet. I'm on Chapter Two. The computer is in the spare room next to Jenna's bedroom, but if you prefer, I'll have Carol set it up in your room."

"I can do that."

"Let Carol. That's her job."

I didn't like the idea of other people waiting on me, especially since I was basically a servant myself, but it was too early to start arguing with my new boss.

"In the meantime, why don't you ask my granddaughter to show you the house and grounds?"

You mean the one who shut her door in my face?

There must have been something in my expression. "Have you met her?" Mrs. Roberts asked.

"Uhm, sort of." For once I weighed my words carefully. "As I was coming up the steps, she opened her door to look right at me then closed it."

Mrs. Roberts made a rueful face. "It's not personal. She's having trouble adjusting to being home by herself."

She's not by herself. She has you.

But I didn't say that. "I sort of got that idea."

"She'll come around. She's a very interesting and intelligent girl with nothing to do. I think she'll enjoy having another young person around the house."

I wasn't so sure. "Okay, Mrs. Roberts."

"Now, we can't have 'Mrs. Roberts' and 'Louisa.' Either you call me Marguerite, or I will call you 'Miss Berry.'"

"Okay, Marguerite." As I turned to leave, something thin and pale blue near the floor caught my eye. I bent down to see what it was. "What…"

"What is it?"

"It's a piece of fishing line." I couldn't break it, so I moved aside so she could see. "It looks like it's tied from one closet door to the other." I opened the door and, as I'd expected, it was a walk-in closet, with sliding doors on rollers, everything immaculately organized at Marguerite's eye level. "So, if you…"

I trailed off. I didn't really want to say, *didn't see it and rolled into the closet, your chair might snag on this, and if it didn't break or come untied, you'd have to catch yourself before you went pitching forward onto the floor.*

Who could have done such a thing?

Just what the hell was going on in this house?

Chapter 2

Marguerite wheeled over for a closer look. "Hmm." Her tone was noncommittal, and I suspected she didn't want to show emotion to someone she'd just met. "I would have seen it before anything happened."

She wouldn't be able to bend down to untie the wire. *I* couldn't untie it, and couldn't break it without cutting my fingers. "Stay away from it until I bring a knife or scissors."

Marguerite waved one hand in complete disregard, but for the slightest moment I caught a twist to her mouth. "It's harmless now that I know it's here."

It was way too early to ask her who in her family might do something like this to hurt or scare her. She didn't even seem scared, but rather almost resigned, as though a mischievous child had done something silly.

Anyone in the house could have done it. It would be easy enough to wait until Marguerite was asleep, or bathing, to tie the wire. Or until she left the room. Even without the elevator, she wasn't exactly a prisoner here. The hallways were more than wide enough for her chair. Carl might have designed the house himself with her in mind.

I was starting to think my job might entail keeping an eye on her as well as typing her book.

I left and knocked on the door I'd seen Tamara peeking out of. No answer. I followed the sound of blasting music to the first floor and found her in a study or office of some kind, sprawled over a sofa, listening to the *La Bamba* soundtrack on a boom box. I hadn't seen the movie, but the music was all over the radio. I was already tired of it.

I had to ask her twice to turn it down before she did. "I'm Louisa, your grandmother's secretary." No response. I hadn't expected one. "She wants you to show me around the house. It can wait, if you're busy."

She gave a snort that might have been her idea of a laugh. "I'm never *busy*. I was in bed all of June and July and I'll be *recuperating* all term."

"Did you catch those UVs in bed?" Her skin was tanned nearly as golden as her hair.

She got up and stretched languidly, tugging an oversized pink sweatshirt down over stone-washed Jordache jeans. "My big brother takes me to the tanning spa. I don't have to look like I spent the summer in bed, do I?"

She didn't. She was thin, but too pretty to look sickly. "Do you model?"

She shook her head. "I'm too short. I'm the family shrimp."

Shrimp? She was a head taller than I was. "How tall are you?"

"Five-seven. What about you?"

"Five feet."

"Don't you hate being short?"

I smiled as serenely as I could. "Not a bit. I'm a gymnast."

"Don't you have to stand on chairs to get things out of cabinets?"

"All the time."

"Does your hair get in the way?"

"Constantly." It had to be tied into an elaborate bun during gymnastics, and every once in a while, I looked at someone with a little pixie cut with envy. For about one second.

"How come you don't cut it?"

"Because I love it."

"I guess I would too. Come on, if you want to see the house."

"Where does your brother work?"

"Why do you want to know?"

I wanted to stick a paintbrush into her smarmy smile. "Just asking."

"Know how many times he's made the *Most Eligible Bachelor* list?"

"You think I read that crap?"

She looked me up and down. "No, I guess you wouldn't. He sells electronic stuff at the Silo in Bellevue."

I wondered what a marketing major was doing with a job like that. Nothing against Silo, but if I had a bachelor's degree I would aim a little higher.

Tamara showed me the downstairs, all of which was covered in the creamy carpet except for a music room with reflecting hardwood floors and a baby grand. I pointed to it. "Do you play?"

She shook her head and her hair flopped into her eyes. "Mom's the only one who can, and she almost never does. Grandmother did before she got sick."

I wondered what illness Marguerite had. But there was no polite way to ask. "Why don't you play?" I touched a couple of keys. I didn't know anything about music, except for bluegrass, but even I could tell this was an instrument worthy of a concertmaster. It seemed a shame not to enjoy it.

Tamara made a face. "I've got better things to do."

"Like what?"

"Swim, if I ever get to again. Or go boating or water-skiing. Mom's best friend has his own mini-houseboat and dock, and he used to take us out in it all the time. She won't even let me do that now. I'm not sick anymore. I don't need all this dumb medicine I'm on. Mom's so overprotective she makes me sick—uh, mad."

I smiled. "I guess she loves you."

Tamara shrugged as though dismissing a particularly absurd notion. She didn't walk as much as weave as she led me toward the foyer. As we passed the staircase, I stopped to look more closely at the family pictures. Tamara gave me a funny look, like she didn't want me to see them, as though I were…invading her privacy? I ignored her and gaped at what I assumed was Jenna's senior picture from high school. She hadn't smiled for the camera, but made a lips-parted, almost pouting face with wide, expressive green eyes. "God, your mother was gorgeous."

"Put up with her shit for nineteen years and she won't impress you anymore."

I almost fell down the steps. "*What?*"

"I didn't say anything."

I took one last look at a family portrait taken probably ten years ago. A dark-haired Tamara with slightly bucked teeth rested in her father's arms, both smiling happily. She looked a lot like him, especially with her hair dyed, since his had been a butter-swirled chocolate blond.

"Do you want to see the room you'll be staying in or not?"

I started. "Uhm, sure."

I paused on the landing and pointed to the tarp-covered pool. Seattle's August weather was mild enough to keep even an unheated pool in use, and I wondered why this one wasn't. "Is the pool covered for the winter already?"

"Mom did that when I was sick 'cause she said I'd go swimming and catch a big bad cold."

"In August? In a heated pool?" Maybe Jenna was overprotective.

"Oh, that's just what she said. The real reason is she's afraid I'll go skinny dipping when she's got some of her rich friends over."

"Have you ever done that?"

"I had a suit on. She didn't stay around long enough to find out." She smirked. "Oh, I forgot to tell you, Mom says if you need anything special to eat or drink, there's a list in the kitchen for Mrs. Wharton to do the shopping." She pointed to a closed door at the end of the hall. "That's your room."

"Thank you." But I was talking to the stairs. She'd already taken off, probably to return to her music.

It was a beautiful room, with a four-poster bed covered with a blue and brown quilt. Cream-colored lace curtains at the windows matched the carpet—how long would it take me to track in mud?—and blended with the pale blue walls. Pretty nice digs for a secretary.

Or a bodyguard? I thought, remembering the fishing line.

Chapter 3

*G*age watched Paul run off with his cap, the Dodgers cap he'd saved for weeks to buy. Authentic MLB merchandise. Real wool. Fitted to his 7 3/8" head.

And now it was gone. No point in trying to get it back unless he wanted to fight Paul and his four friends. No point in pleading with them to find something else to do. Gage knew that from experience, because four years ago, he had been Paul.

He was getting what Dad would call a taste of his own medicine, and it tasted like ~~boiled shit~~ ~~he'd ordered dessert~~ ~~and~~ ~~someone had boiled dirty socks and served them to him for dessert~~.?!

Come up with some way to say how it feels/tastes to have the tables turned on him

ᐱᐱᐱ

Marguerite and I spent several hours on my first day working on her book and getting to know each other. She told me about her previous books and how her writing kept her from being bored and depressed. I told her about my grandfather and the powwows and bluegrass festivals we used to go to.

"I suppose that answers my question." She held a ballpoint pen in her left hand and a pile of notes in her right. I'd asked if I could see them, but she laughed, shook her head, and showed me the top page. It was a mess of scribbles, strikeovers, and margin notes, all in smudgy blue ink. I'd never be able to read it. "I was curious as to why someone your age would enjoy someone my age."

We'd talked about it a little over the phone. Just a little. I hadn't been sure how to explain to a stranger that my culture valued elders and that's how I was raised, that my grandfather was my hero and my boat had drifted pretty far out to sea since his death earlier that year. "I always have. There were some younger people at the festivals, but mostly I always hung around my grandfather and his friends. That was, I guess, the biggest influence in my life. The most stable thing."

Maybe it was too much information for someone I'd just met. But I already felt more at home with her than I did with my own parents.

"You seem like a bright young woman, if a bit of a free spirit." She chuckled and I smiled back. "I think the advice most people my age would give you is to stay in school. You may not see the rewards of an education now, when good jobs are hard to find, but someday things will turn around again. They always have."

I didn't want to tell Marguerite about the advisor who thought I wasn't ready for college and should be evaluated for ADD. Or what I'd said to her. "I was wasting my money in college."

"How so?" Marguerite's tone was brisk, and I got the idea she might not be sympathetic to my inability to fit in.

"Well, you know, I told you about the curriculum not being…" I trailed off. Elders are hard to BS. They've heard it all.

"Did you think of trying another major? Maybe something that would allow you to work with elderly people?"

One of the elders I'd known for years had suggested the same thing. She'd pushed me to *play the game*, as she called it. "It's a white man's world, Louisa. Getting angry about that isn't going to change it. Becoming the change might."

I wasn't sure why I'd never taken her advice. "I guess that's something to think about if I go back."

"No, dear. *When* you go back."

It had taken a long time, but I'd found a job that was more than just a job. A chance for me to do something worthwhile, for someone I could care about.

Marguerite gave me a contract she'd already signed and asked me to do the same. It outlined what my duties would be—no mention of protecting her from fishing line or of fixing elevators—and that I was expected to stay for the duration of the novel in progress, including revision and preparation for the publisher. About six to eight months' work, Marguerite advised me. After that we could evaluate the situation and decide whether I would stay with her for another book.

There was, however, a question of what my role in the household would be. Marguerite wanted me to eat meals with her family rather than with the servants.

"You're kidding," I said. "I'm not a family member. I'm more like one of the servants."

"Nonsense. You aren't wait staff. You're an assistant to me. I'm sure Jenna eats lunch with her secretary at Airtech."

"I doubt it," I said bluntly. "I've never had a boss who mingled with the peons. Uh, I mean, employees."

"I'd like you to," she said in a tone that didn't invite further discussion. "I think it'll be good for Joel and Tamara to have another person their age. Especially Tamara, since her mother won't allow her to go to school this term."

I started to say I wasn't sure Tamara wanted my company, but stopped when I realized the opportunity hanging out with the family would provide.

There was a broken elevator no one seemed to be in a hurry to fix. Someone had tied a wire across Marguerite's closet that had taken a knife to remove.

The culprit had to be one of the family members—the people Marguerite had told me *went their own ways*. If I got to know them, maybe I could figure out what was going on.

സ‍

I changed clothes before dinner, hoping my painted T-shirt and slacks weren't too casual. When I went into the dining room, the family was already seated at the table. A redhead wearing a bright turquoise blouse that made her look as though she was on sabbatical in New Mexico half-rose and held out her hand for me to shake. "Hello, Louisa. I'm Marguerite's daughter-in-law, Jenna. This is my son Joel, and you've met my daughter Tamara." She gestured to Tamara at her right and to a young man on her left.

Was I supposed to call everyone by their first name?

"I guess you already know, I'm Louisa Berry, Marguerite's new secretary."

Carol had set a place for me with china, real silver, and a crystal water glass. She handed me a patterned cloth napkin in a fan shape with a gold ring around it. How did they eat off finery like this? It was like wearing an ultra-expensive outfit you were sure to drop a saucy meatball on.

I could see reflections of the chandelier in my plate. Out of nowhere came a memory from my early teenage years, when I was just coming into my own as an artist. I'd painted a decorative plate for one of the elders who'd always cared for me like her own granddaughter. Rather than hanging it up to look at, she had it treated so she could use it, and every time I saw her at a powwow she was eating off my plate. When I was eighteen and went back to my first powwow in three years, I learned she'd died. I never saw my plate or found out what happened to it.

The china in front of me was worth more than anything I would ever make or own, but not to people I loved, people whose values I shared.

"Relax, Louisa." I looked up at Joel, whose warm brown eyes were laughing even if he wasn't. "If you drop something, you won't be the first person. We probably won't even kill you."

How encouraging.

"I'm sure that's very reassuring to her, Joel," his mother said.

To avoid staring I looked around the room and a framed prayer caught my eye, Hebrew lettering on the top and English on the bottom. I squinted but could read only the first of the English words, *Lift.*

Joel followed my gaze. "'Lift up your hands toward the sanctuary and bless the Lord. Blessed art Thou, O

Lord our God, King of the Universe, who bringest forth bread from the earth.'"

He looked like something out of GQ magazine, only I'd never seen anyone that sexy in GQ—or any other magazine. His black hair was combed behind his ears and grazed the collar of his shirt, and his full lips turned into a smile to match his mother's. I assumed he was still in his work clothes and that his job didn't encourage the grunge look popular with a lot of Seattleites—torn jeans, dirty Green River T-shirts, and clunking Doc Martens. He favored the neat look, a crisp white dress shirt and power tie. Not exactly family dinner attire these days, even for the rich. Silk tie, no less. I thought about touching it and turned away quickly.

I motioned to a cloth-covered basket. "Mrs. Roberts, could you pass me the muffins, please?"

She handed me the basket. "You may call me Jenna."

Now that I saw her in person, I recognized her from the news, where she'd been featured regularly over the past few years. When her husband died, she promptly took over Airtech while earning a BA and MBA from the University of Washington, or U-Dub, as Seattleites called it, in night school. She was probably the richest and definitely the best-known woman in Seattle.

Who would have ever thought I'd sit at a table the size of Pier 70 while she invited me to address her as though I were an old friend?

I grabbed three muffins and slathered them with whipped butter. I weighed ninety-eight pounds, and I kept hoping if I ate enough I'd get bigger.

"Real blackberries," I said through a mouthful of them. A seed stuck in my back teeth, and I wondered what they would do if I reached in to pluck it out.

"Picked by our own little hands," Joel said. "Our property's covered with them, and this is their peak season. Get ready for blackberry everything."

"Where'd you get that cool shirt?" Tamara interrupted, pointing to my T-shirt with her fork.

"I made it."

They stared.

I did too. "Did I say something wrong?"

"You painted that yourself?" Joel asked.

I glanced down at it, a sunrise scene with an Indian girl's face in the foreground. "In high school. This is one of my older works."

He whistled. "A boho, huh? Be nice to me and I'll show you a shortcut through the woods to Ben Franklin."

I perked up. My favorite art supply store, and a bonus was the odd candy you couldn't get anywhere else.

I was sitting on my hair. I pulled it at the base of my neck and draped it over the left side of the chair. Joel smiled at me and I couldn't quite meet his eyes. "How long did it take you to grow your hair?" he asked.

"Twenty-two years."

He took his knife and spoon and began to drum a rhythm on the tablecloth. *"Gimme a head with hair, long, beautiful hair, shining, streaming, gleaming, flaxen, waxen."*

Jenna laughed. "I haven't heard that song in a while."

But I had, on the oldies station. *"Oh, say can you see, my eyes? If you can then my hair's too short."* I couldn't sing worth crap, but it didn't matter. Joel was beaming at me, still drumming the rhythm, and a kind of current, a jolt, was running between us, lighting the room with electricity.

Joel put the silverware down. "You said twenty-two? I would have guessed you to be about eighteen."

"Thank you. Most people think I'm fourteen or fifteen."

"You've never cut your hair in your life?" Tamara said.

"Never."

"Mom, I—"

Jenna held up one hand to signal an end to the sentence. "Please don't consider it. Your hair looks like a bowl of spaghetti already."

I laughed. Joel did, too, but Tamara's dirty look was directed at me. Joel saw it and quickly changed the subject. "So what do you do for a living? Are you a secretary between jobs?"

I could tell them I'd been selling my paintings, T-shirts, and jewelry at the powwows since I was twelve. Grandpa would get a booth for me, and I would make enough spending money over the summer to last all year. But I doubted any of the Robertses had ever set foot at a powwow and I wasn't ready to explain it them. "I'm a freelance typist. I do mostly students' term papers."

"That's interesting," Jenna said.

My eyes rolled before I could stop them. "No, it's not. You wouldn't believe how bad some of the writing is. And you run out of patience with boys who can't type and think that's a girl's job."

Joel's hand gripped his fork. "So? That's good job security for you, right?"

Ah, the old Puritan work ethic, coming from someone who would never have to worry about a job or money. I tipped my head in mock apology. Maybe disparaging the male populace of U-Dub in front of someone who was outnumbered at home wasn't a good way to start off. "It is, of course. But two years of it is enough, thanks. And working in an office isn't any better."

"Why not?" he asked.

"I always get fired."

"How come? Are you stupid?" Tamara said.

"*Tamara!*" Jenna looked aghast.

Maybe this was why Marguerite had asked for *discretion*.

Joel coughed into his hand and said something I didn't recognize, maybe "Shake it." He turned to his sister with a smile that had just enough love in it not to be condescending. "That's 'hush,' for those family members who don't speak Hebrew."

"No, it's not. It's 'shut up.' I know all the everyday words." Tamara looked directly at me. "I know all the curse words. Want to hear them?"

"No, thank you," I said as politely as I could.

Jenna looked uneasily at me. I pretended not to notice. I was quickly getting the idea she had her hands a lot more full than you would expect for a mother with grown children.

Not that I was anyone to talk. I addressed Joel. "To answer your question, I have a smart mouth and no control over what comes out of it."

He grinned. "I'd like to hear more about that."

What could I say? The truth? Sometime in the months since Grandpa's death, my tolerance for fools had plummeted. My last boss had ordered—or rather, *suggested*—that I cut my hair into a "businesslike" style and leave my hair ties at home. When I suggested he go to hell, he hinted I had "personal problems" that should be dealt with as soon as possible. He did a good job of making it sound like concern, but all I heard was *Get out*.

The job before that wanted me to miss the Yakima Nation Festival because the office would be open that weekend and I was expected, not asked, to work the overtime. Never mind that I'd missed all the festivals since Grandpa's death. I wanted it to be my decision.

I would never lump all wealthy white people, or even just all white people, into the same category of *Who-gives-a-crap*, especially since I was technically as much white as Indian. But I seriously doubted this particular group of wealthy white people would understand.

I decided on the safest answer. "Well, one job, the boss wanted me to make a phone call. I mean, just dial the phone, as though he was too good for such a lowly task." They were all ears. "I told him, 'The doctor did such a good job of bandaging your finger I can't even see the cast.'"

"What'd he say?" Tamara asked.

"'You're fired.'"

Jenna joined in the laughter. "But that's what secretaries do. They manage the employer's time—including making phone calls."

"It was a joke. A mistake, I guess, and not my first. But I don't need someone to act like mine is the only screw-up he ever saw. One boss did that to me, and I told him the last time I celebrated my birthday it wasn't December twenty-fifth."

"Hmm, you're right," Joel said.

"What do you mean? How do you know when my birthday is?"

"About not being able to control your mouth."

I was saved from having to reply to that when the doors that led into the kitchen banged open and an older woman in a white apron came through them. I almost laughed out loud. She looked like a throwback to the gothic novels I'd read in junior high, gray bun and all, and a face as cheerful as though she'd eaten a bowl of bullets for breakfast. "Will that be all, Mrs. Roberts?"

"Yes, thank you."

Bullet-eater didn't even glance at me. "Ma'am." She turned abruptly and left. I stifled snickers, but gave up when Joel began to laugh, then Tamara. Even Jenna smiled.

"Mrs. Wharton, our beloved cook," Joel said.

"Wait till you taste her apple pie," Tamara said.

She was right. The apple pie damn near made me swoon. Jenna excused herself from the table after dessert and glided away. I saw that her blouse was not a blouse at all, but a tunic that hugged her slim waist under a huge silver belt and covered the hips of shiny matching slacks. Not exactly your typical CEO togs—she looked more like a twenty-five-year-old model. I would have expected her clothing to be a little more conservative and in line with her position, but to paraphrase Rhett Butler, when you're rich enough, you can tell the world to go to hell.

But no one had been anything other than polite and welcoming—well, Tamara was a little off, but that could be explained. Mrs. Wharton wasn't friendly, but she wasn't paid to be.

I couldn't picture either of them—or the others, for that matter—sneaking into Marguerite's room and tying a trip wire. And the elevator was a completely different mystery, beginning with *how was it broken* and moving on to *who knew about it* and *why hadn't they done something*.

Discretion was the least of what I would need to work here. Maybe Marguerite should have hired a private investigator.

Chapter 4

The next two days went smoothly. The family didn't seem to mind or even question my presence at their table, and both Jenna and Joel went out of their way to be gracious. Tamara ignored me, but since she ignored her mother as well, I didn't take it personally.

Thursday night I was in the dining room with Joel and Tamara. It was just the three of us, since Jenna had a business meeting of some kind. Tamara came to the table with a Walkman hooked to one of the front pockets of her jeans, cooing softly to whatever was playing. Joel politely pulled out both our chairs before taking the same seat he always did. "How's your work coming along?" he asked me.

"Ah ah ooh wooh, ooh ooh ooh yah, yah yah yah yah yah," sang Tamara.

Joel cleared his throat, reached across Jenna's empty chair, and tapped his sister's shoulder. "Please, Tam."

"Please what?" she retorted. "Let me listen to this without having to hear bitching. It's my only chance."

As if on cue Jenna glided in, shimmering in a red and gold dress with matching clips tucked into her hair. "Tamara, I've asked you not to wear headphones at the table." She leaned over and plucked them from her daughter's ears.

Tamara snatched at them. "Who cares? You're not even going to be here. Joel doesn't mind. Neither does Louisa, do you, Louisa?"

"No," I said. It was the only possible answer. "What are you listening to?"

"Uhm…" She glanced at her mother. "The Temptations."

My ex-boyfriend had listened to KBSG, the local oldies station, and after two years of it, I knew the Temptations' music pretty well. I didn't think they had a song with that riff. "I Wish It Would Rain" had an ooh—ooh introduction, but the melody wasn't right.

But what was the point of lying? Was she listening to something her mother had forbidden?

And why control her choice of music at nineteen?

Jenna put the Walkman down at the end of the table. "I'll be home by ten."

"We'll wait up," Tamara mumbled into her salad.

"That isn't necessary."

Tamara paused, a forkful of greens an inch from her mouth. "Who's this hoo-hah with?"

Jenna's eyes narrowed. "Bill's firm."

"Not that slimy accountant?"

"I beg your pardon?"

"Mom, I can't stand that guy. He—"

"I'm not interested," Jenna interrupted her with a nervous glance in my direction.

"Tam, would you pass me the cracked pepper?" Joel asked, maybe a little louder than necessary. He'd already used it, so it was clearly a distraction. But Tamara did as he asked. She also retrieved her Walkman.

Jenna took a breath. "I'll be home around ten."

Joel smiled. "You said that, Mom."

Jenna blushed, looked from one of her children to the other, then left.

Tamara shut off her tape with a *click* and addressed me. "You were talking about her picture before, and I said I wasn't impressed. Did you see that dress?"

It was a rhetorical question. "What about it?"

"Even I don't wear stuff like that."

"Well, you could," I told her. "I would, too, if I looked like her." *And could afford it.*

Tamara muttered something I couldn't hear.

She was right about one thing, though. Jenna didn't look like any businesswoman I'd ever worked for. Her clothes were as colorful as the wingdress I'd worn to my last Fancy Shawl Dance. "I guess she could do the power-suit look, but maybe she doesn't like shoulder pads and drab colors."

Joel was trying to look as though he weren't interested and almost, but not quite, succeeding.

"Would you like her better if she were ugly?" I finally said.

"No."

Joel nearly choked. "Tam!"

I wasn't sure if he was scolding her for disrespecting their mother, or cautioning her not to do it in front of a relative stranger.

It didn't matter. She ignored him. "Hey, Joel, we better hurry. It's almost six. You heard her. We have four hours."

"She said by ten, not at ten."

Tamara jumped up, dumping her Walkman on the table. Her brother sighed, but got up and followed her out of the room, leaving both their full plates untouched.

Of course I went with them.

They hurried down the hall past the music room and study and out through French doors, not seeming to notice me behind them, and began to remove the tarp from the swimming pool.

Tamara looked up and saw me. "Did you bring a suit?"

"No. Uh, is your mother going to like this?"

They stared. "Is that any of your business?" Tamara snapped.

"I guess not, except I need this job."

Joel laughed. "You won't get in trouble. You don't work for Mom. Besides, who's going to tell on us?"

"One of the servants?"

"So?" Tamara said. "What can Mom do?"

"Drain the pool."

She snorted. "You can't just drain this kind of pool. This isn't a municipal pool with concrete. It's fiberglass. If you drain it, pressure would build up and break it. You'd have to fill it in and close it permanently, and Mom's not about to go through that."

The pool was uncovered by then. Tamara turned to Joel. "You turned on the heater, right?"

He nodded. "This morning."

Joel was way ahead of his sister. The outside temperature was a seasonable fifty-four degrees, which would make the pool water cold enough to stop her heart. *Assuming she has one* popped into my head before I knew it would.

"I'm going to go change." Tamara started for the pool house.

"I already did." Joel stripped off his shirt, exposing chiseled shoulders and biceps that had probably seen a few hard tennis matches. My head swiveled away so fast I almost gave myself whiplash. I didn't want to get caught staring.

I went inside and put on my oldest shorts and a T-shirt. Why not? It would be a good chance to hang out with the kids and get to know them better—not a bad idea if I was going to be living in their house indefinitely.

Funny how I thought of them as *the kids*, even though we were all adults, and Joel was two years older than I. But I'd always spent more time around elders than anyone my age. Well, almost always.

Tamara came back out in a red one-piece and her hair tucked neatly into a white swimming cap. She dived in from the bank and did an expert breaststroke to the shallow end. "Anybody want to race?"

I couldn't see the point. "No, thanks."

"Not me," Joel said.

Tamara smirked at her brother. "You know you can't compete with me."

He hooted. "I don't want to be responsible for your getting water on your brain."

"Ha! You get water on your brain every time you sit on the john."

"Oh, yeah?" He did a cannonball into the pool, grabbed his sister, and dunked her. A long time.

"Joel!" I yelled after about twenty seconds. "Are you crazy? You'll drown her."

He let go and she bobbed to the surface, not even out of breath. "Don't worry, Louisa," he told me. "I've seen Tam hold her breath for two minutes."

"Why don't you hold yours for twenty?" she taunted.

He grabbed at her but she ducked away, laughing, and did the crawl up and down the length of the pool several times.

"What song do the Temptations sing that goes 'Ah ah ooh ooh yay yay'?" I asked Tamara when she stopped to rest.

Her saucy grin was clearly visible in the yellowish pool lights. "I don't know."

"What were you really listening to?"

"Three Dog Night."

Late '60s-early '70s hippie feel-good music. Harmless enough, surely, and nothing R-rated in their repertoire that I could remember. In fact, they were one of the few racially mixed bands from that era, and sang about social harmony and the environment.

Not exactly head-banging rock. I'd been expecting Black Sabbath or Judas Priest.

She noticed my puzzled look. "Mom sort of hates them."

"What does she care what you're listening to if she can't even hear it?"

"What does she care about anything I do?"

Joel nudged her.

I switched gears. "That's pretty unusual. I mean, when Three Dog Night was big you were on training wheels."

She shrugged. "Good music is timeless."

I had to smile. Most of what I listened to predated KBSG's oldest song.

"What kind of music do you like?"

It was too soon to tell her my tastes were even more off the wall than hers. It was going to be hard enough to earn her trust or even tolerance. Better to try and establish some common ground. "My last boyfriend liked the same kind of stuff you do. He listened to KBSG. I got pretty used to it." It was time to change the subject while she was still in a gregarious mood. "Tell me about the slimy accountant."

"What for? You won't ever meet him. He only works with Airtech, not Grandmother's books."

"How come you think he's slimy?"

"He is!"

"You're just hard to get along with." Joel's words were softened by a teasing tap to his sister's nose.

"You didn't see him that time I did. He looked at Mom and he licked his lips. I saw him."

"Really licked them? Did she see him?" I asked.

"No, she had her back turned. He wasn't real obvious about it. Just kind of like this." She touched the tip of her tongue to her lower lip. "It was gross."

Joel was laughing. "Maybe they were chapped."

"Yeah, right!"

"Is she dating this guy?" I asked.

"No. Mom doesn't date. But I guess Mr. CPA Slimeball hasn't figured that out yet."

Joel retrieved a beach ball from the pool shed, and we played and swam and splashed around for close to an hour. Then we heard a car coming up the drive.

"Oh, God, Mom's home early!" Tamara vaulted over the side of the pool. "Come on, Joel. No, Louisa, you stay here," as I started to follow. "We don't have time to cover the pool again, so we'll tell her we fixed it so you could swim." She pulled her cap off and ran across the lawn, hair flying behind her. Joel followed, leaving me alone.

I didn't know how long they wanted me to stay out by myself, alibiing for them, but I didn't mind. The water was pleasantly warm and I floated on my back for a few minutes, wondering how I would get the tangles out of my hair. I hadn't taken the time to braid it and it would be a mess when I got out.

But I would never cut it.

It had cooled off outside and when I got out of the pool I was shivering. I hadn't thought to bring out a towel. Fortunately, Joel had left the shed unlocked and there were plenty of towels there. I took two and put one on my head and wrapped the other around my wet shorts and shirt. I started inside but stopped when I heard a loud pop coming from the house—a second-floor window to my left, maybe?

The bay window at the top of the stairs? Or Marguerite's room?

I'd been to enough rendezvous to know a gunshot when I heard one. And I was pretty sure it had come from the second floor.

Chapter 5

I took off across the lawn at a dead run. Both towels fell somewhere in the grass. I paused outside the patio door long enough to wring the worst of the water from my hair and T-shirt, then burst inside and tore up the stairs.

Marguerite's door was closed, but the light was on. I tapped on the door and opened it. "Marguerite?"

She was sitting up in her chair, watching TV and going over her notes. She gave me a bemused and maybe slightly affronted look. "Is everything all right?"

"That's what I came to ask you," I gasped. I couldn't remember the last time I'd run that fast. "I heard a gunshot."

She put the papers down and stared at me.

"I thought it came from up here." I paused to get my breath. "I thought someone was shooting at you."

Her head tipped–to one side as though she were hearing the words spoken in a foreign language that she almost, but not quite, understood. "I'm afraid not. I've been here all evening, and I didn't hear any shot."

Had I gone crazy? "Is there a gun in the house?"

"Yes. But only Jenna knows where it is." Her eyes widened as she saw me trembling. "My dear, relax. I'm fine. Could you have heard fireworks?"

I didn't think so.

But who was the target? Not Marguerite, if she hadn't heard a shot.

Was someone shooting at me?

I didn't know where Jenna was—or, yes, I did, for I could hear the front door closing and her voice calling to Joel and Tamara as she came up the steps.

I'd been in the pool for almost ten minutes after she'd come up the drive. Where had she been all that time?

I backed out into the hallway in time to see Joel step out of his room, headphones hanging around his neck. "Yeah, Mom."

I blew out a gust of air. *He's okay.*

The only one unaccounted for was Tamara.

Jenna saw me in Marguerite's doorway and looked up and down my wet body. "Were you out in the pool?"

No, I shower in my clothes. "Yes. Joel uncovered it so I could swim."

"Was Tamara out there with you?"

"I was alone." It wasn't a lie. I didn't say I was alone the entire time.

Nor was I too damn concerned about Jenna trying to keep her adult daughter out of a swimming pool. "Did anybody hear a gunshot?"

Jenna's eyes narrowed in a bemused frown. "No."

I turned to Joel. Did I imagine it, or did his whole face seem to shut down? "Are you sure?" he said after a moment's silence. "You might have heard fireworks from town."

It was almost exactly what Marguerite had said. But I had the feeling Joel knew better.

If he had heard it, he would hardly be sitting calmly in his room listening to music while someone ran around the house shooting.

But he knows something.

What did he know? Where Jenna hid the gun? Who had the gun? Who was the target?

"Did your car backfire?" I asked Jenna.

Her expression was tolerant. "No."

Of course not. She would never drive anything in such poor repair.

The smile Joel turned on me radiated charm. "Maybe it was a car on the road. If you're done in the pool, Louisa, I'll go cover it now."

"Go ahead."

Tamara appeared in her doorway. She had changed into a nightshirt and pink bathrobe, which she tied around her waist as she addressed her mother. "Were you looking for me, Mom?"

"Yes. Where have you been?"

"I didn't go anywhere!"

"That's not what I meant. You weren't in the pool, were you?"

Tamara came into the hallway and waved a strand of her tawny hair near Jenna's face. It was dry and freshly brushed. "Does it look like it? Does it smell like it? Louisa was the one in the pool. I was listening to music."

"Who turned on the pool light?"

"I did. I wanted Louisa to be able to see."

She'd showered or Jenna would smell chlorine on her skin. Could she have fired the shot from the bathroom between her room and Joel's? Not likely. The shot—if there had been one—had come from this end of the house, so the most likely spot was the bay window on the landing.

But then why hadn't Marguerite heard it? Had the shooter been downstairs?

Tamara wouldn't have had time to shoot from the first floor, come back up, put a cap on her hair, and shower. She'd have to shower first, then go downstairs and shoot, then hurry back up to her room and pretend she'd been there all along.

No. She would be cutting it too close. If Jenna came straight into the house, Tamara was busted. It almost couldn't have been her unless she'd known Jenna would be delayed.

So if the shot had come from downstairs, Joel had to have been the culprit.

'*Only Jenna knows where it is.*'

Or Jenna.

But why? What motive could she have?

For that matter, what motive could any of them have?

Was I wrong? Had it been a car backfiring, or was someone in town setting off fireworks?

No one else heard anything.

That could be explained. Jenna was in the garage, on the other side of the property. Tamara was in the shower. Joel had headphones on.

Except he heard his mother calling him.

Maybe the song ended just as Jenna started up the stairs.

But Marguerite should have heard it, and she didn't.

It had been a long time since Grandpa took me to rendezvous, and the guns we saw and heard there were usually powder rifles—not something I would expect to find in suburban Seattle. But even though it had been years since I'd heard recognizable gunshots, I knew how deceptive sound could be. An echo or reverberation could make a person think the noise came from the other direction.

Maybe it really hadn't been a gunshot. Or maybe it had come from a nearby property.

The last thing I wanted was to have them all think I was crazy.

"Louisa?"

I jumped. "Yes?"

Jenna looked wary and not entirely patient. "Hadn't you better change out of those wet clothes?"

"Yes." I moved past Tamara and Joel without a glance and shut the door to my room behind me.

My hands shook as I changed into a purple sweatsuit. I'd never know what happened unless I found a gun—which would mean searching through a house the size of a junior high, and probably getting caught and fired in the process. Even then, I wouldn't know who'd used it and how recently. Maybe no one knew how to shoot.

I had no idea who might be responsible. I didn't really want the kids to be antagonistic toward me, and making an enemy of Jenna was out of the question.

It wasn't like this was some Movie-of-the-Week. No one had any reason to shoot at me, or at Marguerite, who clearly hadn't been the intended target, if there was a target.

But I would be looking over my shoulder. A lot.

ഛഝഛ

The next morning, I was up long before Marguerite, thinking about the fishing line, and now the maybe-gunshot.

Something in this family was off-kilter.

I decided to find out what I could about them on my own. It wasn't anything I felt comfortable talking to Marguerite about. Not this soon. I didn't want to frighten her unnecessarily or worse, offend her by implying that someone in her family was missing a few ingredients in her—or his—cake.

What could have happened, or be going on now, that would make any of the family members hostile toward one another?

Maybe Carl's death wasn't what it seemed. As far as I knew, that was the only event that had really rocked them.

I knew almost nothing about him and hadn't yet had the nerve to ask Marguerite. I'd have to research. It was Friday, and the nurse would be with Marguerite most of the morning, so I was free for a few hours.

I took off for the Bellevue library, where I spent a few minutes with the *Reader's Guide to Periodical Literature* and wound up with a fat stack of magazines and microfilm. I tossed the newer ones aside, not really interested in how Airtech was coping with the aftermath of the Challenger disaster. The articles from the early '80s didn't have much on Carl, but instead focused more on how Airtech worked with Boeing after its big layoffs. By contrast, there was a lot more to be found about Jenna. With only a high school diploma, she was expected to turn the company over to another officer when she inherited it in 1981. She didn't. She went out of her way to make a name for herself, recruiting new employees aggressively, visiting area high schools and colleges and offering fat scholarships—particularly to blacks and women. I remembered two of my college classmates switching majors to take advantage of them.

Two years after her husband's death, she was named Seattle's Woman of the Year, and people were standing in line to work for her.

So at least one person was probably better off without Carl.

Of course, that didn't mean anything. Certainly not that she would do anything to knock him out of the way. In fact, it was a thought I'd better move to the trash bin of my mind as fast as possible.

No. Not the trash bin. Just an out-of-the-way shelf, till I figured out what was going on with the family.

A *Forbes* magazine from a few years ago featured Carl on the cover, beaming confidently. The article described him in flashy adjectives like "dynamic" and "forceful" and made a tongue-in-cheek comparison of his loud-mouthed, hands-on managing style to that of the Yankees' Billy Martin. But one thing I could tell about Carl Roberts without reading anyone else's opinion—he knew what he wanted from life and he got it.

The microfilm of the *Post-Intelligencer* had a lengthy article on his death and a picture of the family at the funeral, Jenna's face hidden behind a lacy black veil, and Joel with one arm on her shoulders and the other around his sister's waist. Marguerite stood in the background, her head averted from the camera.

According to the story, when Carl made his funeral arrangements, he'd insisted on Three Dog Night's "One" being played. No wonder Jenna didn't want to hear their music anymore.

But every indication was a death of natural causes. He had high blood pressure, which led to kidney problems. One article pointed out that renal failure was a not-uncommon side effect of both hypertension and the drugs used to fight it.

According to a spokesperson for the Roberts family, efforts to locate a suitable kidney donor were unsuccessful.

There were still things money couldn't buy.

෨෨෨

When I got back to the house, Marguerite's nurse was still there, sitting with her on the balcony. I took advantage of the free time to see the rest of the house—

whatever wasn't closed off or private. The room that Tamara had been in on my first day appeared to be her father's study, and it didn't look as though it had changed in the six years since he'd been gone. Several photo albums and yearbooks took up one bookshelf, and I settled in a recliner to look at them.

I didn't get far. "Oh, there you are." I looked up to see Joel standing in the doorway, wearing tennis whites. He didn't seem to notice, or care, that I was looking through his family photos. Of course, he probably figured Marguerite had given me free run of the common rooms. "Thanks for covering for us last night."

"No problem." I looked carefully at him. "Did you really not hear any weird sounds last night? Like fireworks?" *Or gunshots?*

He gave me the same bemused look his grandmother had. "Not that I can remember. After you came in?"

"No. Like, right about when your mother came home."

He shook his head. "As soon as I got out of the pool I went to my room. If Mom knew I was swimming, she'd know Tam was, too." He shrugged. "I don't want her to get yelled at. She's bored. She's only nineteen and she's pretty athletic, and between Mom and her doctor, she doesn't get to do anything."

That was the same thing Marguerite had told me, and it probably explained a lot of Tamara's attitude. "I guess her getting a job is out of the question?"

Dark eyes rolled to the ceiling. "Yeah."

He'd changed the subject, and I'd allowed it. I'd gotten all I was going to get out of anyone about the maybe-gunshot. "Speaking of, why aren't you at work?"

"It's my day off." He gestured to his clothes. "You play tennis?"

"Not since high school."

"Want to play?"

"Let me see if your grandmother needs me first."

The nurse was leaving and Marguerite was ready to start working on the book. I went to tell Joel I'd play with him later, but he was already on the court, hitting the ball against a backdrop, his lean body moving as easy as water.

If this house wasn't so *off*, I could think, and feel, a lot of things that wouldn't be wise under the circumstances. Or maybe I was already thinking them anyway, wise or not.

I watched him until Marguerite called me into her room.

Chapter 6

Marguerite's new book was coming along well. Like her previous ones, it featured a misfit kid, only this one was a high school freshman, not a grade schooler. There was an undertone to the prose that I couldn't really put my finger on—kind of like my first conversation with Marguerite, that feeling of *What's really going on here?*

One thing that struck me was how well she depicted an ordinary and plain middle-class family. Marguerite clearly hadn't forgotten where she came from, and knew that type of background would appeal to a lot broader audience than what she lived now. I tried to think of a way to tell her that without sounding patronizing or rude. Finally I gave up and just said it.

"The advice is always 'write what you know.'" Her smile was wistful. "I'm seventy-two, and I've been wealthy—or lived in a wealthy household—for only fifteen years. Remember, I grew up, and came of age, during the Depression."

I did some quick mental math. She was born in 1915. I kept silent, hoping it would encourage her to tell me more.

It did. "Chris and I married in 1935. I was all of twenty years old." This time the smile lit her entire face.

"We'd survived the worst of the Depression, and the war hadn't come to America yet, but it was a hard time for many people. We didn't have a handful of change to jingle in our pockets for years."

"How did you get by?"

"Very frugally." She pinched the page she held with her thumb and index finger. "We squeezed every penny until it was the width of this paper. But you know, Louisa, we weren't unhappy, and we never felt 'poor.' As newlyweds, the promise of the life we would have together kept us going. We never envied people who had more than we did. Rather, we appreciated what we had."

I kept quiet and listened, a skill I'd developed from hanging around Grandpa and his friends.

Marguerite sighed. "When I look back at my life, that's the richest time. Not now, when I can buy anything I want, but when we saved for a month to buy a better cut of meat for Sunday dinner and apples for a pie. Nothing has ever tasted as good."

I couldn't think of anything to say.

"You're very quiet."

"I'm listening."

"Good," Marguerite said. "You haven't made a fuss about it, but I've gathered that your living situation is a concern to you."

I lifted one shoulder in a careless shrug to hide my embarrassment. She'd fronted me enough money to pay the rent through September, but I didn't know what I would do when my lease ran out at the end of the year. My rent was going up twenty-five percent. There was no way I could stay there, and I knew better than to think for a moment my parents would help. They'd made it clear what they thought of my *refusal to grow up*. "Only that finding a new apartment in January is going to be, uhm, interesting. Rents have gone wild the last couple of years. And that's on the few places that are even available."

She shook her head. "I've heard, and it amazes me. I remember the recession of the early 1970s, when people your age were leaving the city in droves."

I knew we'd had a recession, but it hadn't affected my family, so it hadn't registered in my eight-year-old brain.

She went on. "Please don't let your apartment occupy your mind."

I thought she was concerned about whether I'd be distracted from my work for her. But then she added, "We'll work something out. I'm sure this won't be my last book." She kept the moment from getting mushy by thrusting a handful of papers at me. "But it might be if we don't get busy. Here are Chapters Two and Three."

I finished them by three o'clock, when Tamara knocked on my open door. "Joel and I are going downtown. You want to come along?"

"Downtown Issaquah?" Not only was it bike-riding distance, it was little more than a collection of business offices, quaint shops and fast food places. Picturesque, but hardly, I would think, Tamara's idea of fun.

"The city. Joel promised Mom he'd pick up her car and take it in for cleaning."

There was a gleam of genuine excitement in Tamara's dark eyes. The car wash wasn't my idea of a good time, but I guess if you're stuck at home all day, any sort of outing sounds fun. I was curious enough to say, "Okay. Give me a second to ask Marguerite."

"Meet us downstairs in five minutes."

I figured out what was going on when we got to the garage and Tamara held up a set of keys with a wicked grin. "We're taking my car."

"Where did you get those?" Joel asked. "I thought Mom took them away from you when you got that ticket last spring."

"The one for careless and impudent driving?" Tamara dangled the keys playfully in front of him. "The one she wouldn't get fixed for me?"

Fixed as in *it never happened*? I wasn't sure. I'd never been ticketed.

Joel looked like a parent with a misbehaving child. "Yes, *metuka.*"

"She's not very good at hiding things. When we take her car in, we'll have to leave ours behind. You know she's threatened to have this car towed if she ever finds it in the Airtech parking garage. Let's see if she really does."

Joel covered his face with his hands. "It won't matter, Tam. We'll have it back from the detailer's before she leaves the office."

"Then what's the problem?"

"The problem is that you haven't driven in three months."

"Nuh-uh. It's just been three months since you and Mom knew about it."

"Did you ever get your license back?"

"Oh yeah. I told you. I know all her hiding places."

Joel sighed. "Okay."

This was starting to sound like a bad idea. But my curiosity won.

We piled into the Nova. The engine turned over with a disturbing *rawr-rawr.* As Tamara put it in gear, it backfired with a *blam!*

I jumped and swallowed a curse. Good thing I'd been to the bathroom before we left or I'd have wet my pants.

"Sorry!" Tamara said, not sounding at all sorry. "I should have told you this car backfires."

Uh-huh. And did she start it up the night I thought I heard a gunshot?

I wished, but I didn't think so.

Tamara shot down the drive in reverse. I checked my seatbelt as she took one hand off the wheel to flip on the radio. "Walk Like a Man" blasted through the speakers.

Joel flipped to KUOW—public radio. I didn't know anyone our age who listened to that.

"Hey!" Tamara yelled as she changed gears. "It's my car. I get to pick!"

"You know I hate that station."

"It beats Fish Heads in the Toilet, or whatever that crap was you were listening to that one time."

"Who?" I asked.

"Fish Heads in the Can," Joel corrected. He turned to me. "It's a punk band from U-Dub. And Tam, you're wrong. *Anything* beats Frankie Valli and the Four Freaks."

I had to laugh. The Four Seasons wasn't my thing either. "Why don't you turn on KJUN?"

"What's that?" Tamara asked. Her left hand dangled out the open window and I hoped she would let Joel work the radio.

"Bluegrass."

"Where are they?"

"Fourteen-Fifty."

"AM and country? You want to clean puke up off the seat?"

"That might be an improvement in this car."

"You want to walk?"

"Louisa was just kidding," Joel said.

No, I wasn't. "I guess you're the one responsible for *Chiffons.*" The security gate password and the name of a sixties rock group.

Joel shook his head. "Mom is."

Tamara interrupted. "How come you like country music? I don't know anyone who listens to that."

Bluegrass wasn't exactly country, but there was no point in correcting her. She'd think I was picking an argument. "My grandfather used to take me camping and to bluegrass festivals, and that's what he always played. It brings back good memories."

"Are you pretty close to him?"

"Yeah."

"Where's he live?"

I pointed at the sky. "He died last winter." Just for a second, that *alone* feeling hit me, as though Grandpa's death had taken not just him, but everyone I had ever known or ever would know.

I'd thought I was doing better.

"Sorry," Tamara said. I hadn't known her voice had any volume other than eleven. "I guess his music would make you feel better."

"Maybe that's why Mom's still a rock and roller." Joel pointed to the radio, which was once again on KBSG. "This is what was playing when she—" He froze during the intro of the next song, eight staccato notes, but I didn't recognize it until the vocals began. "*One is*—"

Joel's hand shot out. *Click.* Silence.

"No!" Tamara screamed. We were just entering the tunnel over Lake Washington, and her right hand left the steering wheel to grab at the radio. "Turn it back on!"

I had visions of us smashed against the tunnel walls.

"Turn on your lights." Joel's voice was quiet but firm. "And don't ever take both hands off the wheel when you're driving."

"Let me hear it." She jabbed at the radio dial.

"Get both hands on the wheel or pull over," Joel said just as quietly. "I'm sorry, Tam, but I agree with Mom. I never want to hear that song again."

"So? Please, Joel. She won't let me play it! She won't let me play any of their music." Spit and tears burbled her words. "This is my only chance."

The car swerved as she made another grab for the dial. My jaw was on the floorboard. If he didn't let her have her way, "One" would be playing at all our funerals. "Let her hear it."

Joel flipped it back on.

Tamara relaxed.

I didn't. My mouth had gone so dry I couldn't swallow.

I'd almost forgotten the maybe-gunshot, the trip wire, the general eeriness of the house and this family. They could almost pass themselves off as normal until I spent enough time to see who and what they really were.

Tamara was someone who didn't care if she put us all in danger as long as she got what she wanted.

Joel slumped in his seat, his cheek resting in one hand so I couldn't see his face even when we left the tunnel and were back out in the light. When the last note faded away and a Supremes song came on, his entire body sagged as though someone had stuck a vacuum hose in his mouth and sucked out the tension.

Tamara glanced at him as she turned onto Rainier Avenue. "Thank you," she said in a small voice.

Joel took a deep breath. "You know Mom's not the dragon you make her out to be."

"She yells at me for listening to Three Dog Night. She threatened to throw all their records away."

"You know as well as I do the only time she did that was when you danced on the coffee table to 'Joy to the World' and broke it."

I believed it.

"She wasn't even home when I did that. How'd she know that's what happened?"

"You didn't think she'd believe it was me, did you? It's not exactly something I'd be dancing to."

"Carol could have kept her mouth shut."

"Tam, Mom's her boss. When she's asked a question, and she obviously knows the answer, she can't just say 'Duh-ee, Mrs. Roberts, I dunno.' Mom would fire her, or any of the servants, for lying. They can't cover for you and you know it."

I leaned forward, my chin on the back of the seat between their heads. "Who cares if she throws those records away? I'll take you to Golden Oldies and you can get them all replaced—at probably about a third of what your father paid for them."

They turned to look at me. Tamara turned back to the street just in time to honk at a bicyclist who was too far into the traffic lane and wasn't wearing a helmet to boot. "It wouldn't be the same."

She was right. It wouldn't. If the music meant that much to her, maybe her mother shouldn't give her a hard time about listening to it. Especially if she used headphones or played it during the day when Jenna was at work. "Hide them."

"It's her house. Where do you think I'm going to hide records where she won't find them?"

I settled back in my seat. "Marguerite's room. I'll bet she never goes in there."

They glanced at each other. Then both looked away as though pretending they hadn't.

A lot of Seattle's architecture is fairly new. Most of the city was rebuilt after the Great Fire, and a lot of the rest, including the entire Seattle Center, was built for the 1962 World's Fair. Airtech was part of Rainier Square, a downtown business area south of Seattle Center that included IBM's towering skyscraper and the library with its collection of sculptures. I hoped I could persuade Joel

and Tamara to let me walk down to Pioneer Square and
stop in at my favorite bookstore, one that specialized in
mysteries and was next door to an Indian art shop. It was
a part of town I loved, and the comedy of watching
exhausted tourists chug up Cherry Street's ninety-degree
angle was an added benefit.

Joel's voice broke into my thoughts. "Tamara!"

"Will you quit yelling at me?"

"I will if you pay attention to the bicycles. You almost
ran that one over."

"Tell him to buy a car."

We made it to Airtech, and Tamara waved cheerfully
to the uniformed security guard as she pulled into the
garage. She headed for the RESERVED PARKING
spots, pulled up behind a sedate gray Chrysler and tossed
a spare set of keys to Joel. "You get to move Mom's car."

Once he did, Tamara parked her Nova in its spot. Joel
did not surrender the keys to Jenna's car, nor the driver's
seat. I expected Tamara to put up a fit, but she said
nothing. Neither did the security guard as Joel drove past
him and out onto Fifth Street. I settled in the plush back
seat and leaned against the upholstery. It was as soft as a
feather bed.

Jenna had a car phone, something I knew about, but
had never actually seen. Maybe that was what delayed
her the night before. If she'd been on a call when she
pulled into the garage, she would have wanted to finish it
before coming inside.

Maybe.

We took the car to one of those fancy places that
washed, waxed, shined, and vacuumed it, and gave it
back looking like it just came off the assembly line. The
employees addressed Joel as "Mr. Roberts" and did
everything but spread rose petals under Tamara's feet.
Apparently they were regular customers. By the time the

car was done, it was nearly five o'clock. So much for the bookstore.

Tamara didn't wear a watch, but she'd been watching the clock carefully. "It doesn't make any sense to take Mom's car back to Airtech. Let's just take it home, and she can drive my car. I left the keys in it."

"Like Mom's going to want to drive your car."

"By the time we get back to Airtech, she'll be on her way home already, and then we all get stuck in downtown rush hour traffic. What's the point?"

Joel considered that. "Is there some other motivation for this? Like, maybe, you just want Mom to get stuck driving your ugly Nova home?"

Tamara grinned. "If she hates it that bad, she can take a limo."

"That's true." Joel took the keys from the attendant and handed him a twenty-dollar bill for a tip.

The car phone rang almost as soon as we were back on the road. Joel answered. "Hello?"

Pause. Then, "Well, we're just leaving the car wash. Tam said she left her car with the keys—"

I could hear faint squawking. Whatever Jenna was saying, she was dangerously close to her *outside voice*.

Joel turned to his sister. "Uh-huh. Okay, Mom. We'll see you there." He hung up and glared at Tamara.

"What?" she said.

"Did you know she had a dinner meeting?"

Whoops. We were all in trouble. There was no way Jenna could use Tamara's battered Nova for a business get-together.

"Well, uhm, she might have—"

"Why didn't you tell me?" Joel sounded stern and parental.

"You would have made me take her car back to her."

"Of course I would have."

"I thought it would be kind of funny for her to come out and find my car there. She'd just hire the limo."

"I don't think that's the point, Tam. You could do that to me and I might laugh. But you know Mom won't. Why do you do stuff to make her angry and then wonder why she gets angry?"

Tamara glanced at me.

I pointed out the window. "Hey, look at the outfit that lady's dog is wearing."

They weren't fooled, and they stopped talking.

We dropped off Jenna's car and took Tamara's. Jenna managed to be nowhere around for the switch, and I was relieved. The tension between her and her daughter was too much for me. I was ready to get back to Marguerite.

Chapter 7

Is there some reason you're so quiet tonight, dear?" Marguerite asked me as we worked on the book that evening. Her reading glasses rested on her nose and she tapped her pen thoughtfully against her bottom lip.

"Yes. No. Never mind."

"I'm here to listen if you want to talk about it."

I smiled at her. I'd talked to her about a lot of things I wouldn't have been able to say to anyone else. "Not really. It's none of my business."

"Jenna and Tamara?"

Was she a mind reader? "Huh?"

"I can't walk, but that doesn't mean I can't see or hear. What is it that's bothering you?"

"Uhm, nothing."

"Out with it, Louisa," she replied crisply. "What upsets you about Jenna and Tamara?"

I explained the car switch as briefly as possible, including Jenna's reaction to it. "Tamara's not as funny as she thinks, but it sounds like Jenna might have overreacted. From what Tamara said, she has a limo at her disposal. Some people don't even have a crappy Nova to drive."

Marguerite was silent.

Bad move. I'd walked into her house and insulted her daughter-in-law. I tried to laugh. "I've been here a week and already I'm running my mouth. I guess this is why I have a hard time keeping a job."

"Maybe you can learn a valuable lesson from this. Do you plan to have children?"

"Yes." I wondered what she was getting at.

"I know you have good intentions, but I daresay you'll make mistakes with your children, too."

"What do you mean?"

"I mean, Jenna hasn't had an easy time with Tamara. Tamara was completely her father's daughter. When he was home she would sit in his study with him for hours, listening to the music he liked or playing checkers. He was teaching her to play chess before he died. They enjoyed each other's company, and she's never had that kind of relationship with her mother. Jenna tried to teach her to play the piano, but she gave up when Tamara got upset over the constant mistakes any beginner makes."

I could picture that, and hear what Jenna would say. Something like, "If you throw tantrums like a child, you'll always play like a child."

Maybe Jenna wasn't the one who'd given up.

Marguerite nibbled the end of her pen. "Tamara had a terrible time dealing with Carl's death. I don't believe she's come to terms with it yet, or that she ever will."

"I can relate. I still go to sleep at night, and wake up in the morning, missing my grandfather." As soon as the words were out, my entire body felt like one huge spontaneous combustion of embarrassment. Marguerite had hired me to type her book. She wasn't my counselor. Or confidante.

But before I could apologize for crossing a line, her face softened and she closed one hand over mine. "I know. When my husband passed, I wondered if I would ever smile or laugh again. But you do. Time passes, and the sharpness of the hurt dulls a little."

"He must have been so young."

"Sixty." I saw her throat work as she swallowed. "He also had high blood pressure. Back then, the only thing he could take for it was sulfur. It wasn't a very effective medication. He had a stroke and died the same day."

Wow. So much tragedy in one family. I didn't believe in curses, but it wasn't a stretch to think they might be living under one. "What kind of work did he do?"

"He was a corporate lawyer." Marguerite shook her head as though discussing an errant child. "Not quite as much a workaholic as our son, but enough of one. And now I see Jenna going down the same path. I'm actually relieved neither of my grandchildren is interested in Airtech. I want it to be successful, but I prefer they outlive their father."

"You'd think Tamara and Jenna would be closer, since Jenna's now the only parent Tamara has."

Marguerite laughed. "Dear, is human nature ever that simple? I'm not sure Jenna would welcome a closer relationship. She's been too busy with Airtech to pay any attention to her children, so Tamara grew up on her own. She's not an easy girl to deal with, and they don't have anything in common."

"I don't with my mother, either. I guess I can understand that. But Tamara doesn't have to pretend she doesn't have any sense." I wasn't sure how I knew Tamara was pretending.

Marguerite smiled. "Tamara is a very clever girl. She has a lot of her father in her, including his stubbornness, but not, unfortunately, his knack for charming Jenna."

"A deadly combination, huh?"

"No, not deadly. Just very tiresome. I've lived with their bickering long enough. I wish one of them would grow up—and I'm not certain which."

∽∽∽

The next couple of weeks passed without incident. I was starting to wonder if I'd imagined, or exaggerated, my unease about Marguerite's family. Then I was awakened one Saturday morning by Jenna's and Tamara's voices carrying down the hall.

Not this again.

"Tamara, there is no reason on earth for you to go to the center today. You were just there last Sunday—*after* your doctor told you to take it easy and put that aside for a while."

"I worked there every other day before I got sick!"

"Yes, and that's why you came down with mononucleosis—or at least one factor. You do too many things—"

"I have to do things. You won't let me go to school. You won't let me swim. You won't let me drive. Please, Mom. At least at the center I feel useful."

"I don't want to argue with you and have you get all upset—"

"Yeah, because I might get sick again and then you're not being the perfect mother!"

"*Tamara.*"

Did she ever say her daughter's name in any tone other than *exasperated*?

"I'm sorry, Mom, but I'm a prisoner here. Maybe Joel hates his job, but at least he has a place to go and something to do. The center needs volunteers. I'm doing something worthwhile there. Here I'm just stuck in this—

this *catacomb* with that old bat." I could hear Tamara crying in teary, gaspy sobs.

"They don't need sick—"

"I'm not sick. I'm fine. Let me have a life!"

"I'll discuss it with you when you're calmer," Jenna said in the kind of tone usually reserved for hysterical four-year-olds in the grocery store. Her footsteps started down the stairs.

Something smashed.

I jumped.

"Did you just throw that at me?" came Jenna's shocked voice from the bottom of the stairs.

What kind of nuthouse had I wandered into?

Tamara's door slammed hard enough to disrupt the San Andreas Fault two states away.

Huh. So she thought of her grandmother as *that old bat?*

Quickly I got up and dressed in jeans and a Supersonics T-shirt. I stopped in the bathroom then went downstairs, veering around Carol, who stood at the foot of the steps sweeping up the pieces of whatever Tamara had thrown. I couldn't tell what it was and Carol didn't even glance at me. I did look at her, and there was no expression at all on her face.

Jenna sat at the dining room table, staring at her coffee. I wondered if I should pretend I hadn't heard the argument, but decided that would be disingenuous, not to mention impossible. Besides, I wanted to know what the center was and why it meant so much to Tamara.

"Morning," I greeted Jenna.

"Hello, Louisa." She sighed.

"Uhm, I couldn't help hearing some of what Tamara said, and I was curious about what kind of center she works at." Sometimes the direct approach was best. I held my breath to see if she would get angry or offended.

She didn't. "She volunteers at a rape crisis center. Apart from swimming, it's the major interest in her life."

"Is she a counselor?"

"Not officially, because she doesn't have a degree, but she serves that function. She's considering a career in social work."

I tried to choose my words carefully. "That's an admirable goal."

"Yes, it is, but Tamara tends to go overboard, and that's exactly why she got sick. I want her to do something productive, but not that stressful."

I must have looked confused, for she went on as though I'd pressed her. "I work with dozens of people who are on every kind of nonprofit board imaginable. They could all use a dedicated volunteer. I've talked to Tamara about some of them, but she won't consider anything except the crisis center. I'm afraid if she made a career out of immersing herself in other people's trauma, she would probably have a breakdown. That's not an easy job—for anyone."

"I guess not. But it's an important one. Rape victims have to have someone to talk to."

"I'm not sure Tamara is the person for them. I really wish she would quit. She's been at the center for almost a year, and I've seen the change in her. Seeing the abuse that some men can inflict on women has made her wary of all men. She never dates anymore."

I didn't want to say there could be more than one reason for that. Maybe she was afraid someone would go out with her just for her money or because she was the daughter/granddaughter of well-known people. "Do you think she'll ever learn to disassociate herself from it?"

"I doubt it. Tamara is the type who takes on all the world's problems. Once we sheltered a battered wife, and the husband came out here, scaled the security gate, and tried to break in with an axe." She said this so calmly I could only gape. "Tamara got her father's gun and shot out nearly every window in the kitchen aiming at him."

So there was a gun in the house. Tamara had access to it and could use it. *I knew it. I knew I heard a shot.* Marguerite had told me no one knew where the gun was except Jenna, but Tamara had made it clear she could find things her mother tried to hide from her.

Means and opportunity.

Jenna misread my face. "She didn't hit him. I still don't know if she really intended to do so. He didn't file any charges, of course. He would have had to explain why he was trespassing on our property and trying to beat down the door with an axe."

Wow. "Poor Tamara. I'd get mono too."

"She's a Type A personality, just as her father was. I don't want her to meet the same fate." She stirred her coffee slowly and pensively. "This isn't the only cause on her list. Last Christmas, she and Joel dressed up as Santa and Mrs. Claus and went to a homeless shelter to pass out toys to the children. They both came home crying. They told me some of the children had nothing except what they had been given that day."

I wasn't sure quite what to say to that. I'd assumed they were stereotypical spoiled rich kids, but it seemed there was a lot more to them than I had thought. I felt a twinge of shame for having misjudged them, and not even for any good reason except the feeling that *something in this house was not quite right.*

Jenna broke into my thoughts with a snort that was supposed to be a laugh but didn't quite make it to the finish line. "I'm sorry you had to hear our argument. I wish I could pretend it was an unusual occurrence, but it's not. I hope you'll be discreet. I don't know if Marguerite talked to you about that or not."

"It's okay. I'm not going to sell any stories to the *Times*." I felt bad for Jenna, whose daughter clearly hated her, and who seemed to have no one she could really talk to. Marguerite was old and unwell, Joel couldn't really do anything to bridge the gap between his mother and sister, and of course most of Jenna's time was spent with her employees at Airtech.

But what was Tamara's problem with her?

And why would Marguerite bring an outsider into this with no warning?

Jenna managed a smile. "The *P-I* would be all right. They'd be kinder to us."

Joel came in then, smiled at me, and poured himself a cup of coffee before addressing his mother. "What's the matter with Tam?"

"What makes you think anything is?" Jenna nodded her thanks as he topped off her cup.

"I heard you talking about her when I came in. And she's in her room right now blasting some excuse for music."

"She's upset because I won't let her work at the center every day of the week."

"Maybe you should let her make her own decisions, Mom."

"Joel, I already argued it through with her. I am not going to argue with you as well." Jenna took a punctuating sip of her coffee. Joel wisely kept quiet.

We were almost through with the meal when Tamara came in with a glittery cobalt blue blouse in her hand, which she laid on the table next to her place setting. She ignored both her mother and brother and flopped into her seat. Carol came in and poured a cup of coffee for her. As soon as she set it down, Tamara held the blouse up without looking at her. "The third button broke."

"I'll fix it, Miss Tamara," Carol said with no change of expression.

Jenna gaped at her daughter. As soon as Carol and the blouse were gone, she said, "Tamara, I am ashamed of you."

"Yeah, I know." Tamara slurped her coffee. "What'd I do this time?"

"What did you do?" Jenna repeated. "It's what you didn't do. You could have sewn that button yourself. You treat Carol as though—"

"As though she were a servant?" Tamara laughed. "She is, Mom. What's the point of having servants if you do everything yourself? Grandmother hired Louisa 'cause she's too lazy to type her own books." She turned to me with a hostile smirk.

Jenna practically spluttered.

"She's not lazy," I said. "She's disabled. If you want to be a social worker, you need to develop some compassion." *Whoops.*

Tamara turned to Jenna.

Jenna just looked at her.

I stood. "Excuse me. Maybe I'd better go eat in the kitchen with the other *servants*, since my presence here seems to upset the hell out of Tamara."

"Good idea," Tamara said. "We never asked you to eat with us. But Grandmother said that's the way it's going to be, so here you are."

There wasn't much point in telling her Marguerite hoped that her grandchildren and I would be friendly, if not friends.

"You'll do no such thing," Jenna said to me. "I apologize for my daughter's manners, Louisa."

"I didn't mean anything," Tamara said. "I'm just—I feel weird. It's this medicine I'm on."

Jenna jumped on that and began drilling her about doctors and sleep patterns and diet. I was relieved, for that took her mind off me and let me escape from the table.

It wasn't much of a reprieve, however, because I had barely finished making my bed—I couldn't get used to the thought of a maid taking care of me—when Carol came to tell me that Jenna wished to speak with me. "She's in the music room," Carol told me. As usual I couldn't tell from her face what was going on, but I could guess. I was about to get reamed for the way I'd spoken to Tamara.

I followed the faint sound of piano music—an old doo-wop or R&B number I didn't quite recognize—into the music room. The chandelier's light shone down on Jenna at the piano. Her eyes were half-closed and a faint smile made her look like a teenager. A teenager in love, maybe, although that wasn't the song. She played by ear, like the bluegrass musicians I'd seen. A closed book of fifties classics lay on the bench next to her.

She finished the song and turned to me just as I recognized "The Great Pretender." I braced myself to be told off, but to my surprise her tone, when she spoke, was almost humble. "I'm asking you to please not repeat what Tamara said about Marguerite."

"I hadn't even thought about it," I said truthfully. "I'm not a tattletale, and it would probably hurt Marguerite to be called *lazy*."

"Tamara knows better. I wish she were as 'lazy' as Marguerite, with something productive to do with her time."

Maybe you could let her go to school.

"Productive without being foolish. Her doctor cleared her for two classes this semester." I jumped a little. I hoped it wasn't obvious what I'd been thinking. "Six hours. She signed up for five courses, seventeen hours, and refused to drop any of them. I had no choice but to take her out of school."

I doubted Tamara would tell the same story. Or even see the situation the same way. "One of the reasons Marguerite hired me is that she wanted someone else Tamara's age in the house. I've tried to tell her I don't think Tamara's really warming up to me."

"I hope you're not offended. I'm sure you've figured out that she's lonely, and bored, and angry at me, and her illness, and she's taking it out on everyone else."

"That's why I'm not taking it personally. But maybe she's right and I don't belong at the table with the family."

Jenna shook her head, and her coppery hair swished with a light flowery scent, just enough for a relaxing day at home. "Marguerite asked that you be allowed to spend time with us, and I understand why. I offered years ago to hire a secretary for her, but she wanted to do everything herself. Now I suppose that's getting harder." She touched the piano keys. "This is her piano, but of course, she can't play it anymore. Even when she comes downstairs, her hands just don't cooperate with her."

I nodded. "Her handwriting's hard to read. She told me she did the typing until the last book, but it was too much for her." I paused before asking my next question, which was probably none of my business, but I wanted to know exactly what I was dealing with. "What does she have? I mean, why is she in a wheelchair?"

"Multiple sclerosis."

"How long has she had it?" These were questions I would have liked to ask the nurse, but of course, she wouldn't tell me the date without Marguerite's okay.

"It was diagnosed when she was fifty-seven. That's older than the typical case, and I believe she had symptoms long before she admitted it and saw a specialist."

Based on what I knew, it was the same attitude Carl had taken with his own illness.

Jenna went on. "As you may know, it's a degenerative disease, and the victim gets progressively worse. She's been in a wheelchair for the last three years."

"I'm sorry."

She shrugged that off. "It would be a tragedy for anyone else, but she's done well. I'm glad she has her writing. It's kept her busy, and relatively happy."

But why don't any of you have anything to do with her?

How long had it been since Marguerite had been able to come downstairs? I wondered if Jenna noticed. Or cared.

Nothing I could ever ask, of course.

Or maybe I could. "We're getting a lot of work done with the elevator out of service. Do you know when it might be fixed?"

Jenna played a soft glissando. "It's an unusual elevator, so it's difficult to find a repair company that has the right parts. But we'll get it taken care of as soon as possible."

It wasn't really an answer, and she knew it as well as I did. But I couldn't call her on it.

I glanced up at the chandelier and instinctively moved away from it. It was a strange fixture. Most chandeliers are in the middle of a room, but this one was almost in one corner, as though it had been hung with the expectation that a grand piano would be placed under it. If it ever fell on anyone they would probably be flattened.

"May I be excused?" I asked. "Marguerite should be up soon."

"Of course." Jenna turned back to the piano and began playing again. She was on a Platters kick—I recognized "You've Got the Magic Touch."

Marguerite was up early, for her, and sitting up in her chair eating the breakfast Mrs. Wharton had brought her. She put her cup down and smiled at me. "Are you ready to get to work? I have the latest chapter." She handed it to me.

"You have worse handwriting than a doctor." I laughed, but could have hit myself, remembering what Jenna said about her hands "not cooperating" with her. I opened my mouth to apologize when I saw a frown light between her eyebrows, but as quickly as a mosquito it disappeared.

"One of the curses of being left-handed," she said lightly, then carefully eased a spoonful of fruit compote to her mouth.

I changed the subject, fast. "I think I might try to get a look at the elevator today. Hey, why don't the steps have a banister? It seems kind of dangerous for such a long flight. Think of how easy it would be to fall down the steps, and there's nothing to hold on to."

Marguerite hid a tolerant smile behind her coffee cup. "Carl installed banisters when he had the house built. He later had them removed."

"Let me guess. The kids slid down them."

"Close. Joel and five of his friends broke them."

I gasped. "My parents would have killed me."

She laughed. "I think we were all too relieved no one was hurt to be angry. Speaking of getting hurt, I wouldn't mind if you left the elevator up to a professional. I'd rather you weren't taking that kind of chance."

I waved away her concern. The elevator looked pretty simple, like one of those old-fashioned ones in movies where the floors were visible through a cage. "How far does it go? Just between these two floors?"

"From the first floor to the third. I'm not sure why it goes to the third. No one uses that floor except Carol and Mrs. Wharton. It was meant for servant's quarters, but they're the only servants who live in."

"Even if I fell, it's not that far. And I won't. I'm a gymnast. I can climb like a cat."

"Let's focus on this first," she said with a nod at the pages. "Why don't you go read it and come back here, in, oh, an hour?"

I practically ran to my room to read the latest chapter. Marguerite wasn't kidding about trying something new. I'd glanced through her books when I took the job, and the earlier ones had been the Beverly Cleary type—full of humorous but realistic childhood scenes that were so true to life I could almost smell the mystery meat and spilled milk in the school cafeterias. *I'll Take The One On Either End*, the Newbery winner, was about a boy who had to be the world's most hapless misfit. The stuff he did—and others did to him—was so true to life and well portrayed that I laughed my head off when I read it.

But there was nothing to laugh at in the new book. The main character was a fourteen-year-old boy whose major problem, topping a list as long as a Union Pacific train, was that he was afraid his father was abusing his twelve-year-old sister. Each chapter had a disturbing beginning where Gage, the boy, played with a different lethal weapon, the obvious conclusion for the reader to draw being that Gage was going to kill his father.

Gruesome—but arresting. The psychological suspense was almost unbearable. If I'd bought the book at a store I might have cheated and flipped to the end—which I'd *never* done.

The teenage dialogue was good, too. Marguerite was

adept at picking up on it. Having Joel and Tamara around was probably a big help.

I finished typing the new chapter and went back to Marguerite's room with both sets of pages.

"I'm still wrestling with Chapter Eight," she told me. "Why don't you go spend the rest of the day doing something fun? It's Saturday, after all."

Which was the Jewish Sabbath, come to think of it. Other than Joel's spoken Hebrew, I hadn't seen any religious observance by the family. "I was thinking of going to the Art Museum and the library."

"By all means, go. I should have Chapter Eight done by tomorrow morning."

"How does the book end? Is Gage right? What's going to happen to him? To Sharon?"

"I can't tell you that. You'll have to read it as we go along." Her eyes gleamed with her secret.

Maybe she hadn't plotted that far ahead. I'd read an interview with one of my favorite mystery writers in which she admitted she didn't outline and frequently changed major details of her novels mid-story.

The house was too chilly and quiet for me. I hadn't brought much music with me and wasn't really in the mood for the few tapes I had. I went downstairs to the study and looked through the albums, tapes and CDs to see if there was anything I might like.

Tamara came in as I was flipping through some old folk records. "You like that hippie stuff?"

I was holding one of Peter, Paul and Mary's albums. "Some of it." A couple of their songs were campfire standards that I'd first heard at music festivals with Grandpa. People would stay up till past midnight jamming—playing and singing whatever anyone wanted.

Of course, I wasn't going to share that memory with Tamara.

She pulled up her father's desk chair, shaking her long hair off her shoulders before straddling the chair and resting her chin on its back. She was wearing pink again, a fuzzy pale rose sweater, and her khaki pants sagged in a way that didn't look like a style choice. I figured she'd lost weight during her illness, and rather than spring for a whole new wardrobe, Jenna was waiting for her to gain back the weight. "Me too."

I stared.

She stared back. "What's your problem?"

"I guess I didn't expect you to."

"I like a lot of music. Just not country. Dad used to make fun of it, all those twangy steel guitars and stuff."

I grinned. "That's a defining part of the sound. But most of what I listen to is acoustic."

"Yeah?"

I nodded. "Bluegrass. Your father wouldn't have liked that, either. It doesn't have steel guitars, but it has Dobros, which sound similar."

"What's a *Dobro?*"

"A resonator guitar. It looks sort of like a regular guitar with an aluminum plate over the sound hole. It's held perpendicular to the body and played with a pick."

"Do you play?"

I made a face. "I have about as much musical talent as that paperweight."

"Me either. I mean, I don't play any instruments. Mom tried to teach me piano when I was a kid, but I couldn't get it right and she gave up."

"How long have you worked at the rape crisis center?"

She looked startled at the abrupt change of subject, but replied, "A little more than a year."

"Really? And you haven't picked a major yet?"

She gave me a funny look.

"I mean, Marguerite told me you were undecided, and your mother said you were thinking about social work. I would have thought you'd have decided by now if you've been a counselor that long."

She shrugged. "I can't decide between social work and sports medicine. And it's not like I can just wait and take a general ed program until I make up my mind. If I'm going into sports medicine I have to start focusing my classes in that direction."

"Would you be a doctor?"

"More like a trainer. Or a coach. That'd be cool, I think. A swimming coach. But I'd kind of like to do both."

"What about a double major?"

She rolled her eyes. "Do you like school that much?"

"No. I didn't make it through community college."

"Me neither. Like school, I mean. I'm ready to finish up and get out—" She stopped.

Get out of here? "Why don't you go away to college?"

She looked down at the floor.

I mean, I sure would if it meant getting away from a mother I hate and a grandmother I never seem to have anything to do with.

But of course I wouldn't say that. For all I knew, she was completely dependent on her mother's money, which gave Jenna veto power over Tamara's schedule and course load.

There was also the chance Jenna would refuse to let her headstrong adolescent daughter out of her sight.

"I guess if I were you I'd go for the sports medicine degree. You won't make any money in social work."

"Who cares?"

"You don't want to be poor, do you?"

She snickered. "What are you talking about? I already am. I don't have any money."

I gestured around the room. "I guess people with no money live in three-story houses with twenty-something rooms and a swimming pool and tennis court?"

"The house is Mom's. Mom and Grandmother have money. I don't even work. Mom doesn't give me any spending money, 'cause when she did, I sort of spent it on stuff she didn't like."

"Uh-oh. Things to smoke?"

"No. Drink."

"I got in trouble for that too." Maybe she and I had more in common than we thought. "When I was fifteen. I got grounded for the next three years, literally."

"I think Mom would like to do that to me. She's trying to." She got up and moved the chair back under the desk. "Mom went somewhere. I'm going to the center before she gets back. If you tell her that, I'll tell her I told you I was going shopping and that's where I went." She gestured to the Kingston Trio album in my lap. "Your parents listen to that?"

"No. Sometimes my grandpa did."

Her face softened. "Isn't that kind of music great? Music that connects you with people you love? That's why I like Three Dog Night so much. When I listen to them it feels like I'm being hugged."

She started to walk away.

"Tamara?"

She turned.

"I'll tell Jenna you're out shopping, but you'd better buy something or we'll both look pretty silly."

She gave me a look that could pass for a smile and left.

Was this even the same person who had been so nasty to me at breakfast?

☙❧❧

I probably should have offered to drive her, but that might have been too much togetherness for both of us. Anyway, before I left to go anywhere, I wanted to check on the elevator. Joel was working, so with everyone gone, this would be an ideal time.

Marguerite was right about the third floor. No one was there. I propped the door open and shone a flashlight on the shaft. Climbing on the shaft wouldn't be necessary. I wasn't a mechanic, but I didn't need to be one to see what the problem was.

The steel cable had been jammed at the top. With, of all things, an ordinary pair of pliers.

I clutched at the door with sweaty hands while I thought about what this meant. Someone had jammed the elevator so Marguerite would be unable to come downstairs. They'd deliberately turned her into a prisoner.

Chapter 8

I couldn't reach the pliers, but that didn't mean the family members couldn't. They were all six or seven inches taller than I was, at least. With a stepladder, it would be no problem at all.

I'd picked up a tape measure at Ben Franklin a while back. It went to the bottom of my handbag, and I'd never used it, but I would now. By measuring my own reach and doing simple arithmetic, I calculated that Jenna and Tamara would have a reach of about eighty-three inches. Joel's would be eighty-seven or eighty-eight.

The women would need a stepladder. Joel wouldn't.

I wanted to find the gun.

Maybe before this I could have convinced myself I'd imagined the gunshot, or that it was a firecracker or a car or a TV show, but not anymore. Someone had fired a gun, and I wanted to know who and why.

No—I *needed* to know. If there were too many scary things going on, maybe it was time for me to get out and find another way to make a living.

And leave a helpless old woman in a wheelchair?

Who was I kidding? I wasn't going anywhere. Marguerite needed me. And I wouldn't admit it to her, but the chance to solve a real-life puzzle was intriguing, even energizing. I'd picked the Criminal Justice program thinking that one day I could be a private investigator, like Sue Grafton's fictional Kinsey Millhone. Of course, Kinsey had a law enforcement career for a while before hanging up her shingle, and I didn't think I'd follow that path. But nothing was stopping me from doing my own investigating.

Since Jenna and the kids were gone, it was a prime chance to search their rooms for the gun. But I couldn't get into Joel's. Both the door from the hallway and the one leading to the balcony were locked. Tamara's was such a mess of clothes, CDs, and textbooks that I shuddered and left promptly. I'd never find a gun—or anything else—in that chaos. The only thing that caught my eye was a light therapy box. I'd seen them used to treat Seasonal Affective Disorder, which wasn't an uncommon problem in our rainy and overcast climate. It was one of the reasons my parents had moved to Arizona.

Jenna's room was the opposite, so pristine I was afraid to take too deep a breath. The only personal touches were a five-by-seven picture of her and Carl on the bureau and a Discman on the pillow. Otherwise, it would have looked like a sample bedroom at Masins, if the average bedroom had a real wood-burning fireplace with a daybed in front of it.

There was a hope chest next to the bed. I raised the lid, expecting to find spare linens and maybe the gun nestled between them.

What I didn't expect to see was a veritable KBSG studio of music. The Grass Roots. Ricky Nelson. The Chiffons. The Shirelles. Elvis. The Platters. Buddy Holly. Dion. The Crystals. Top Hits of 1960, 1961, 1962, and 1963. A second Discman and a Walkman to play them in, spare headphones and a stash of enough batteries to start a Radio Shack, hidden in the chest like a secret obsession. Like a fat girl would hide her candy bars.

I ducked out of there.

Ↄ∞ↄ

"I figured out what's wrong with the elevator," I announced at dinner that night. Joel and Tamara continued to eat, saying nothing, but Jenna looked up with interest.

"Oh? What is it?"

"The cable's jammed on the third floor." I wasn't about to tell her with what. "You'll want to call a repairman to fix it."

Jenna hesitated for a fraction of a second. Then she gave me a smile so fleeting I wouldn't have seen it if I hadn't been watching. "Thank you. We'll take care of it."

Joel's attention was on his own plate. Tamara paused with her fork in her hand before loading it with enough long grain rice to fill three mouths.

One of them was guilty. But I couldn't figure out who. Nor why the others didn't seem to give a crap.

Marguerite had mentioned Tamara was afraid of heights, so I didn't think she would climb even a stepladder. Jenna was an unlikely prospect as well—Miss Executive risk breaking one of her manicured nails?

That left Joel—who wouldn't need a ladder. Maybe a stepstool, to get the pliers in the exact spot.

It didn't make much sense for him to screw around with the elevator to keep Marguerite trapped upstairs. As the only male in the house, he was likely to be the one prevailed upon to carry her downstairs if the need arose. I wondered if she'd ever asked him to do that and what his response might have been.

It was impossible to guess. I didn't know Joel well enough.

I spent the evening on the manuscript. Even though

Marguerite hadn't asked me to do so, I decided to play "editor" and pencil in a few minor changes and a major one. *Gage needs to be more sympathetic/likeable. What about a scene showing him in a more positive light? Make him a little stronger, less passive. So far everyone is doing unto him and the only thing he* does *is play with weapons. What about a couple of scenes from his sister's head? What makes Sharon tick?*

Maybe it was overstepping, but I'd been known to read two to four books a week, and I knew what I was talking about. It was a good book, maybe the best one Marguerite had ever written, but it was dark. Very dark.

Well, what would you write if you were trapped in one room with no one to talk to except a stranger?

Because despite the bond growing between us, that's what I was. The nurse had made her scheduled visit the day before, and she'd been pleasantly surprised by how well Marguerite was doing. I'd tried to be modest and not take credit, but even the nurse knew Marguerite was lonely. All she'd needed was someone to sit with her and talk to her, take some interest in what she did. She had her writing, but as I knew from my art, the creative process was a solitary activity.

Marguerite didn't need a secretary, or even a companion. She needed a family.

At about eleven-thirty I got hungry and went down to the kitchen to make a bowl of popcorn. I melted shredded cheese on it and sat in the kitchen eating it and drinking a Dr. Pepper, but stopped in mid-crunch when I heard piano music.

I set my bowl on the table and tiptoed through the dining room and across the hall to the music room. The door was open and someone was playing "Bridge Over Troubled Water," the melody plaintive, the chords resplendent. I looked in, expecting to see Jenna, the only person in the house who could play the piano.

But even in the darkness I could make out Tamara's slim form and wavy long hair.

Chapter 9

*G*age picked up the blowtorch and turned it over in his hand. It looked like a hobo's cup with a bugle glued on top. He guessed the gasoline would go in the cup ~~and~~ but what would he light to make the flames come out of the business end?

How would Gage say that? Is there a name for the end of a blowtorch? Would an ordinary 14YO kid know it?

He slammed the contraption down on the metal shelf with a clang. It wouldn't work if he didn't know how to use the damn thing.

⁏⁘⁏

Sunday morning I was up early, as usual, waiting for Marguerite to awaken so I could show her some ideas I had for the book. I thought she'd created a pretty naïve kid, young for fourteen, and she was doing well at showing his lack of even basic sophistication. *Business end* was a great way for him to describe the blowtorch, and if she tinkered with the phrasing, the scene might lose its punch.

I didn't go to breakfast with the family, but sneaked down to the kitchen ahead of everyone and got a cup of coffee and a blueberry muffin. The kitchen smelled warm and toasty and rich, like a high-class diner. It was almost the size of a small restaurant. Pots and pans hung from the ceiling, there were several cutting islands, and two steel refrigerators gleamed next to a stove twice the size of the standard one in my apartment. My stomach growled and I knew the lone muffin wouldn't be enough food, but I couldn't sit at the table and look at Tamara. Not without asking her a lot of questions.

"Why did you pretend you couldn't play the piano?"

To Jenna—*"Why did you tell me she couldn't play? What a ridiculous thing to lie about."*

To Joel—*"Didn't you tell me the same lie? What in the name of God is wrong with this family?"*

Of course, it was possible Jenna didn't hear Tamara play. I wouldn't have if I hadn't been on the first floor. The house was too big, and the ceilings too high, for sound to carry from the music room to the back rooms on the second floor. And if Jenna went to sleep playing sixties rock on her Discman, she wouldn't hear anything from the first floor—or probably even the second.

I wondered if Marguerite could hear her.

It wasn't any of my business, and it probably wasn't a big deal, but it gave me the creeps.

I took my food back up to my room, but I got cabin fever quickly. I wondered how Marguerite tolerated living in her room every second of every day, with only the trips out to the balcony to break the monotony. Once the elevator was fixed maybe I could take her out for real.

I went down to the study, shut the door, and put one of my tapes into the stereo system. Bill Monroe's mandolin filled the room and I breathed in the sound. The study was filled with family artifacts, and since I was alone in the room, I felt more comfortable examining them than I would if Tamara was in there. I walked around the room, my moccasins sinking into the plush carpet. The cool air settled on my skin as I picked up photos, trinkets and mementos. Carl's diploma from U-Dub, with a summa cum laude degree in Aeronautical Engineering. On the desk, what I guessed was a wedding picture, Carl and Jenna gazing besottedly into each other's eyes as they clasped hands.

On one of the bookshelves, two trophies held up opposite ends of a row of thick engineering texts. One was a swimming trophy that Tamara had won in sixth grade. The other was for a tennis championship that Joel had won his senior year in high school.

The door opened and I turned to see Tamara. Her lip curled as she saw me standing by the bookshelf, and I took an instinctive step back.

"Mom's in the bathtub," she said without preamble. "She'll probably be there for the next hour. When she gets out, tell her Joel's taking me to Northgate."

Marguerite had told me she probably wouldn't have anything new for me to type until Monday. This would be a good chance for me to try to figure out what made these kids tick. Maybe they'd let down their guard and give me some clue to what was going on around here. "Can I go with you?"

She shrugged. "I guess. You'll have to ask Joel. He's driving."

Joel appeared in the doorway. "Sure you can. Tam, I'll tell Carol to tell Mom where we went. I want both of you to be ready to leave in about five minutes."

"What's the hurry?" I asked. "Most of the stores aren't even open yet."

"We have to get out before Mom catches us and tells Tam she's too 'sick' to go anywhere."

"The only thing I'm *sick* of is her," Tamara muttered. She pulled the headphones off my head and put them to her own. Her nose turned up and she tossed them back to me. "What is that hokey shit?"

"It's called bluegrass, and this is Bill Monroe, who invented it."

"Someone ought to take him out and shoot him."

If she was trying to offend me, she would have to try harder. "Maybe we can do that to you, too, after you get a museum named after you." I shut off the tape and headed upstairs for a jacket and my handbag. Just before I got to the steps I heard Joel say, "Stop giving Louisa trouble."

I paused, but I couldn't hear Tamara's answer—if she had one.

I offered to drive, since my car spent most of the time sitting and I'd been advised by a mechanic to take it on at least one decent drive a week. When we approached it, Joel's head tipped and he knelt to look under it. "Maybe next time." He stood. "You have a small radiator leak."

"Not that hose again." I'd had it patched in June. "I guess it's time for a new one."

He was already opening the hood and poking around. "This hose here?" He examined it. "You don't need a new one. Let me put some sealer on it and top off your radiator."

"Joel, let's get going." Tamara hopped from one foot to another like she had to go to the bathroom.

"Take it easy, Tam. This'll just take a minute." Joel got a tube and a jug of antifreeze from the garage. He handed the jug to me.

I watched him apply the sealer to the hose, breathing through my mouth so I wouldn't smell its sickly chemical odor. "How do you know so much about cars?" I asked.

"I don't. But I can do the simple stuff." He traded props with me and poured some of the antifreeze into the radiator, his hands so steady he didn't even use a funnel. "I took auto shop in high school and learned how to take basic care of a car. That was one of my more useful classes."

He shut the hood and smiled at me. "You're good now."

Yes, I am. Maybe the sealer didn't have the rubber-cement smell I'd thought, or expected, because all I could smell was Joel, and it was a clean, soapy, guy-smell. The vibe, or connection, was back, and I felt as though we were touching each other even though we were about two feet apart. One lock of black hair fell across his forehead and he brushed it aside with a smudged finger. "You might want to wash your hands," I managed.

There was a sink in the garage. Of course.

"I'll drive," Joel said as he dried his hands on a clean rag. "I'd rather you test that hose on a shorter drive, and maybe when I'm with you."

I nodded. Out of the corner of my eye I could see Tamara watching us.

"Can I drive?" were the first words out of Tamara's mouth when we got in Joel's car.

"No."

"How come?"

"Because you're not supposed to. Because your medications have a warning label that says *Do not operate machinery*."

"Don't tell me you're going to start going along with Mom's rules."

"You don't even know how to drive a stick."

"Yes, I do. You taught me."

"That was last year."

"You think I'm stupid and I forgot?"

"It takes practice," I interjected from the back seat.

Tamara didn't turn around. "Who asked you?"

"Oh, you're just as sweet as an angel food cake today, aren't you?"

"Ladies, please," Joel pleaded. "Tamara, maybe I'll let you drive a little later. Let me see how the traffic looks. It's Labor Day weekend, so there will probably be a lot of tourists, and you know how they drive."

The way we would if we were in their towns and didn't know where anything was.

Tamara giggled. "Let me run some of them down so they won't take up all of Pike Place with their dumb cameras. See, there's one now." She pointed to a sporty red Pontiac with National Rent-A-Car tags.

"Keep talking and I'll make sure you never get a set of car keys in your little hands again." Joel squeezed one as he spoke. Theirs was an unusual relationship, less brother-and-sister than best friends. Maybe even only friends, for I hadn't seen either spend time with anyone our age.

Or, perhaps, parent-child. Certainly Joel seemed to take a lot more responsibility for his sister than Jenna did. Perhaps because he knew her better.

Perhaps because he cared.

"At least turn off the geriatric station." Tamara pointed to the radio, tuned to the sixties oldies station.

Joel laughed. "Maybe later. Mom's music is better than most of what's out now."

"What do you mean, 'Mom's music'?" I asked.

"I told you before, Mom's a rock-and-roller. Tam, do you remember that time Grandmother was in the hospital?"

"Which time?"

"The first time. I came home from school and Mom was playing Dion and the Belmonts. Loudly. And singing. You could hear her all over the house." He began to sing, off-key, but even so I recognized "I Wonder Why," an upbeat doo-wop number.

Tamara gasped. "Mom singing? To Dion? When? Why didn't you tell me?"

He shrugged. "It wasn't that important."

Then why did he still remember it? And why did Tamara care?

"Anyway," Joel continued, "as soon as she realized I was in the house she stopped. Like someone pulled a cord on her."

"I only hear her play the piano about once a year. I've *never* heard her sing."

She hadn't? I'd looked through their high school yearbooks, and in addition to Carl being voted *Most Likely to Succeed* and being selected *Cutest Couple*, Jenna had been voted *Most Musical*.

The *Most Musical* of her high school class never sang in front of her family?

"She told me once she used to sing to me when I was a baby," Joel said.

Tamara snorted. "I don't remember that."

He laughed. "You weren't born."

"No, I mean, she didn't sing to me."

"When you were a baby? How many things do you remember from when you were a baby?"

"I remember you. I remember your face sticking in my crib all the time and Mom and Dad telling you to get it out before you scared me."

I wondered if she really remembered it or if it was a story someone had told her.

We were early and the mall wasn't open yet, so we stopped at Lake Union and enjoyed the view. Tamara gazed at the sailboats with longing. "I need to get out on the water again. Even Bill hasn't been over lately. He always takes us out on his boat a few times each summer, but not this time. I'll bet Mom told him not to so I couldn't go."

"Who's Bill?" I asked.

"Mom's best friend." Tamara turned to Joel. "Well? Did she?"

"I don't know." Joel sounded tired. "She might have. You know I don't hang around much when he's over."

"Oh yeah?" I knew I shouldn't, but I couldn't resist. "Is he another slimy guy?"

"No," Tamara said. "He's been Mom's best friend since, since Dad was here. He was Dad's best friend too. We hung out with their family all the time when Dad was alive, but..." She trailed off to watch one of the yachts go by. "I can't stand this. I really can't stand just looking at the water. Let's go."

"I have an idea," I told her. "If you know Bill that well, why don't you just get on the blower and ask him to take you out on his boat? What's the worst thing he can do?"

She just looked at me.

I looked back. "It sounds like maybe you like complaining about your mother more than anything else."

"Why don't you mind your own damn business?"

"Ladies," Joel said.

"It's okay, Joel," I told him. "We understand one another fine, don't we, Tamara?"

"Each other," Joel said.

"What?"

"The three of us are *one another*. You and Tam are *each other*."

I took a deep breath and tried to count to ten. I got to four. "I don't like people who make me feel foolish."

His face fell. "Sorry."

If Tamara had corrected my grammar like a fourth-grade teacher, I would have wanted to deck her. But somehow, looking at Joel's black hair, mussed from driving with the convertible top down, and his warm brown eyes, I couldn't really be angry. He had an air of someone who needed an understanding wife to welcome him home from work every night with a hot dinner and a fresh-baked apple pie. At the same time, I could see him taking her orange juice in bed and reading the funnies to her when she had a cold.

I hadn't seen any sign of a girlfriend. I wondered why.

I got a surprise when we passed Woolworth's. We stood there debating whether to go in and buy some home de-improvement items when a pretty strawberry blonde walked by and stopped short. Her face softened as she looked at Joel. "Hello, Joel."

He glared at her.

She looked taken aback and maybe a little hurt. "You don't have to—you could say hello."

He gave her a tight grimace a blind person wouldn't have called a smile. "Hi, Val."

Val looked embarrassed. She fiddled with a name badge that hung around her neck and turned to Tamara. "Hi, Tamara."

"What's up, Valerie?"

"Uh, not much." Valerie ducked into the crowd without another look at Joel.

"Either of you ladies want a pop?" Joel jerked his head in the direction of the snack stand.

"Yeah. Pepsi."

"Dr. Pepper for me, please." I started to dig in my handbag for money, but he was gone before I had my hand on the tie.

"What was that about?" I asked Tamara.

"That was Joel's old girlfriend. They went together for two years in high school."

"Why does he act like he hates her?" But I could guess.

"She dumped him."

"I don't guess you want to tell me why."

"She said he was too moody."

"I don't think Joel's moody." *You, on the other hand...*

She snorted with wry laughter. "You haven't known him for two years. What's going on with you guys?"

"What? Nothing!"

Joel returned with our drinks and the conversation died a quick death. My curiosity didn't, however. High school for Joel had been six years ago, certainly long enough to get over even a major heartbreak. Maybe I'd ask Marguerite what she knew. If she'd lived with her son's family since its beginning, she was bound to have some recollection of a girl Joel had dated for two years.

We shopped for almost two hours, Joel's mood improving only slightly despite Tamara's and my attempts to cheer him. He kept looking around defiantly as though preparing to do battle with Valerie if she dared to violate his personal space again. However, once we were back in the car he seemed to relax a little.

"I get to drive now," Tamara announced.

Joel hesitated. "All right, but I want you to take it easy and do what I tell you."

They switched places. Joel pointed to the clutch. "The first time you switch gears without putting your little foot on that I'll break it."

"The clutch?"

"No. Your foot."

I wanted to break both of Tamara's feet before we were out of the parking lot. She stalled the car about eight times trying to back out of the parking space then lurched around like a drunken inchworm making her way to the exit. Two elderly people getting out of a car with handicapped Nebraska tags had the misfortune to be in our path. Tamara elbowed Joel. "Look, Joel, Elmer and Mabel from the sticks. Ten points!" She threw the gearshift into neutral and gunned the engine, scaring the Nebraskans' life out of them. They practically leaped back to the safety of their car. I was sure they could hear Tamara's shrieking laughter.

"Foot on the clutch!" Joel howled.

I hid on the floor. I didn't want the couple to think I had anything to do with Tamara's behavior. Not that they knew who any of us were, but treating elders with disrespect made my stomach turn.

"Tamara, that wasn't funny," Joel scolded. "What if you'd done something wrong and put the car in fourth gear and run those people over?"

"I wasn't going to. They got out of the way."

Joel shook his head. "Shithead." But his tone was more affectionate than annoyed and he rubbed his sister's tousled hair with one fine-boned hand.

I couldn't wait to get back to the house and Marguerite's book. It unnerved me too, but at least it was fiction.

So, apparently, was a lot of stuff in the Roberts family. I'd been thinking about asking Tamara why she said she couldn't play the piano when she played like a session musician. But it was one of the rare times my mind put the brakes on my mouth, and I closed it before the words could come out. Clearly it wasn't something Tamara would talk about, at least not with me.

Maybe not with anyone. If she played only in the middle of the night, she wanted to keep it a secret, and asking her about it wouldn't do anything except open the monster's cage.

Jenna's car was in the garage when we got back, but she was nowhere in sight. Joel and Tamara escaped to one of the back rooms on the first floor, presumably hiding before she saw them and figured out Tamara had been out.

I went up to Marguerite's room. She was propped up in bed with a small stack of the book's pages on a clipboard in front of her. She smiled at me as I came in. "You're just in time. I just finished Chapters Eight and Nine."

I held out my hand for them. She gave me the clipboard, but touched my hand to keep me from leaving. "Please don't leave yet. Sit down."

I did.

"I tried to write a little more carefully. I'm sorry my handwriting gives you trouble."

I'd been thoughtless. "I'm sorry. I shouldn't have said anything. It's not that bad."

"White lies aren't necessary, my dear. My hands, as well as the rest of my muscles, are not what they used to be."

"That's not your fault."

"It's not yours, either. But that's not what I wanted to ask you. It seems like you've been spending a lot of time with my family. What are your perceptions?"

I hesitated.

She chuckled. "You won't hurt my feelings, Louisa."

I wasn't so sure. "Tamara's weird. Or just plain immature. She behaves like a twelve-year-old. Literally. Maybe she's trying to get Jenna's attention, but it doesn't seem to be working. Joel is growing old before his time babysitting her."

"How do they treat you?"

"Tamara can go either way. Jenna goes out of her way to be nice. Joel—well, he's not around much. He's polite and—it's an old-fashioned word, but he's gentlemanly." I hoped I wasn't blushing. "Most of the time, anyway. He ticked me off today when he corrected my grammar."

Marguerite chuckled. "I'm not surprised. He has a little arrogant touch in him. Much like his mother was, once upon a time."

I wanted to hear more about that. I kept silent, hoping that was the best way to encourage her to elaborate. But she didn't take the bait.

"Why don't you eat meals with them?" I said finally.

Marguerite gave a little shrug that made her look not unlike Tamara. "I can't go downstairs because of the elevator."

"I'll bet you didn't even when it was working. I bet you won't after it gets fixed. Why not? It has to be lonely in here by yourself."

Her face softened. "I'm not lonely. That's why you're here."

"I'm not your family. They are."

"My dear, hasn't it occurred to you yet, this—" She pointed to her chapters. "—is not a full-time job?"

It was a weird question, but I gave her an honest answer. "Of course it has. It's barely even a part-time job. I keep hoping you won't get angry that I spend so much time with Joel and Tamara, but you said you want them to have someone their age."

"That's part of the truth. The rest of it is…" She paused and looked down at her blue patterned lap blanket. "I could use the company too. The truth is, Jenna and I don't see eye-to-eye on a lot of matters, and that makes things uncomfortable. And Joel and Tamara aren't interested in spending time with a sick old woman." Her matter-of-fact tone kept the words from sounding self-pitying.

"What matters don't you and Jenna agree on? Airtech? I thought you weren't interested in it."

"I'm not. I gave Jenna complete control of Airtech. I haven't even been to a board meeting since 1983. No, just—personal things."

I prodded. "Like the kids?"

"Yes, partly."

"And?"

"The house. Which is none of my concern, since Carl left it to her. Investing the remainder of his assets. Which holidays to celebrate and how. We're two completely different people, and there are no two ways about it. Jenna, as a teenage girl, fell rear end over teakettle for my son. That did not automatically translate into affection for me."

I wondered what Marguerite's husband had thought. What role had he played in the household? Was he like Carl, and now Jenna, rarely home? Had he left the household to Marguerite? There was no real way to ask that, of course. Maybe one of the kids would tell me. "But you're both reasonable adults. You can compromise on most things."

"Jenna's idea of a compromise is the other person recognizing no one could possibly know more than she does. She's a fine woman, but she seems to bring out a querulous streak in me, and I in her." Her smile went clear up to the few crinkles in her forehead. "Under that soft exterior is one tough woman."

I must have looked puzzled. It wasn't really the impression I'd gotten.

"You don't know her the way I do." The smile was gone and replaced by an expression I couldn't quite identify.

"Well, no, of course not. But even in the short time I've been here, she seems…well, like she doesn't know what to do with Tamara." *And puts up with way too much.*

"It's a power struggle. And she's the one losing, by having such a contentious relationship with her daughter. I love Tamara dearly. She's a delightful girl when she's in a pleasant mood."

"She keeps things interesting," I admitted. Between her pizzazz and Joel's warm grace, the job was proving to be a lot more interesting than I'd thought.

I shuffled the papers in a silent signal that I was ready to get to work, hoping Marguerite wouldn't be offended. But she just waved her hand at the door. "Enough of this. Go read."

I couldn't dismiss myself that easily. My mind was still wrapped around the book. The story was getting really involved and Gage was flipping out more and more. His latest weapon, besides the blowtorch, was a chainsaw from his father's tool shed. He was a disturbed boy who didn't get along well at school and had no friends—he'd been a bully in grade school, and it was the sort of small town where no one forgot or forgave. He was big and blond and bulky, and everyone expected him to be a football player or wrestler, and his only real interest was drama. It was starting to depress me, for I was wondering how the story could possibly have a happy ending, and suspecting that it wouldn't.

In just a few years, Marguerite had made a good name for herself in children's books. Not quite Beverly Cleary or Judy Blume, but if she stayed with the genre, she could expect to see her books' shelf life outlast her own. What she was doing with this book was what Judy Blume had done—her main characters got older and their problems more intense. Interesting if you could make it work, but like jumping off a high bridge, there wouldn't be any way to turn back. Once she'd written *Forever* and *Tiger Eyes*, it must have been hard for Judy Blume to go back to writing about Peter and Fudge.

I was relieved when I finished Chapter Nine. It was an emotionally draining book and my eyes hurt by the time I put it down.

Marguerite was dozing when I went back to her room, but she came awake quickly. "Are you finished already? You *are* a fast typist."

"That's a heck of a book." I sat down in the wingback chair. "How did you come up with this idea?"

Marguerite covered a yawn with her fingertips. "A news story."

I perked up. Being a part of creating something was really kind of fun. "How close are you keeping to what happened?"

"Oh, not very. Playing what-if is more fun than sticking to facts. I have some ideas, but I want to see where the story takes me."

I would know soon enough. Meantime, I had to change the subject before I lost my nerve. "About the elevator…"

"Yes?"

I'd thought about it long and hard before deciding that hiding things from her, as though I were dealing with a small child, was pointless. I'd spent enough time around elders to know the one thing they hated above all was being treated like children. "I think someone broke the elevator on purpose."

She just looked at me.

I looked back. It wasn't easy to hold eye contact.

"Okay," Marguerite said slowly. "And…"

"The cable was deliberately jammed. And, well, I'm

sorry to put it this way, but it's got to be one of your family members."

"Deliberately jammed *how*?" Her voice sharpened into a whip.

I felt like a tattletale. But she needed to know this. "They put a pair of pliers on the third-floor cable. It's out of my reach, but anyone taller than I am could do it easily with a stepstool or small ladder."

Her face tightened in fury, but she recovered immediately. "It wasn't Tamara. As I believe I told you before, she's afraid of heights. She won't climb even the smallest ladder. So that leaves Jenna and Joel."

I wasn't so quick to let Tamara off the hook. She was the only one of the family who seemed unbalanced. "When did the elevator stop working? Was Tamara in the hospital, or could she have done it? Or paid someone to do it for her?"

Marguerite's eyes narrowed to pencil slashes. "That implies one of the household employees."

I'd known she wasn't going to like what I had to say, but I still had to swallow hard and take a slow breath before continuing. "I'm sorry if that sounds disrespectful. But I have to look at any possibility."

"No, you don't, my dear. You're not a private eye."

It would be the wrong time to tell her I'd toyed with the idea of being a criminal investigator. "When did you first notice you couldn't use it?"

She paused. "This is Labor Day weekend? Early August. Not long before I hired you."

"When did Tamara come home?"

"About the same time."

Marguerite had a good mind. I would bet money she knew the exact date but didn't want to tell me. Which meant one of several things—A, Tamara was nowhere around when the elevator was broken, so Marguerite knew as well as I did that the next likely suspect was Joel.

Or B, Tamara was home by then, and had summoned up the courage to climb a ladder. Meaning her hatred of her grandmother was stronger than her deepest fears.

None of it made sense. Tamara didn't have anything to do with her grandmother, but other than calling her *lazy*, she hadn't done anything to make me think she hated Marguerite. It was her mother she hated. If Tamara were going to cause trouble for anyone in the household, it wouldn't be Marguerite.

The culprit had to be one of the others.

Chapter 10

Marguerite leaned forward. "Louisa? What are you thinking?"

I had to say it before I lost my nerve. "Why didn't you tell me?"

"I didn't know."

"What? What do you mean, you didn't know?"

She was very still. "I spoke clearly. I didn't know the elevator had been jammed."

"That's not what I meant. Why didn't you tell me…" There was no way to say it kindly. She was already angry, and probably hurt, and anything I could say would make it worse. "You have to know that at least one person in your family is out to make your life hell. But you never told me that when you hired me. You made me think this was a normal family. Well, it's not."

Dead silence. I could hear myself breathing.

This was the point where anyone else would tell me to hit the road. I hoped Marguerite wouldn't do that. She needed me, or at least an ally.

When she finally spoke her voice was almost a whisper. "Now you know why I wanted discretion."

I couldn't look at her. If her face was as despondent as her voice, I would start crying, or something equally pointless.

Who would be this cruel? Didn't they know that isolating Marguerite from contact with other people might make her not just lonely, but eventually a little…off? I wouldn't even think the word *crazy*. Although it would make a lot of people crazy to live in a place like this. "Sorry. I was thinking. Maybe I could try to figure it out."

She managed a smile. "My dear, you're doing the job I hired you to do quite well. There's no need to moonlight as Sam Spade. You'd have to be very clever to get anyone to admit to deliberately breaking the elevator."

Clearly she wasn't ready to talk about it. "You're right. I'm sorry."

"Don't be." She smiled at me, and this time, it was a real and a warm smile. I pretended not to see the redness in her eyes. "I'm touched that it's so important to you. That elevator's been broken for a month and you're the first person who's bothered to find out why."

I was probably the only person who cared. "Do you have anything else for me to do? Joel and I had talked about going to the art museum today."

She rubbed the corners of her eyes as though removing sleep crumbs. "I'm still a little tired. I think I may lie down for a while. Go, and have a wonderful time."

I probably would, and not just because the art museum was one of my favorite places on Earth. While it was true that spending time with the family might allow me to earn their trust, it was also true that the house was a dark place, and Joel lit it up.

God, I hoped he wasn't the one who'd jammed the elevator.

I went outside to where he was washing his car with a rag made of someone's old underwear. I pointed to it. "Whose was that?"

He held it up, filthy, stained, and dripping dirty soap. "Try them on and find out."

"You're sick. When are we going to leave? The museum closes in less than two hours."

He shook his head. "It's open later tonight because of the holiday weekend. But we can leave as soon as I finish this, if you're ready."

I looked down at my jeans and terry pullover. "Give me a minute to change clothes."

"Uh-oh. When Mom or Tam says that it means till next Thursday."

"I'm not talking about a business suit or three pounds of makeup and hair spray. Should I just wear this?"

"No, put on something a little dressier. I might want to take you to dinner."

"You might?"

"If I get hungry enough." He winked then pretended to squirt me with the hose.

None of my jeans could be called *dressy*, so I put on black slacks and a white blouse and tied a black bow in my hair. I felt silly and overdressed, but Joel's smile when he saw me made up for it. He whistled softly and took my hand. "That white blouse with your dark hair looks good enough to eat."

I hoped I wasn't turning red. Getting that sort of compliment happened to me about as often as finding a hunk of diamond in the middle of Pioneer Square.

"I hope it's all right with you if we make a stop on the way there," he said. "They'll probably be closed by the time we get back."

"Who will?"

"I want to stop at that little perfume boutique on Front Street and pick up some bubble bath for Mom."

"Is it her birthday?"

"No. It's just something she really likes."

At the store, he sniffed everything carefully before selecting one with a rose scent. "Do you want some?" he asked me as he took it to the counter.

"No, thanks. I don't do baths. I'm a showerer."

"So is Tam. I don't think she's taken a bath since she was about four. Mom, on the other hand, could soak in the tub for two hours."

"It's too hard to deal with my hair in the bathtub."

He touched it. "How does it not get in the way in the shower?"

"I have to tie it up and put it under a shower cap."

"You haven't thought of cutting it, have you?"

"My mother did, once. I saw the scissors and screamed. And ran. She got the message."

"How old were you?"

"About six. It was already down to my waist."

We were back outside. He fluffed my hair gently before opening the car door for me. "I'm glad you didn't let her cut it. You have the most beautiful hair I've ever seen."

Was he flattering me?

Did I care?

Maybe a little. He was the obvious suspect to have jammed the elevator, especially if it had happened when Tamara was in the hospital. Maybe he'd also fired his father's gun. Unfortunately, since he'd had no interaction at all with Marguerite in the almost three weeks I'd been with the family, it was almost impossible to figure out what kind of relationship they had—other than *none*.

But even a woman who knew she wasn't a natural beauty enjoyed a compliment every now and then.

I brightened even more when we got to the art museum. Even when I was feeling bad, seeing beauty created—whether from positive or negative feelings— made me feel good. Someone had stuck a Christmas-style gold bow on the nose of one of the lions that flank the entrance, and Joel pulled it off and handed it to me with a flourish. "*Zahav, ahuva.*"

I had to smile. "What's this, a Hebrew lesson? What did you just say?"

"*Zahav* is the Hebrew word for gold. It has an alternate meaning, which is, something of brilliance or splendor."

"What about the other word?"

He motioned me inside ahead of him without looking at me. "Nothing, really."

The first room we went into had a religious display. Joel pointed to an oil painting. "I've always wondered how they preserve these for so many years. Every once in a while you read that some art work had to be restored, but not as often as you would expect for something that's hundreds of years old."

"It's pretty simple." I'd studied art on my own enough to know more than most people. "A lot of what we refer to as 'oil' painting is really encaustic—that's a process where melted beeswax is used. That lasts forever. And on some of them, there's a final coat of removable varnish, almost like shellac, that's put on to protect against age and handling. That's a pain, though, because it takes about six months to dry and has to be reapplied periodically."

"So does someone like you use that stuff?"

"Are you kidding? That's for paintings that are going to be on display for years. I just buy oil paints if I want to work with them, and most that are made now are specially treated anyway."

"Is that your favorite way to paint?"

"No. I like pencils and fine-point markers best. When I was younger and more ambitious I used watercolor, but you wouldn't believe how much trouble it is. It's good for Monet-style landscapes or painting where the color is more important than the detail, but not for anything like portraits. I used to do a lot of fabric painting, and my grandfather would set up a booth for me at the powwows—" I stopped.

"The what?"

"Powwows. Indian gatherings. The Yakima Nation—that's what I am, Yakima—has one in September during Native American Observance week, and they also have a summer retreat in July that's a big deal. My grandfather used to take me to them and get me a booth so I could sell the shirts I'd painted. I'd earn enough spending money for the whole summer, at least."

"You said your grandfather's not around anymore."

I shook my head. "He died last March." *Wow*. It was still hard to say.

"I'm sorry." His voice was a gentle caress. "Those must be good memories."

I smiled. "My favorites."

"September? I'd like to go with you."

"I'm not going."

"Why not?"

I didn't answer. It should have been obvious.

Joel took both my hands in his before saying, very softly, "If I'd given my granddaughter the best memories of her life, I'd want her to do more than remember. I'd want her to keep our heritage alive."

"Someday I'll go back. It's just too soon." What I didn't tell him was that not all the memories were good, and that a lot of the good ones had been spoiled—by stuff I'd done, that I was finally realizing I couldn't blame on my parents or anyone else. I'd done it, knowing it was wrong, and stupid.

Joel squeezed my hands then released them and followed me to the Asian art exhibit.

"You're in the wrong business," he told me as he watched me examine the pattern on a piece of jade. "Don't you think you're wasting your time typing third-graders' books?"

"Her new one is a lot different. It's definitely not for third-graders."

"Oh, yeah? What's it about?"

"A fourteen-year-old boy with a lot of problems." He wasn't really paying attention, and I got the idea he'd asked just to be polite. "I guess you haven't read any of her books."

He shook his head. "No. They don't interest me."

I wondered what did interest him. "Tamara says you hate your job. Why didn't you get a different degree? Isn't there anything you'd rather be doing?"

"Of course. But a man, if he plans to have a family, has to be prepared to support it."

"I guess you plan to have one."

"Yes. I love kids. I'd like to have three, at least."

I laughed. "At least? I've always wanted four. I'd like my own family to be the kind I always wanted when I was growing up."

"Didn't you say you're an only child?"

"Yes."

Joel chuckled. "That has its advantages. I love Tam, but sometimes she's such a pain in the butt I spend five minutes with her and can't sit down for a week."

I believed it. "I know brothers and sisters fight as children. But I wish I had them now, as an adult. I don't have anyone who's shared my history to spend time with or talk to, and I don't make friends easily."

"Maybe you should spend more time around people like you. Get a job at a gallery or something."

"That's easier said than done. There are a lot more artists than jobs for us."

"Maybe there are. But one way to be sure you never make a living doing what you are, being an artist, is to settle for a typing job."

"Oh yeah?" I wasn't too crazy about the path the conversation was taking. "What about your job? Do you love it?"

It was a rhetorical question and he knew it. "There wasn't much out there for marketing majors."

"But is that who you are?"

He didn't answer.

I didn't give up. "What are you good at? Never mind. I already know. Taking care of your sister. Keeping peace in your family. What's the professional term for a peacemaker?"

He almost smiled. Almost. "A mediator? Arbitrator?"

"You could do that kind of work with a business degree. You could do it just by being who you are."

His face softened. "I kind of like who *you* are." He turned me to face him and brought his lips down to mine.

When I opened my eyes, the security guard was grinning at us. Joel was giving me the same adoring gaze I'd seen on Jenna's face in her wedding picture. If this was lust, it was the strongest I had ever felt it. If it was love, it was the quickest it had ever happened in recorded history.

I wasn't sure which it was. But something was making my legs tremble and the rest of me tingle.

I scooted away from Joel as fast as I could. He caught up with me in the next room. "What's wrong, Louisa? Did I make you angry?"

"No."

"Then why did you run away from me?"

"We're in a public museum."

"Are you embarrassed? Ashamed?"

"Of course not."

"Then what's the problem?"

What could I tell him? That I suspected him of clamping pliers to the elevator cable so his grandmother would be trapped upstairs and unable to interact with the family? Or that I wondered if he had lied to me on my first week, claiming not to have heard a gunshot when I was now convinced there had been one? Or maybe I could tell him his sister's behavior bordered on bizarre and his mother acted as though she were on another planet. *Right.*

Nothing I thought could be repeated.

He pulled me close to him and I could feel his heart beating against my chest. Or was that my heart? "You're the most intriguing woman I've ever met."

"Joel, you've only known me a few weeks."

"Doesn't it seem as though we've known each other longer?"

"Yes." Something had definitely clicked between us. Joel's eyes sparkled with it. "Let's finish our tour before they arrest us for public indecency." I moved out of his arms and headed for the regional art exhibit. The security guard was peeking around the corner at us.

"I hate stuff like that." Joel pointed to an abstract of what looked like gray paint mixed with sand.

"You have to know what it's saying," I told him. "Art is contextual. One time I came here with my parents and there was this mural that was just a blob of gray and black, and my immediate reaction to it was 'Ugh.' But it turned out that the artist had painted it as a reaction to the Berlin Wall. This—" I looked at the legend. "This is ash from Mt. St. Helens. It's not really abstract. It's saying something."

"The Berlin Wall, huh?" Joel looked thoughtful. "Do you think that'll come down in our lifetime?" He didn't wait for an answer. "I think part of Mom's family ended up in West Germany after World War II."

"Where are they from?"

"Poland. I doubt there's any of her family left in Poland. It became a place Jews didn't want to be. A place they couldn't be, without being killed or shipped off to concentration camps."

"Does she have any family left? Any who live here?"

"No. Her parents came to this country when it started getting ugly in Poland. I think they were the only ones."

"Are they, uhm, dead?"

"No." He looked grim. "They disowned Mom when she got married at seventeen instead of going to college."

I couldn't do anything but stare.

"She never talks about them, but I think they moved to Chicago before I was born."

"I'm sorry." And I was. I couldn't imagine not having grandparents. Nor being disowned, for anything. My parents were tired of my inability to settle down and keep a job, but if I were in real trouble and had no other options, I could probably call them.

Who was it who'd once said "Home is where, when you have to go there, they have to take you in"?

Except my parents had moved, and their home wasn't mine. So Jenna and I had something in common.

Joel gave a dismissive shrug and turned away from the Mt. St. Helens picture. "I guess that explains a lot of why Mom is the way she is. Why she's hard to get close to. She's been burned pretty badly." He made a show of looking at his watch. "Are you hungry? Why don't we go somewhere for dinner? I have the perfect place in mind."

"Where?"

"McDonald's."

He had to be kidding.

He was. "My second choice was Ivar's."

Would I ever turn down Ivar's?

Would the Mariners ever win the World Series?

I hadn't realized how much I missed my own apartment until we were heading north on I-5 toward the U District. Ivar's was in the opposite direction, in Wallingford, and when Joel turned left onto Forty-Fifth, I couldn't help staring out the window at my neighborhood, several blocks east. He glanced at me but didn't say anything until he was maneuvering his way around the circular esplanades that punctuated Meridian. "Do you live around here?"

"In the U District."

"You could ride your bike here, if you have one."

I grinned. "I've done it a couple of times, in the summer. The weather has to be perfect and I have to be feeling pretty ambitious."

"It's just about perfect tonight. Do you want to get an outside table?"

Ivar's had a deck that overlooked Lake Union. The sun would be setting soon and the lights on the water from the city skyline would be hard to pass up. But it was the inside décor, designed to look like an Indian longhouse, that I really loved. I shook my head. "We can go outside after we eat."

When we got inside, I inhaled the alder smoke for several moments before pointing to a set of portraits on the wall. "Does she look like me?"

"Sort of," Joel said, examining it carefully. "But you're prettier. Softer. *Yakima Woman*—that's what you are, right?

"Yeah. Hey, for all I know, that could be one of my relatives." I gestured to a totem pole. "You know that expression *Low man on the totem pole*? They've got it backward. It actually went from top to bottom, so the low man was really the high man."

We got a window seat and watched the dusk while we ate. The food was terrific, as usual, and I stuffed myself with barbecued salmon and cornbread.

Joel watched me with a mixture of amusement and approval. "The last three girls I went out with were on diets and wouldn't eat anything but lettuce and diet pop. I'd rather see a woman enjoy her food."

"You don't have to worry about that. The only kind of diet I'd ever go on is to gain weight."

He smiled at me over a forkful of cole slaw. "I like you just the way you are."

"Are you feeding me a line?"

"How could I? Your mouth hasn't been empty for the last half hour."

"Oh, funny man." I pretended to shoot water at him from my straw. "I can look in mirrors. I'm hardly the vision you make me out to be with your compliments."

"But you're real."

I wasn't sure what he meant. "As opposed to what?"

"A lot of women." He took another bite. "I think women get confused about what we—guys—look for. I don't care how beautiful a woman is if what's on the inside isn't the same. It'd be like opening a package and finding a rock or empty pop can."

"Speaking of." I'd be broaching a tough subject, but I was curious. "Why doesn't your mother ever go out? I mean, she's relatively young; she's gorgeous. I would think she'd have a line of suitors, to use an old-fashioned term."

"I don't know why." Joel set his fork down and rested his chin on his folded hands. "Maybe it's her choice. Maybe she's too busy with Airtech. And maybe no one wants her."

"*What?*"

"It's what I was just saying. She has an unapproachable air."

"Maybe she's afraid some guy would just want her money."

"I think it's more of a defense against outsiders. Unfortunately, Mom's forgotten the difference between an outsider and her own family."

"Was she always like that?"

"I don't think so." He picked up his fork and jabbed it at his plate without spearing anything. "My parents took us to their fifteen-year high school reunion when I was fourteen and Tam was nine, and that's the most fun I think I've ever seen Mom have. She giggled with her girlfriends and danced the Loco-Motion and the Mashed Potato. The DJ played 'Can't Help Falling in Love,' you know, that old Elvis song, and everyone cleared the floor for my parents. I didn't even know that was their song. They danced to it like they were still seventeen and eighteen and in love. Tam and I kept looking at each other like, who are these two strangers and why did our parents leave them behind?"

I didn't know what to say.

"My father told everyone about when they met. They were the only juniors in a calculus class and Mom was the only girl, and I guess she had put some smart-aleck in his place who thought girls didn't belong in calc. Everyone roared with laughter over that story, and my father preened and Mom blushed. She was very beautiful that night. I saw what my father fell in love with. And vice-versa."

I poked at my coffee with the spoon.

"I haven't seen it since. I don't think Tam needs to worry about the slimy accountant. If Mom treats him the way she treats everyone else, he wouldn't spend five minutes more than he had to with her."

I almost choked on my coffee.

Joel stared into his. "Don't misunderstand me. I love my mother. I would do anything for her. I just hate what my father's money has turned her into."

"She doesn't strike me that way at all. She's been really nice to me."

"You're not a threat to her." Joel tipped his cup as though he was going to take a sip of coffee, then set it back down. "Besides, none of us want you to go to Grandmother and tell her we haven't made you feel welcome."

Well, hell.

Joel saw me staring at my plate and his head tipped to one side. "What?"

"Thanks, Joel. That makes me feel good. Here I thought maybe you actually liked me."

He reached across the table for my hands, but I put them in my lap. "You know I do. We all do. I'm just saying Grandmother made it clear you were to feel welcome. So we did what she wanted. Why is that offensive?"

I couldn't explain, and what he said made sense. But it also made me feel as though I was living in a houseful of phonies.

But it was different for them. Every step—or misstep—had the potential of being front-page news. Any kind of normal life was out of the question, and for Tamara especially, Jenna was an impossible act to follow.

Joel seemed to read my mind. "Do you know what I would give to be any regular guy? Do you know how much I hate being rich? I hate every damn minute of it. One thing I'm really enjoying about this evening is not having to wonder, *does she like me or my money?* Correction—Mom's money. Grandmother's money. Tam and I don't own a thing."

Someday they would, but there was no need to point that out.

He went on. "You're too good for that. I love the way you say whatever you want. You don't treat us any differently because we're rich. I can't remember the last time someone did that."

"Money doesn't impress me."

He smiled at me for several moments before saying, "I know."

We walked out onto the deck and watched the sunset and the blinking city lights bouncing on the water's surface. The Space Needle towered in the distance, and the trees in West Seattle made imposing shadows along the skyline. The boats glimmered. I watched them and basked in the smell of Ivar's food and the warmth of Joel's arm around my waist. This time, when he turned my face to his to kiss me, we didn't stop for a long time.

When we finally broke it off, I was trembling. I opened my mouth and what popped out of it was, "Don't you have a girlfriend?"

I couldn't imagine that he didn't.

"Yes," Joel said softly. "You."

He pulled me close and nothing else existed.

It was foolish. I knew I should be more objective about someone I suspected of jamming the elevator and maybe even shooting at Marguerite—or at me—but I couldn't. All I could think of was how long it had been since I'd felt the way Joel made me feel. And how much I needed it.

I pulled away from him while I still could. "Let's go. Can we stop at my apartment? I want to pick up some music." I also wanted to pick up my drawing pencils. It was too late to stop at U-Dub's bookstore, where I did a lot of my shopping.

"A gentleman never turns down a lady's request." Joel

took my arm and led me around the deck and back to the parking lot.

We didn't talk on the way to my apartment beyond the essentials of how to get there. Joel broke the relative silence as I was opening the door. "What kind of music are you picking up?"

"Some mix tapes of bluegrass favorites. Nothing you'd know."

"Why don't you play some of them for me?"

"It's sort of an acquired taste. Unless you've grown up on it, like I did, you probably won't like it." That was an understatement. I couldn't even picture what his reaction to Bobby Osborne's distinctive Kentucky tenor would be.

"Try me."

I glanced at the telephone long enough to remember I hadn't talked to my parents since before I'd started this job. They didn't even know where I was. I didn't have an answering machine. People who wanted to get hold of me could usually do so eventually.

But not now.

Guilt twisted my stomach. I hadn't gotten along with my parents for a while. They'd been angry and disappointed when I dropped out of the community college and even more so when I did it again. When they moved to Scottsdale, they'd made it clear I wasn't welcome to come with them—as if I'd even thought of leaving Seattle—and they expected me to make my own way.

I hadn't even told them about this job, much less the three before it. I didn't want to hear what they would say—or not say. I didn't really think they'd been trying to call me. But if they had, it was disrespectful to leave them wondering why I never answered the phone. I'd have to call them.

But not with Joel here.

I rummaged through my tapes and records, trying to find something I thought he could tolerate. Finally I selected Bill Monroe's "Watson Blues," a mournful instrumental, and put it on. "This is the guy Tamara thinks ought to be shot."

He tried to laugh. "Don't pay any attention to Tam."

"Why? Because no one else does?" Had Joel realized how much alike his sister and I were? Rough around the edges, or maybe all the way through, trying to find our way in a world that didn't seem to have a place for us, using music to cope with a loss that had taken over our lives.

He didn't answer. He helped himself to a seat on the sofa and listened to the song in silence, studiously examining a spot on his crisp jeans. When it was over he looked up at me. "That's very melancholy."

"That's why it's called 'Watson *Blues*.'"

"Is that what you listen to all the time?"

"Not that one song, or artist, but the same type of music, yeah. Most of it's pretty upbeat, I guess because of the kinds of instruments you find in a bluegrass band. Even the sad songs have a hard-driving beat. 'Rockytop,' which is one my favorite songs, is a real toe-tapper. But when you listen to the words it's a sad song, about a guy who grew up in the country and now lives in the city and feels displaced and homesick."

"Doesn't it depress you? If I listened to that all the time, I'd feel worse—I mean, it would depress me."

"It doesn't. Nothing is more comforting."

"Tam's like that. Maybe you and she have more in common than you think."

Yes, he had realized.

He rose and examined the books on my shelf before tugging one free. "This is one of my favorites, too."

I couldn't see what he was holding. "Which?"

"*The Diary of Anne Frank.*" He pronounced it properly, *Ahn Frahnk*, not the Anglicized way.

That was a surprise. "I thought only girls read her."

He shook his head. "It was required reading in eighth grade. Then when Tam was about fourteen, she had chicken pox. No one else would go near her, so I brought her meals and medicine to her and read to her. This was one of the books we read."

It didn't surprise me that he was the one taking care of his sister.

He put the book back. "I've always thought I would someday name my daughter after Anne. Her given name was Annelies." *Ahn-uh-leez.* "It's a pretty name and she was a real heroine. She never lost her spirit, even looking evil in the eye." He pointed to a couple of my paintings on the wall. "Did you paint these yourself?"

"See my signature?"

He gazed at my favorite, an eagle and a wolf with a background of snowy mountains, for a long time. "These are incredible."

"Thanks." I turned away before he could see my face.

Too late. "What's wrong?"

I tried to laugh. "Nothing important."

He took a step toward me and laid one hand on my arm. "It is important. Can you tell me?"

I gestured to the painting. "I was painting that for my grandpa. He died before it was done." Another piece of unfinished business. "So I finished it and kept it. But every time I see it I think, *that wasn't supposed to be mine.*"

Silence. I couldn't look at him.

I'd never said anything that personal to anyone.

Then he was next to me, his hands warm on my shoulders. "Maybe it was."

How could he understand? When, as far as I could see, he never even spoke to his grandmother?

Maybe I could find a way to tell him that someday she wouldn't be there anymore, and he might feel the same way I did about my grandfather.

You can't get the time back.

He stepped away and pointed to a photo on the coffee table. "When was that taken?"

I smiled for the first time since dinner. "Three years ago. That was my first Fancy Shawl Dance as an adult."

"Do you still have that dress?"

I pointed to the bedroom. "In the closet."

He hesitated in the doorway. "May I see it?"

I nodded.

He took the wingdress and matching shawl out of the closet and held them up. His mouth hung open. "Wow. These are stunning."

I grinned. "There's matching boots, too." One of the elders had made the outfit for me.

"I'd like to come the next time you do this dance."

The grin dropped off my face.

Joel flinched as though I'd slapped him. "You wouldn't want me there?"

"I told you, I don't go anymore."

He sat on the edge of the bed. "You're kidding."

I didn't answer.

"Is it too hard without your grandfather?" His voice was as soft as the cotton shawl in his hand.

I didn't know how to explain why I hadn't gone to any of the Indian Society meetings or events since Grandpa died, except to say that it wouldn't be right without him anyway.

"If this—" Joel tipped his head toward my dress. "—is that important to you, I want to be a part of it."

"Maybe." That sounded dismissive. "I mean, maybe

I'll go back. And if I do, you can come with me." I turned away and dug through a desk drawer for my colored pencils.

"Louisa?"

"Yeah?" I didn't look up from a box of art supplies.

"Why don't we lie down for a little while?"

I stopped and turned to stare at him. "Are you joking?"

His arms, which had been half extended to me, dropped to his sides. "I didn't think I was that bad. I mean, the only time I cover the mirror is when I'm sitting *shiva*."

"Huh?"

"Nothing."

I felt bad. "Don't take it personally. I just think if we lie down, neither of us will want to get up."

"I promise I'll be a gentleman," he said quietly. "I just want to hold you."

I put my dress and shawl away, shut off the lamp, and lay down next to him.

Joel was true to his word. He didn't try anything, and I didn't know if I was disappointed or not. As I lay with him in the darkness, feeling his heart beat beneath my cheek, I thought of my ex-boyfriend. Paulo was Polynesian and had the kind of family I'd always wanted—huge and happy—and the kind of house I loved—noisy, warm, and messy. When he broke up with me, not long after I dropped out of Seattle Central for the second time, I missed the companionship of another artist and the feeling of a family far more than I missed whatever romance we'd had. In my embarrassment at being dumped, it took me awhile to realize I'd loved Paulo's place in my life a lot more than I'd loved him—if I ever had.

I'd go back to the Roberts' house with Joel, but it

would be hard. It was a somber house and being in it dragged me down. If I continued to see Joel after the book was done, it would be in spite of his family and not because of it.

"Louisa?" Joel whispered.

"Hmm?"

"You don't have to go back."

I sat up and stared.

He toyed with a strand of my hair that fell over his chest. "Why are you looking at me like that?"

"What makes you think I don't want to go back?" How did he know what I was thinking?

He snorted. "Who would?"

"I can't just walk out in the middle of the book."

"Why not?"

Because that's what I've done all my life.

Because every time I lose a job or do something stupid, I see my grandfather's face, and I know how much better he thought I could be. But I'm not.

But I wasn't ready to say that to Joel. "Because it's my job. Are you going to support me if I walk out on it?"

He stroked my back and neck. "We can talk about that."

No, we couldn't. I could walk out, but to do so would be to leave Marguerite alone with whoever was responsible for the elevator and the gunshot.

I'd never replace Grandpa, but for the first time in months I had someone to care about. To care for.

But how could I know if I was falling in love with…not a *murderer*, but someone vicious enough to neglect and mistreat a disabled old woman?

I had played the wrong song. "Where Do We Go From Here" would have been a better choice. I didn't know if we could—or would—go anywhere.

Joel's hand rested on my stomach, discreetly below my breasts. I shoved it aside and jumped up. "Let's go."

I half expected an argument, but got none. Nor did I get a goodnight kiss when we got back to the house. I put one of my tapes in my Walkman and played it for a long time, but for some reason, the music didn't comfort me the way it usually did.

Chapter 11

Monday was Labor Day. I went downstairs to breakfast and walked in on a simmering scene. Jenna was dressed in slacks and a light sweater, prepared to go to the office and take advantage of the empty building and silent telephone to get some extra work done. Tamara was apparently trying to talk her mother into staying home so they could spend the day together as a family.

I couldn't wait to hear what Jenna had to say about that.

Tamara dumped sugar into her coffee and stirred hard, slopping some onto the table. She ignored the stain. "Mom, listen to me. Please, just this one day, don't go to work. Let's do something together. All three of us. You don't have to work."

"Unfortunately, I do. When that Northwest plane crashed in Detroit last month, the FAA changed its requirements, and now all planes will have to have devices that tell air traffic controllers their altitude." She sounded like she was giving a stockholder speech. My eyes were already glazing over. I could only imagine what Tamara's reaction would be.

I didn't have long to wonder. "Mom. This isn't the boardroom. Talk to *me*."

"I'm trying to." Jenna's voice had taken on the familiar edge. "Our engineers have to work with the FAA and the airlines on that technology."

"But you don't. Why don't you do like everyone else and pass that job on to some underling?"

Jenna set her spoon down. "I'm trying to set an example. Be a role model, for you and other young women."

"What? How?"

Good question.

"When I inherited this company, everyone expected me to delegate all responsibility and become a figurehead CEO. But I didn't, because I didn't want to be the woman who's afraid to enter what's traditionally been a man's field. A lot of people thought I couldn't handle it, and I wasn't going to prove them right."

"No, you just didn't want to face Grandmother and tell her you couldn't keep Dad's legacy going."

Joel sat so still he might have been playing freeze tag.

Jenna glanced at me, her cheeks fuchsia.

"Never mind," Tamara said. "This isn't about Dad or Grandmother. It's about you. You don't ever want to be with us. Why can't we be a real family, just for one day?"

A moment of silence, then Jenna said, "All right. I have a lot to do, but I'll try to come home a little early."

Tamara muttered something unintelligible as she shoved a forkful of French toast into her mouth.

Interesting. They'd both made good points. I liked Tamara, most of the time, at least, but her headstrong attitude was the polar opposite of Jenna's gentleness and grace.

I didn't blame Jenna for preferring to use her holiday to work rather than spar with Tamara.

On the other hand, Tamara was right. Jenna wouldn't lose anything by spending the day with her daughter, and if it was what Tamara wanted, maybe Jenna could make more of an effort.

"Aw right!" Joel crowed from behind the *P-I*.

"What?" Tamara asked.

"There's a Stoogefest going on at the drive-in. Let's go." He turned to me. "Do you want to come with us?"

"Not on your life. The Stooges are for idiots."

Joel flapped his hand on top of his head and jabbed two fingers in the general direction of my eyes. "I resemble that remark."

"We know," Tamara said to me. "That's why we're asking you."

"Tamara!" I half expected Jenna to start fanning herself like a southern belle.

"Oh, Mom, Louisa knows I'm kidding. Don't you, Louisa?"

"I certainly hope so," Jenna mumbled. "Joel, which drive-in is showing the Three Stooges?"

"Puget Park."

"You're going to drive all the way to Everett?"

"It's not that far."

"No, but it isn't a pleasant drive." Jenna was right. The scenery, if it could be called that, was little more than marshland, and the lumber mill near Everett smelled foul enough to sear the stripe off a skunk's back.

"It's not so bad. At least I'm not talking about taking the girls to Midtown."

"Why? Where is that?"

The three of us just looked at one another and snickered. If Jenna wasn't in the habit of hanging around porno shows, I wasn't going to be the one to enlighten her.

"Now that I think about it, that's a good plan." Jenna nodded at Joel. "You won't have to attend the dinner—or try to avoid it."

Joel saw my questioning look. "Mom's having a dinner party tonight. One of those fancy ones where everyone dresses up like the Stooges in *Hoi Polloi*." He picked up a spoon and held it to his eye like a monocle. "By the bye, how is the countess?" he asked Tamara in a faux-British accent.

"It'd be okay if they all ended up having pie fights like they do in the Stooges," Tamara said.

Jenna gave her a Look. "That's why I'm glad you're going to the movies."

c/ɔc/ɔ

After breakfast I went to the music room. Along with my tapes and drawing pencils, I'd brought the small harmonica Grandpa had bought me during my forced exile from the powwows and bluegrass festivals. I don't have much musical ability, but lots of practice had brought about a recognizable version of "Boil the Cabbage," and I wanted to hear how it would sound in a room with such good acoustics.

Jenna heard me playing and came in. "I didn't know you could play the harmonica."

"I can't." I wiped it off on my T-shirt and put it in my back pocket. "That's really the only song I can play."

"What's the name of it?"

"'Boil Them Cabbage Down,' but most people just refer to it as 'Boil the Cabbage.' It's kind of a bluegrass, old-time standard, especially for fiddlers. If you can play it, you can get by in just about any jam session."

"How did you come to like bluegrass? That's unusual for someone your age, not to mention in the Pacific Northwest. Are you from the South?"

I shook my head. "Native Seattleite. And it's not as unusual as you'd think. In Darrington, there's a lot of transplanted North Carolinians, and they have a bluegrass festival in July. My grandfather used to take me to it every year." I didn't need to tell her why he stopped.

"Do you come from a close family?" There was a hint of wistfulness in her voice that surprised me.

"No, not really. But I was close to my grandfather."

I waited for the inevitable response, something along the lines of *Too bad my kids aren't close to their grandmother.* Or better yet, *My kids aren't close to their grandmother because...*

But of course she would never share such a thing with a relative stranger.

"What does *ahuva* mean?" I finally asked.

Her head tilted slightly to one side and a faint smile touched the corners of her mouth. "Where did you hear that?"

All of a sudden I wished I hadn't brought it up. "Uhm, well, it's nothing."

The smile blossomed. "It's an endearment. It means 'beloved.'"

Oh.

I needed to get away from her before my face gave me away, more than it probably already had. "Well, uh, I'll see you later, I guess."

I went upstairs and knocked on Marguerite's door, and she called for me to come in. She was awake and sipping coffee. "Is your nurse coming today?" I asked her.

She set her cup down and brandished her ballpoint. "No. She's off for the holiday. You're just in time. I was thinking about some of your suggestions. Bring me the entire manuscript and we'll work on it now." She smiled at me. "You seem to enjoy my family's company. However, we're getting to the meat of the book, so you might be busier than you have been for a few days."

"That's okay. This is my job." Good. I was off the hook for going to the Stoogefest.

⎰⎱⎰⎱

Except I wasn't. Marguerite was worn out by early evening. She dismissed me a few minutes after five and told me to go enjoy the evening. "The new season of *Designing Women* starts next Monday, so tonight there's a Season One recap." She already had the TV remote in her hand. "I don't know who's in worse trouble, Suzanne or Mary Jo."

I had to admit I'd never watched the show.

"It's for Women of a Certain Age." She patted my hand indulgently. "And you have a long way to go, Louisa."

I told her I would rather sit and watch *Designing Women* with her, but she was adamant. "You've earned a night out. It might do you some good to be around young people instead of spending all your time with me."

At least I would be relatively safe. Joel would be driving. And both Jenna and Marguerite knew where we were going, so what could Tamara do to me?

Joel had borrowed a friend's pickup truck for the excursion. It was ready and waiting by six o'clock, in all its hideous glory. One could only guess what its original color had been, because the current color was rust. It was dented in several spots as though its owner had taken it to a bumper car arena and let ten other cars hit it. The pass-through window was long gone, but a jagged hunk of it haunted the corner by the passenger's head. It made the worst Indian car I'd ever seen look like a Rolls-Royce.

I looked at it, and at Tamara in a pair of old jeans, a huge Sea U sweatshirt that obviously belonged to her brother, and white Reeboks with yellow laces, and laughed without amusement. "So this is how rich kids have fun—you pretend to be commoners."

She looked me up and down, pausing to stare pointedly at my suede fringed top. "It must be nice not having to pretend."

"After living with this family, I'm proud to be common."

"Ladies," Joel entreated, putting an arm around each of us. "Let's get on the road before Mom's guests show up. They're due any minute." As Tamara climbed into the truck he whispered in my ear, "No 'rich kid' jokes, please. They're not funny."

No, they wouldn't be. I looked into his dark eyes and felt even smaller than my five feet. "Sorry."

He squeezed my hand.

The drive-in was jammed, and it was easy to see what kind of crowd it was. Beer cans peppered the ground, and every second car or truck was full of young men who were full of their contents. Joel swung into a spot next to a group of five rowdies who were washing down their Skipper's with something that came in a bottle too big to be beer.

There was no point in asking Joel if he knew what the heck he was doing, so I kept quiet and monkeyed with my 3-D glasses.

We nestled into the pickup bed among a pile of blankets and Joel reached into the cooler for a Bud Lite. "Beer, Louisa?"

"I don't drink, thanks."

"Nothing?"

"Not a drop."

Tamara leaned around Joel to gaze curiously at me. "How come?"

"Why should I?"

"To relax."

"I don't think that's the way the Great Spirit intended for us to relax."

"Are you an alcoholic?"

"No!"

"I hear that happens to a lot of Indians."

I wanted to take the proffered Bud Lite and shampoo her dyed hair with it. "And it was offensive to you when I made smart-cracks about rich kids? This is what happens when you watch the Three Stooges. You see Indians jumping around yelling and talking about 'take-um paleface scalp' and you think that's what we're all—"

"Chill. I didn't mean anything. That's just what I've heard. I didn't say it was true."

"Well, it is. For more people than I want to know about. I don't drink because I don't want to take any chances."

She shut up.

I stared down at the dirty metal of the pickup bed. "My grandfather caught me drinking at a festival when I was fifteen." The Spilyay Native and Western Art Show in Toppenish, long a favorite of Grandpa's and mine. "The festivals were no-alcohol, but someone sneaked some in anyway, and we, the kids, kind of got out of hand. Booze, tobacco, uhm, some legal and some not." *Just say no* was not part of our vocabulary. "Grandpa caught me and snatched me out of there and took me home, reaming me the whole way about why I would want to end up like some of the people he'd known for years." People on the reservation, although I didn't really want to say that to Joel and Tamara. They'd never get it.

Grandpa had been smart enough—and lucky enough—to get away from the reservation. People tried to make good lives for their families, but a reservation was a reservation, and the poverty, dropout, unemployment, and alcoholism rates were at least double what they were in the general population. Tribal bingo was promising to save us all, but I wondered whether it would deliver anything but addiction and despair. It sounded like the kind of con job you would never see in a wealthy white neighborhood, and I hated that they were trying to do it to us.

It was a tough decision for anyone who chose to move away, because it might mean losing ties to the community and culture. Grandpa decided it was worth taking the chance and had done his best to hold onto our heritage.

Joel and Tamara were listening, waiting for me to go on. "Then when I got home, my parents grounded me from the festivals until I got out of high school. Almost three years. I kept thinking they'd change their minds and let up, but they never did." I'd missed out on three years of Grandpa's life, three years I could never get back. He wouldn't let me blame my parents, and maybe he was right.

"I don't dare drink. Or smoke. Or do anything else. I think if I did, Grandpa's ghost would haunt me." I tried to laugh but it was hard, remembering my mother's face and her words. '*When you get out of high school, you can make as much of a fool out of yourself as you want. Until then, I'm not going to let you ruin your life with drinking and lung cancer. I've seen too much of it among our people.*'

It was the first time I'd ever heard her refer to the Yakima Nation as "our people."

"You call yourself *Indian*," Tamara said. "Aren't we supposed to say, like, Native American or something?"

I almost smiled. "You can. We tend to say 'Indian.'"

Joel rubbed my shoulder. "Do you want me to get you a pop?"

"Yeah. Thanks. Dr. Pepper, if they have it."

He nodded. "What kind do you want, Tam?"

"Beer."

He shook his head. "Nothing doing."

"What'd you bring the beer for?"

"Louisa and me. I didn't know she wasn't going to drink any."

"I'll take her share." She smirked at me. I ignored her.

"Tam, I am not contributing to your delinquency. And you know you can't even have cough syrup with some of that medicine you're on."

"You're not the doctor."

"No, but I can follow her orders—and make sure you follow them." Without another word, he climbed out of the truck and headed for the concession stand.

"He should have taken this with him." Tamara grabbed a beer and glugged it down in about ten seconds.

I watched her, appalled. What could I do? Snatch it from her? Was it my business to take care of her? Joel could have that thankless job with my blessing. He would probably smell the stuff on her breath when he returned.

But no, she'd thought of that, too. She took a package of Certs from her hip pocket and emptied about four of them into her mouth.

Joel returned laden with pop and candy. He sniffed suspiciously. "Tam, why have you been eating peppermints?"

She was all wide-eyed innocence. "My medicine gives me bad breath. You know that."

He glared at her but said nothing. It was a convincing enough story. Tamara did have an odd smell sometimes, maybe a little yeasty or fruity.

The show started and they forgot about arguing, beer, and everything else except howling with laughter over every word and slap. Joel went through the beer at such a rate he didn't notice Tamara's sneaking at least two more cans. Great, I would have to drive, and probably argue with them first. Although, maybe that was why they'd wanted me along, why they'd actually pressed for me to go—to be a designated driver.

Except Joel had offered me the beer.

Or maybe they just wanted me away from Marguerite. Maybe they were afraid she would tell me something they didn't want me to know.

If only she would.

Tamara reached behind Joel to nudge me and point to the screen. The Stooges crept through a haunted house while Moe assured the others that while there was nothing to be afraid of, all the same, they'd better get the heck out of there.

Tamara's smile was closer to a leer. "If I were you, that's the way I'd feel about our house."

I snorted. "I'm not a stooge. I don't scare easily."

They looked at each other.

I went on, sensing an opportunity. "Is that how you feel about your house? That it's scary?"

Joel gestured to the screen. "Let's just watch the show."

"Oh, no. The Stooges aren't near as entertaining as your family is."

"Entertaining, huh?" Tamara shoved Joel's hand away from her mouth. "That's a good way to say it."

I had to get her talking while she was too tipsy to care what she said. "Well, except for the two of you, none of you seem to like one another."

"*Everyone* seems to like you. Especially my big brother."

Joel started to get up. "Tam, let's go get some more candy."

"What for? I still have some."

"Then put it in your mouth and stop talking."

"What? Your burgeoning romance isn't a fit topic of

conversation?" She barely got the words out, and "conversation" sounded closer to *cun-ver-SHAY-shun.*

"*Burgeoning?* Nice four-bit word," I told her. "Did they have vocabulary class in your fancy private school?"

"Who says we went to private school? Is that one of your rich-kid stereotypes?"

Whoops. I remembered the trophies in Carl's study, labeled ISSAQUAH JUNIOR HIGH and ISSAQUAH HIGH SCHOOL. She was right. "Sorry."

"It's okay." Tamara tossed a handful of M&Ms into her mouth and talked through them. "We would have if Grandmother'd had her way."

I reached for the bag. "Why? Public school was good enough for her son."

"That's why! She learned a lesson from what happened to him. She didn't want us to meet any Jewish girls and get married too young."

Joel almost spilled his beer. "Tamara!"

"What, Joel? It's true."

"Tam, just be quiet and watch the Stooges."

But Tamara had long passed the border of sobriety and restraint. "It's not like it's going to hurt anything if Louisa runs back to Grandmother and tells her we said that. Grandmother'll just say, 'Yeah, so what?' Anyway, Mom asked you not to tell anyone our business, didn't she, Louisa? Did you have to sign something like the other servants did?"

"No." *Huh.* Sign what?

Joel was up and tugging on Tamara's hand. "Louisa, I'm taking Tamara to get something to eat. Do you mind staying here?"

I clambered out of the truck bed. "Don't bother, Joel. If you want to talk to her in private, you go right ahead. I'm going to the bathroom. And when I get back, maybe it's time to leave." I held out my hand for the keys. "I'll drive. Both of you have had too much to drink."

"That's cool," Joel said, although he did not give me the keys. He began gathering up the blankets. "We'll be in the cab."

As I walked to the bathroom, I wondered what the hell they'd been talking about.

Marguerite had never said one word regarding her son's mixed marriage. In fact, a lot of people didn't even consider a marriage that crossed religions to be *mixed*. Maybe it had been different in the early sixties.

And maybe Marguerite would know better than to mention her disdain for Jenna, if indeed it were based on something so petty. I didn't have any use for bigotry of any kind.

Of course, that was assuming Tamara was telling the truth.

The line at the bathroom was too long and I didn't have to go bad enough to stand in it. It was a clear night and the full moon lit my way. I walked back through the parked vehicles toward the borrowed pickup, but when I was about two rows over, it suddenly started up with a roar and jerked out of its spot. I started running, but even that piece of junk was faster, and it weaved around the rows and sped toward the exit with squealing tires.

Chapter 12

O h, my God," I whispered.
        What was Joel thinking? Why had he done that to
me?

He knew he wasn't in any state to drive. He'd had
about six beers. If he were stopped on the way home he
would get hit with a fat DWI. Not that I gave a sack of
dirt whether he got in trouble or not, but there was always
the chance an innocent person would get hurt in the
process.

But how could I stop them, much less get back to the
house? There was a pay phone by the concession stand,
but since Joel had paid everyone's way, I hadn't brought
my wallet or even any change. Even if I called the house,
what would I say? Interrupt Jenna's dinner party to ask
her to send a cab after me?

Of course, Jenna didn't answer her own phone. I
wasn't sure if Carol could send a cab after me, COD,
without getting an okay from the boss.

Marguerite had her own phone, which she did
answer—at least she had the first time I'd called her. But
that option wasn't much better. Was I supposed to tell
Marguerite the kids had ditched me at the drive-in and
were tearing around in someone else's truck, drunk off
their faces?

Well, it was the truth.

No. This was my chance to get out. No reasonable person could expect me to stay now. I'd put up with a lot more than most people would have.

But I had no way to get back to my apartment. If I took a cab, it would cost a lot more than the maybe thirty dollars I had hidden in the pocket of an old pair of jeans in the back of my closet. Even if I went home, at some point I'd have to go back to the Roberts' house to collect my car and my things.

And that was just what I would do. *Get the hell away from that banana factory.*

I was next to the rowdies' car by then and one of them leaned out of the back window. "Did they leave you behind?"

I tossed up my hands. "It sort of looks that way."

They stopped laughing at the Stooges. The driver reached out and shut off the speaker. "Why'd they do that? Your mom make them take you?"

He thought I was a kid. "Uhm, no. I work for their grandmother."

He gave me an odd look.

I kind of shrugged. "Either they don't like her or they don't like me. Either way, they've ditched me, and I don't have any way to get back to Issaquah."

The back door opened and the guys in back scooted over as far as they could—about six inches. "Get in, babe. We'll take you."

I hesitated. No woman in her right mind would get in a car with five strange guys.

But what else could I do? It wasn't like I had a better alternative at the moment. I couldn't call the house anyway, because I didn't know the numbers, and God knew the Robertses wouldn't be listed in the White Pages.

At least the guys were offering me a seat next to the door. I could always jump out if I got a bad feeling.

Grandpa had once told me the inability to trust people was a reflection on one's own character. Maybe he was right and not everyone was up to no good. It was time to put some faith in someone other than myself.

The one riding shotgun laughed. "It's okay. We're not as harmless as we look."

"Will you shut up?" the driver said. To me: "He means we *are* harmless. Dumb, but nice."

"We wouldn't leave a girl stranded in Everett," one of the guys in the backseat chimed in.

What the hell. I got in.

"Where to, madame?" The driver tapped an imaginary cap brim as we pulled out of the drive-in.

"Just past Issaquah high school." I almost laughed at the thought of bringing the car full of guys back to the Roberts' house. It was hard to say who would be more surprised, them or Jenna and her dinner guests.

"You came a long way out," the guy next to me said as he crunched Cheetos from a crinkly bag.

He didn't know the half of it.

I kept my hand on the door handle in case anything went wrong, but no one did anything to set off my inner alarm system. After the first few miles, I settled in and began enjoying the guys' company. They turned out to be a bunch of childhood friends from Queen Anne. They all went to U-Dub and played baseball for the Huskies. Each one in turn pretended to be the star of the team but would promptly be shouted down by his buds. I watched for the pickup, but never saw it.

When we reached the Roberts' driveway a few of the guys gasped or whistled. "Holy shit," the driver said. "Who's this, the Gettys?"

"No one that normal." I got ready to get out. "Don't

worry about the gate. The owner will lose her—uhm, stuff if she has to change the password on account of me." Immediately, I realized how rude that sounded. "I mean, I'm sorry. You guys are completely trustworthy. Put in *Chiffons*."

He did and the gate opened. He drove up to the curving driveway by the front door. "I don't see your friends back yet."

Neither did I. There was an unfamiliar Dodge parked next to the garage—one of Jenna's guests had lingered.

She was about to be embarrassed in front of whoever it was.

"Thank you." It wasn't enough, but I didn't have any money to give the guys. "Uhm, I'd pay you for your trouble, but I haven't been paid for this job yet, and I—"

"No worries," the one riding shotgun said. "We learned a good lesson tonight. Stay away from rich kids!"

I tried to laugh. "You and me both."

They pulled away with a *beep-beep* and I stepped through the front door. Out of the corner of my eye I could see into the living room, where Jenna, in an emerald green cocktail dress, sat talking with a couple. She glanced up. "Oh, hello, Louisa. How were the Stooges?"

"Stupid," I said without thinking.

The man laughed. He wore wire-frame glasses and had light brown hair and a receding hairline.

"Bill, it's about time for us to leave," the woman said. She was petite and had a fresh-scrubbed look and a peach pants suit. They didn't look anything like what the Stooges had snootily dismissed as the *hoi polloi*. They looked like nice people, the kind my parents might have hung out with.

"Where are Joel and Tamara?" Jenna asked.

The anger I'd felt when I first saw them drive off came

walloping back. "I don't know." I tried not to spit the words. Now that I was safe, it wasn't as big a deal—

Oh, yeah, it was.

Jenna half stood. "What do you mean, you don't know?"

The couple seemed to sense something amiss. "Goodnight, Jenna. We'll see ourselves out," the man said, helping his wife to her feet. They each gave Jenna a chaste kiss on the cheek before hustling out the front door.

I faced Jenna. "I mean, I don't know. They left me at the drive-in. Joel was supposed to give me the keys, but he wouldn't, and when I went to the bathroom, he drove off."

Her mouth sagged.

Maybe the best thing would be to leave it at that, but I couldn't. "They'd both been drinking. If they get home without wrecking or getting a ticket, it'll be a miracle. And I'll tell you another miracle that's not going to happen—me staying in this crazy place. I'm leaving. I came back to get my stuff."

Jenna sank back onto the sofa. "Oh, Louisa, please don't do that." Her breath huffed out. She was scared, of her kids and the trouble they could get in, or what her mother-in-law's reaction to the whole thing would be. I wasn't sure which.

Nor did I care. "No." I stood as tall as my five feet would allow. "I've had it, Jenna. Something in this family is way off. Tamara's not right. I'm sorry to talk that way about your daughter, but she's—"

"She's acting out," Jenna interrupted. "She's angry at me because I wouldn't let her disregard her doctor's orders. You saw that with the car situation."

"Then you deal with her. I can't, and it shouldn't be my problem. Somehow she got Joel to do her bidding, because he had the keys. He has no more control over her than you do, and she scares me. I'm out. Of. Here."

She bit her lips.

"I'll tell Marguerite. If she's asleep, I'll leave her a note."

My stomach felt like a wrung-out dishrag. I could hear myself promising Grandpa I would do something worthwhile with my life, that I would choose work that put food in my soul as well as on my table.

I'd done a crap job every time.

The contract could be a problem. Marguerite would probably be angry and upset with me for breaking it. She could refuse to pay me for the work I'd already done.

But she could be angry and upset with someone else. I couldn't do it anymore. Tamara was bad enough. Now Joel, whom I'd trusted, had joined forces with her.

"How did you get back?" Jenna asked.

"I hitched a ride with the guys in the next car."

Jenna gaped. "You got in a car with a bunch of strangers?"

"What else could I do, Jenna? Stay there until I *grew* some money to take a cab?"

"I'm so sorry, Louisa." She couldn't quite look at me. "I'll speak to Tamara. And to Joel. I can't imagine what they were thinking."

I could. And I would bet she could, too. But clearly she wasn't going to talk about it. "I'm going to go pack."

ɞↄɞↄ

I packed my duffels, carried them down the hall, and set them beside Marguerite's door. I eased it open. She was asleep, as I'd suspected she would be. I laid the note I'd written for her on her bedside table and closed the door.

I took my bags downstairs and stacked them by the door. Jenna still sat on the sofa where I'd left her, and her face had the same stunned look. "I left a note on Marguerite's bedside table," I told her. "It explains what happened tonight, and because of that and other incidents, I don't want to stay here anymore."

She didn't bother to ask what the other incidents were. "I'm sorry," she repeated. "I think you've been wonderful for Marguerite. She needs a companion—"

The front door burst open.

Jenna shot up from the sofa. "Joel? Tamara?"

Joel came into view, looking like he'd accidentally set fire to the Pentagon. "My God. Louisa," he breathed. He strode toward me. His damp shirt smelled of sweat. "Where the hell have you been?"

"What?"

"I drove around for an hour looking for you!"

"No, you didn't." My voice rose and I was afraid I'd wake Marguerite. But I didn't care. Let her hear. "You drove away. You left me there. You ditched me forty miles from here!"

"No." Tamara stumbled into the room. Her face was splotchy with tears and she reeked of beer. "It was me. I drove off."

Jenna sniffed. "You've been drinking."

Look out, Sherlock Holmes.

I turned back to Joel. "Liar. You had the keys."

"I took them," Tamara said. "Don't be mad at Joel, Mom. I did it."

She was telling the truth. The way the truck had screeched out of the lot was the way she drove, not the way Joel drove.

I didn't know why she'd been crying. If Joel had read her the riot act, or if she was genuinely afraid something had gone wrong. *This is what happens when you play pranks. They backfire and you get consequences you didn't plan for.*

Or maybe she did. Marguerite would wake up the next morning to find her secretary/companion gone. In Tamara's eyes, making that kind of trouble for Marguerite could be worth the risk of whatever might happen to me.

Tamara didn't care about me. I was just a pawn in her game.

Joel ignored his sister and mother. "I persuaded Tam to pull over and let me drive. I went back to the movie and looked for you. We looked everywhere. Both bathrooms. The concession line. All around. The roads nearby in every direction. We didn't know where you were, if someone had you, where you could have gone."

"Sing me a sad song," I retorted. "I found a way back. I'm out of here."

Jenna held up one hand. "Louisa, would you consider staying until morning? I'd rather you weren't driving in the dark when you've had a frightening experience."

She had to be kidding. "This house is a frightening experience. I'll drive through hell before I spend another night here!"

Her face tightened and she turned to Tamara. "Come with me, please."

I picked up my bags.

"Louisa." Joel's voice broke. "Let me explain."

"You have nothing to say to me." I didn't want to admit even to myself how hurt I was. I'd thought he really liked me. I'd really liked him, maybe even more than liked, or it could be more under other circumstances. "Do you know what you did? I didn't have a dime on me. No way to get back here, or get anywhere. How was I supposed to know it was just a game and you would come back for me? Or was it? Did Tamara mean for me to be stuck there forever?"

"It wasn't a game. Tam told the truth. While you were in the bathroom, she…" He sighed. "Tam grabbed the keys from me and started the truck up. I was a little slow to react because I didn't think she would do what she did. She threw it into gear and floored it. When I snapped out of my surprise it was too late to grab the wheel or the keys without making an even more dangerous situation. Too late to do anything but try to talk her out of it, calmly."

"I bet you tried really hard. Just like you tried to keep her from drinking the beer. Did you ever think about bringing something to drink that wouldn't cause a problem?"

He hung his head. "You're right. I should have."

"Well, it's okay, Joel. I wouldn't have minded spending the night in Everett if those guys hadn't given me a ride. I would have minded even less if they hadn't been the good guys they were. I got lucky as hell and you know it."

Jenna's voice carried from the dining room. "…have any idea what you did? Do you know how dangerous a situation you put Louisa in?"

Tamara's mumbled reply was indistinct.

"She got in a car with a group of strangers. Do you know what can happen to a young woman who does that? Of course you do. You work at a rape crisis center."

Joel and I fell into an embarrassed silence.

Jenna went on. "If anything had happened to Louisa, she could sue us."

I shook my head. "That's what it's all about for your family, isn't it? Money."

"Mom doesn't mean it that way."

"No? Then how does she mean it? She's afraid I could sue. She's afraid Marguerite will be angry at her when she wakes up tomorrow morning and I'm gone. Well, you know what, Joel? I don't care."

Jenna's voice again. "The only one who looks 'nuts' around here is you. You could have put the whole family in serious trouble."

I didn't take the time to wonder who Tamara was calling *nuts*. "Good," I said. "Let Jenna rip Tamara a new one. Then when she's done, maybe she can put the brat in an institution where she belongs."

Joel jerked back. "Tam's not crazy."

"She's not?" I picked up my bags. "You have to pick, Joel. She's doing things that can hurt other people. Either she doesn't know what she's doing, which is crazy, or she does, and she's evil. Either way, she belongs locked up, and you know it as well as I do."

Chapter 13

I barely made it back to the main road before I wished I'd taken Jenna's advice. It was a long drive home. My right leg quavered like it did the first time I drove in snow, and I had to keep wiping at my eyes when they wanted to tear up.

This *stunk*. I'd failed, *again*.

I'd always believed elders were the cornerstone of any community. Clearly Marguerite wasn't anything of the kind in her house—*Jenna's* house. She was barely tolerated, and sometimes not even that.

What in the hell is going on there? I wondered for the dozenth time.

But what did it matter? The only thing that mattered now was that I'd failed. I couldn't save her, couldn't protect her, couldn't make her family love her or even spend five minutes talking to her. And I'd run like a startled doe at the first threat to me.

Okay, not the first. But still.

"I'm sorry, Grandpa," I whispered. "But you saw all those things they did. At least this time I didn't get fired for being disrespectful. I did everything I could."

Did you? said his voice in my head. *How is walking away any better than being fired?*

But what else could I have done? When Tamara hated me and I had no idea why?

Maybe it wasn't me.

The thought hit me with a chill. Maybe Tamara wanted me gone so she could get to Marguerite.

And maybe it wasn't just Tamara. Maybe they were all in on it.

Jenna had never gone off on Tamara like that before. What if it was all an act? A conspiracy? What if they'd all three planned to drive me away so Marguerite would be at their mercy?

What if Jenna's real reason for getting the kids out of the house was so she could do something to Marguerite before the guests arrived—

No. That made no sense. Jenna had practically begged me to stay. Marguerite was fine when I put the note in her room.

But was she? I hadn't checked. I'd simply dropped the note on the table and closed the door.

Goose bumps covered my arms. *What had I done?*

What was going to happen to Marguerite now that I was gone?

It's not your problem anymore, I tried to tell myself.

I hauled my duffels up to my apartment, opened the door, and dropped everything by the front door. I'd unpack in the morning. It was past two and I was too tired to deal with anything else.

ଈଈଈ

I had an awful night. When I was able to sleep, which wasn't much, my dreams woke me right back up again. In one, I was at a fancy dance wearing the wrong thing and scandalizing the elders. In another, I was back at my last job, and there was some urgent task I had needed to do all along but never touched. I woke up from that one at six-ish, knowing that going back to sleep would be impossible.

I made a pot of coffee and sat at the kitchen table, drinking it and trying not to think. I knew I'd deserted Marguerite. I could have stayed. Just made sure I was never alone with Tamara. Never in a car with her.

The phone rang.

My hand jerked and slung coffee onto the table and wall. I grabbed at the receiver with a wet hand. "Hello?"

I knew who it was even before Marguerite's voice said, "Louisa?"

Crap. "Yes. Look, I'm sorry. That house is just too—"

She cut me off. "My chair is gone."

"Your what?"

It was a stupid question, asked only out of dumbfoundedness, but she didn't seem to care. "My chair. Someone took it last night. I woke up and it's gone."

Air whooshed out of me. "That doesn't make sense."

"No. But it happened." For the first time she sounded her age—in fact, twenty years older. "The elevator is one thing. I can still move about and sit on the balcony on nice days. Without my chair, I'm bedridden."

A sick feeling flooded my stomach. *I knew it.* I knew something would happen to her as soon as I left. It could be anyone in the family, or any two of them, or even everyone. *Louisa's gone. Now let's really give the old bat…*

"I don't understand," I mumbled.

"What's there to understand?" She sounded more like herself. "Louisa, please come back. I know several things have happened here that have upset you."

It didn't take Miss Marple to make that deduction.

She went on. "But I…I need you here."

Oh, sweet Spirit. "Well, I…"

"I'll double what I'm paying you."

Holy crap. "It's not the money, Marguerite. Your family scares me."

Silence. Then, "They scare me, too."

I thought of every curse word I knew and a few I didn't. "Okay. I'm on my way."

I mopped up the spilled coffee, threw my bags back in the car, and headed for Issaquah.

உஸ்உ

When I arrived at the house, it was in an uproar. Everyone—including Carol, who paused only long enough to let me in—was looking for Marguerite's chair.

"It's not a contact lens. It's a wheelchair. It ought to be easy enough to find," I said as I grabbed a blackberry Danish from the sideboard. I hadn't had anything to eat since the previous night and I was starving.

"Louisa!" Jenna backed out of the study. The cocktail dress of the night before had been replaced by a simple sand-colored sheath. "You decided to return."

It was such an obvious point that she could only be waiting for me to explain why. I wasn't going to bother. It wasn't her business. "What rooms haven't been checked? What about the third floor?"

Joel, dressed in khakis and a pale blue shirt, came down the stairs and stopped short at the sight of me. His eyes went to my bags sitting at the front door and his whole body seemed to droop a little. "Hello, Louisa."

He doesn't want me here.

Knowing that, what was it that made my heart play hopscotch every time I saw him? After everything that had happened in this nuthouse? "Joel."

"No one's tried the third floor," he told me. "With the elevator not working, getting that chair up there would be almost impossible."

But not for him. He could carry it.

"The only rooms I haven't looked in are yours, Tam's and Louisa's," he told Jenna. "Louisa would have seen it before she left, and Tam's still sleeping."

"Why don't you go have some breakfast, Mr. Joel?" Carol passed him on her way up the stairs. "I'll search the rest of the second floor."

I started for the stairs. "I'll take the third. Look in my room, too, please, Carol. Maybe the chair was moved after I left last night."

I had barely made it up to the third floor when Carol announced that the chair had been located, stashed in the closet of the spare room next to Jenna's bedroom. Had Joel checked the room but not the closet? Or overlooked the chair?

Or simply not wanted to find it?

I took the steps two at a time "I'll take it to her."

Meanwhile Jenna had come upstairs. Her face was expressionless. "Thank you, Carol. I'll be leaving now."

Marguerite lay in bed, the covers hanging haphazardly over one side. "Oh, thank goodness." She struggled to sit up. "If you leave it in its usual spot, I can get into it by myself."

"Are you sure?" I wanted to help. I wanted to do something to make up for allowing this to happen. I didn't know how dangerous it was, but it had to be humiliating for her to be reduced to a bedridden invalid.

I couldn't even think of how she felt.

She got in the chair, but it was a slow and probably painful effort for her. She repeatedly refused my offered hand. "Would you like to help?" Her eyes were twice their normal size and a dangerous chilly blue. "Find out who did this to me."

"It could have been any of them. Was the chair here when you went to sleep?"

"As far as I know. Did you see it when you dropped this off?" She held up my note.

I shook my head. "But I wasn't looking for it. I probably would have noticed if it wasn't there, because I'd be expecting to see it."

"This is why I need you here."

She wasn't happy about my leaving. In her mind, I had opened the door for whoever wanted to do cruel things to her.

I took a deep breath. Knowing she had every right to be frightened, the best thing I could do was keep quiet.

So of course I opened my mouth and said the first thing I could think of *not* to say. "I doubt one of Jenna's party guests came up here and screwed with your chair. So it has to be one of the family. In that case, you'd have a better idea than I would."

She was silent, her lips tight.

"Don't you lock your door at night?"

Her head tilted as though I'd asked a complete nonsequitur. "No. If something happened to me and I needed help, no one could get in through a locked door."

I didn't want to tell her they probably wouldn't help her anyway. "I think you should start locking it."

No answer.

I went on. "Don't give them easy access to you. Someone wants you immobilized. The elevator isn't enough anymore. Or maybe they just meant for the chair to be hidden for a few hours, or days, and then replace it so you wonder if you're losing your mind."

"I'm not." The words snapped out like popped rubber bands. "How could I imagine a missing wheelchair?"

"I know. So this is purely vindictive. Tell me why your family would be so hostile toward you that they're trying to make you think you've gone crazy."

"What exactly are you saying?"

I might get fired from this job, too. But I had nothing to lose. "Do you think I haven't noticed your family doesn't spend any time with you? Ever? One of them jammed the elevator and no one's fixed it. No one comes up here to see you or talk to you. Someone tied a trip wire across your closet door. Last night Tamara tried to dump me in Everett, and someone took advantage of my absence to hide your chair."

She glared.

"Why do they hate you? Are they afraid of you? Are you afraid of them? If so, why?"

"You're an impertinent little thing."

"Yes, but at least I'm honest."

She glared at me for several moments then chuckled. "Yes, my dear, you certainly are."

I wanted to smile back at her, but I couldn't. I owed her an apology. Or some explanation beyond my note, which lay crumpled on the bedside table.

Or maybe just the assurance that no matter what happened, I wouldn't abandon her again.

I took a deep breath. "I'm sorry I left you alone. I was scared and angry. But I can get around a lot easier than you can, so I promise I won't let them frighten me away again."

"Apology accepted, my dear." She squeezed my hand. "Now, let me freshen up a bit and we can get to work."

I'd need to do more. I'd need to find out what was going on. If Marguerite didn't know, or wouldn't tell me, why her family—or someone in it—hated her, I would find out.

I went downstairs for a pot of coffee, brought it up,

kicked off my moccasins, and got ready for a long morning.

It was. Marguerite got caught up in the story and seemed to put the chair incident behind her. We were so involved in our work that I missed lunch and Mrs. Wharton brought a meal up for both of us. It was leftovers from the previous night's party, and were they ever good.

"Did Jenna hire a caterer for the party or did Mrs. Wharton do all this?" I asked.

"Mrs. Wharton cooked. It wasn't that big a party— maybe eight couples, fifteen or twenty people."

Marguerite couldn't go, of course; the elevator still wasn't fixed. I'd thought about calling a few service places, pretending to be acting on the family's behalf, to see if an appointment had been made. But I didn't need to. Jenna wasn't going to bother. Someone, and I'd bet it was her, knew how easy it would be to fix the elevator. Calling a repairman would cause a situation Jenna wouldn't want.

"Here's your problem, Mrs. Roberts. Someone sabotaged your elevator."

It was bad enough that I knew. An outsider discovering what had been done might require an investigation. So did the stolen chair, but I would have to be the one to raise a cry about it, and I wouldn't without Marguerite's say-so. "I'm sorry you couldn't enjoy the party."

Marguerite waved a hand in dismissal. "Do you think I want to play that silly game?"

"What game?"

"Oh, the 'I'm part of high society' game." She waved her fingers in the air and I chuckled. "Jenna has to do it, of course, but I don't think she's ever enjoyed it. I'm not sure Carl did, either. They were both outgoing in high school, but once you become an adult, partying loses its luster, I think."

"High school sweethearts." I smiled. Marguerite rolled her eyes. *Here goes.* "Where's Jenna's family? Are they all deceased?" If Joel had told the truth, I knew more than I should.

"She hasn't had any contact with them since she married Carl."

"Oh." That wasn't quite what Joel had said. He'd said they disowned her. Marguerite made it sound as though it had been Jenna's idea.

"I agree that to marry at that age was foolish," Marguerite went on. "Chris—my husband—and I tried to talk them out of it, but when it became clear they weren't listening, we had to accept it. We never would have put our son out."

"Her parents put her out?"

"Yes."

So Joel was right. "For getting married? What the hell? I mean, sorry. But that's terrible. They disliked Carl that much?"

"It wasn't Carl they objected to as much as the children's ages and the fact that Jenna gave up a college scholarship to marry him."

Nothing about Carl's religion, or lack of. "I guess they were in love."

"I guess, as well." Her tone was a little sour. "Jenna's parents had high expectations for her, and marriage wasn't included, at least not at seventeen. She skipped a grade and graduated early, as valedictorian, and was an exceptionally talented musician."

One who never played or sang for her family. "So what if she wanted Carl more than she wanted to be a musician? A lot of girls would have made the same choice back then. Maybe now, even."

"Jenna's parents wanted more for her, and I think they thought they could bring her around by being 'tough.' They didn't expect her to call their bluff. And of course, the children could have had a much easier early life if they hadn't insisted on marrying at seventeen and eighteen. Instead of following the appropriate path, they became young, unemployed parents." Marguerite blinked a few times, a sign I had begun to recognize as slight double vision—a side effect of MS. She rarely wore her reading glasses. I wondered if she were too vain to cover her brilliantly blue eyes with any kind of lenses or if she just didn't like the weight of the frames.

"So how did they support themselves? How did Carl go to college?"

Marguerite tapped her breastbone with one index finger. "We supported them. We had no choice. Jenna's parents certainly weren't going to help. They put her out of the house the night she told them she was marrying Carl instead of going to college."

My mouth was practically dragging the floor. "Poor Jenna."

Marguerite's gaze was steady and admonishing. "Jenna has to take some of the responsibility. She told them, 'If I leave, I'm never coming back.' It was one of those cases where everyone, in a moment of anger, says things that can't be taken back. And once they realize it, it's much too late."

I couldn't look at her. Jenna wasn't the only teenager who'd made a bad decision—or put her foot in her mouth. I had something in common with Jenna as well as her daughter.

Marguerite went on. "They thought she was pregnant, but she wasn't. Not until she and Carl married. They were married on June sixth and Joel was born on March twelfth."

She'd counted. But then, who wouldn't? "Since Carl was planning to go to college, couldn't they have waited to have children?"

Her blue eyes rolled upward. "They certainly could have. I took Jenna to a doctor before they were married and got her a diaphragm. They didn't use it because they didn't want anything to spoil the romance of their wedding night."

I tried not to laugh. Something sure had.

"In all seriousness, a child with a child is nothing to laugh at. Chris and I tried to convince them to give the baby up for adoption." She didn't react to what must have been an astonished look on my face. *Give Joel away?* "It would have been best for everyone. That baby would have had two mature parents who were ready for a child, instead of teenagers with no jobs, no education, and no home."

"Well, I guess I know how that turned out. I mean, they decided to keep him."

"Jenna decided. Her exact words were, 'I'll walk through hell before I'll throw my child away.'"

I wondered how Carl had felt about that. Maybe he thought his parents were right and he was better off focusing on college than trying to learn to be a father. "It still doesn't seem right. I mean, I guess I've known kids who were put out of their house, but—"

"Louisa, try to remember, that was twenty-five years ago. Even now, among Orthodox and Conservative Jews, intermarriage is discouraged. Back then it was definitely frowned upon."

I tried to keep my face neutral. Had Tamara told the truth?

Marguerite nibbled her tongue pensively. "Parents who raise their children in a certain cultural environment want the children to adopt their ways. Particularly if their culture is threatened in any way. You probably have some experience with that."

It was more the other way around with me. But I understood Marguerite's point.

"Jenna's parents came to this country from Poland in 1938, just before World War II. As you know, in Poland—most of Europe, really—the Jewish population is almost erased. The concern is that if a Jew marries a Gentile, their religion is put on the back burner. And how do you raise the children of such a marriage?" She pointed behind her, in the direction of Tamara's room. "That's how. By Jewish law, Joel and Tamara are Jewish because their mother is. But Tamara has no interest whatsoever. I don't think she's set foot in a synagogue since she was a child."

"If Jenna's parents had been around, instead of abandoning her, maybe it would have been different. Maybe Tamara would see the value of her heritage. That's what my grandfather did for me."

"They tried."

I jumped a little. "Huh?"

"They knew they'd been wrong. Her mother came to see Jenna when she and Carl had been married a few months. Jenna refused to see or speak to her. Her mother waited for two hours before she finally left. Not long after that they moved to Chicago. They wrote Jenna to give her their new address and phone number in case she ever wanted to contact them."

"Did she tell you why she didn't?"

"She never spoke of it. She threw their letter in the trash unopened. Carl retrieved it and showed it to his father and me. But what could we do?"

What, indeed? "I guess she must have been really hurt. And wasn't over it yet."

Maybe she still wasn't. Maybe she listened to music from her high school years to bring back what was obviously a happy time for her, when she thought she would make a life with the boy she loved. Before it all blew up on her and left her a seventeen-year-old mother, living with her in-laws, fighting to keep her child. Estranged from her own family and so grieved by their rejection of her that she refused to let them take it back.

Marguerite sighed. "You could say that *she* abandoned her parents, since she had the opportunity to get back into their graces. She didn't discuss it with me, so I don't know what she was thinking. But two things you will learn about Jenna if you spend any time with her. She doesn't break her word, and she doesn't give second chances—nor ask for them."

I could have said it looked like she'd given Tamara a thousand chances. But now I understood. She wouldn't give up her son, and she wasn't giving up on her daughter.

Not like her parents had done to her.

Thinking about Tamara reminded me. "Could I be excused for a minute? I want to see how Tamara's doing." I wanted to see her reaction to my return, but Marguerite didn't need to know that.

Marguerite looked at me curiously. "Why? Is she not well?"

"Are you kidding? She got wasted last night at the movies before dumping me there."

Marguerite heaved a troubled sigh. "Drunk? Again?"

"She's done it before?"

"Of course. Sometimes Joel is able to stop her, sometimes not. She seems compelled to get drunk, take drugs, and behave as irrationally as possible. She worries me, Louisa. How do you deal with a problem like that?"

"The first thing I'd do is make Jenna aware of it. Maybe Tamara needs, uhm, professional help."

"Oh, no." I could practically smell the sarcasm. "Jenna is aware. She just isn't interested. She's convinced Tamara does it all to annoy her, and she might be right."

I didn't think the drive-in scene was to annoy Jenna—although it had. Or had it? The whole thing could have been a set-up.

This place was driving me as crazy as it was. I was starting to spout conspiracy theories.

∽∾∾

Joel was apparently off work that day and was, as I'd expected, nursing his sister. He gave me a sober glance then turned back to her. She lay in bed, propped on a generous supply of pillows, holding an ice pack to her forehead. Her puffy face almost made me feel sorry for her, even though I knew better. "How are you feeling?"

"Ughhnnnn…"

"Can I bring you anything?"

"Yeah. Arsenic."

"For who?"

"Myself. Who else? Oh God, Joel, bring me the bowl again. I'm going to puke."

I wanted to ask her if the beer was worth it, but kept my mouth shut.

"Tam, you can't. You haven't eaten anything all day. Try to drink some water."

"Noooo."

I'd seen enough. "Uh, well, I've got work to do. I just wanted to see how you were doing." I started for the door, watching Joel, trying to figure out the look he was giving me. Appraising? No, kinder than that. Approving?

Maybe I just wanted to believe that, because this house was cold and gray, and Joel was warmth and color.

But not today.

Today he matched the house. Something was weighing on him, and I had the feeling it was more than his sister's behavior and state.

I stopped in my room to unpack my bags, but found Carol in there doing the work for me. "Oh, sorry, Carol," I told her. "You really don't have to do that. I can do it."

She smiled as she turned down the comforter and placed my nightshirt on it. "It's my job, Miss Louisa."

"No. It's not. I work for the family just like you do."

"Not quite." She straightened. "I work for Jenna. You work for Marguerite. That puts you on a higher rung."

I hadn't thought of it that way. "Why do you have this whole house to take care of by yourself? I would think there'd be someone else. At least a chauffeur for Marguerite."

Carol shook her head. "Everyone can drive except Marguerite, and the few times she needs to go anywhere, she hires a limo."

"Must be nice."

"Not really." Carol grinned at the surprise on my face. "Would you want to be one of them?"

"No," I admitted. "They don't seem like a happy family."

"They're not." She tipped her head in the direction of Tamara's room. "Tamara's a little beast, but I feel sorry for her. All the money in the world won't make her happy if no one loves her. I've been with this family about six months, and I can tell you no one cares about her except her brother. Jenna's too busy with Airtech, and Marguerite's too busy writing. You're the first person who's bothered to spend any time getting to know her."

She put a folded stack of my t-shirts in a drawer. "I hope you're not doing it to impress Joel."

A more fair-skinned person would have probably turned the color of a raspberry. "Do I look like that type?"

"No." She looked levelly at me. "What about you? What do you think about them?"

"I think Tamara's the youngest nineteen-year-old I've ever seen. Joel thinks he's helping her, but what he really needs to do is wake Jenna up and show her what's going on." I picked up the toiletries bag and hung it on the bathroom door. "But I think his heart's good, and he's doing what he thinks is right."

"But is it right?" Carol said. "If I could talk straight to her without losing my job, I'd tell her why I'm here. I'm washing her family's dishes and doing their laundry and vacuuming the mud they track in on the rug because I lost my daughter when I was drinking."

I gaped.

"I'm an alcoholic," she said softly. "My ex-husband has full custody of our daughter, and I'm working here and staying sober so I can go back to court and show a judge I've changed and I deserve to see my little girl at least half the time."

"I'm sorry." I felt stupid. "I, uhm, didn't know."

"Why would you?" She didn't wait for an answer. It was a rhetorical question anyway. "I'd like to tell Tamara when you start drinking, to make your mother look bad or make yourself feel good, or why ever she does it, you can't always stop. One day you look up and it's cost you something you love. Maybe even everything you love. Then it's not cute anymore. People won't always cut her the kind of slack her brother does. But do you know what she would do if I told her that?"

"Cuss you out?"

"At least. Or make my work harder and my life miserable. I won't let that little girl have that kind of power over me. The only little girl I care about is my own."

She was right, of course. I wished she would speak up, but I could understand why she wouldn't. "Who do you think moved Marguerite's chair?"

"Confidentially?"

"Of course."

"It could have been any of them. Jenna seems to have more class, but since I've been here, I don't think I've heard three conversations between her and Marguerite. They don't like each other, and hiding the chair could be Jenna's way to get back."

Get back for what, I wondered. "But she had a houseful of guests who would have seen."

"Not once you left with Joel and Tamara. The guests hadn't arrived. And once the party was over, and you went home, no one would have seen her."

I pondered that.

Carol went on. "Mrs. Wharton doesn't have much to say to me, but she did tell me she's been here since Mr. Roberts was alive, and she's surprised Marguerite is still here. Marguerite and Jenna have never gotten along, and Mr. Roberts's death only made it worse. They don't have anyone to pretend for anymore."

Yes, they did—me. But I didn't correct her. I still didn't know whether Marguerite had finally given in and hired a secretary because what she really wanted was someone to watch out for her, or if my coming here had brought the animosity to a head. Nor did I know why there was such hatred among the family members.

If I thought Mrs. Wharton would talk to me, I could ask her if she thought Carl's death was as natural as it was supposed to be. But that would never happen.

"What do you think happened with the chair?" Carol asked.

"I think they're all involved somehow. There's too much creepy stuff around this house. It would be too hard for one person not to get caught. Maybe one person is doing everything, or maybe two people, but the others are covering."

She nodded. "That's probably true. Not that Jenna is attached to Tamara. Or even to Joel. But she'd side with them before her mother-in-law any day." She finished with the bed and turned to leave.

"You haven't said two sentences to me the whole time I've been here," I told her.

She smiled. "I've been watching. I've learned to do that before putting my foot in my mouth."

I didn't know what I'd expected her to say, but it hadn't been that. I smiled back. It was good to feel a little less alone.

తించా

Back in Marguerite's room, I picked up my notes on the book but hesitated. She'd told me a lot of interesting things about the family, and I wanted to learn more while she was in a chatty mood. "Is Jenna an only child, too?"

"Oh, no. She had a younger sister who adored Carl. He used to call her 'Pipsqueak.' She became quite a handful at Northwestern."

"A handful how?"

"How was any college student a handful in the sixties?"

"A campus radical, eh?" I shouldn't have, but I laughed. *Jenna's parents got their comeuppance, all right.* I would bet Pipsqueak got bailed out of jail every time.

Marguerite shook her head. "I'm just glad my son was too old for that kind of foolishness. I was lucky to have Carl. My husband died when Tamara was two, and without Carl I would have been alone. Chris and I wanted several children, but I had five miscarriages before Carl, and was never able to get pregnant again after that."

"That's too bad." Meaningless, but I didn't know what else to say.

Marguerite didn't respond.

I had to cover the silence. "I'm an only child too, but I don't think it's because my parents couldn't have any more. I think it's more likely they took one look at me and knew they'd have their hands full." That broke the somber mood. "I don't know if I'll ever get married. I'm too much of an oddball. I haven't found many people who interest me more than my art or my Indian Society activities, so I don't really have friends." It wasn't easy to find anyone who saw the world through the same eyes I did.

"You're making a mistake," she warned. "One that could leave you lonely when you're my age. Or even Jenna's age. She won't admit it, but I think she is lonely."

"When she just had a houseful of friends over?"

"Friends, or acquaintances?"

I didn't know, of course, other than the one couple Joel and Tamara had said she was close to. "The only people I ever felt like I had anything in common with were the ones I met at the powwows my grandfather used to take me to. I haven't seen much of them lately. I wouldn't call them friends, really, not people I could call if I needed someone. I guess I've gotten used to not having anyone like that."

"Have you? Does anyone?"

I didn't answer.

"That's what my son did. He put all of his energy into Airtech. He made himself sick and died much too young."

"Why didn't he see a doctor? Did he know he was sick?"

"He did see one for his high blood pressure. He considered even that an admission of weakness. The only reason he ever went at all, and kept his blood pressure under control, was that Jenna and I nagged him so much he decided the doctor and the pills were the lesser of two evils."

I remembered the news articles. "What about getting a kidney transplant?"

"That's much harder than you think. A kidney donation can't come from just anyone. Jenna had all of us tested, and the only ones who matched were Tamara and I. My doctor wouldn't allow me to donate because of my MS, and Carl refused to put a thirteen-year-old through the operation." Her head slumped.

This family was one surprise after another. "How did Jenna feel about it?"

"Jenna never argued with Carl." Her voice dropped to a near-mumble. "He could have lived if she had been stronger, put her foot down."

I sat silently, processing that.

Marguerite went on. "Of course, he left us both a fortune, and we'll never want for anything as long as we live. Except a cure for the disease I have. Believe me, Louisa, I would give up the money to have my son back, and for the chance to walk down those stairs again."

I didn't move.

She coughed quietly. "Jenna hates this house. Half the rooms aren't used, she's tired of paying a landscaping company to tend the grounds, and the swimming pool is an irritation. She can't impress her clients by bringing them here because Tamara's behavior is too unpredictable. If Joel hadn't offered to take Tamara to the movies last night, Jenna would have paid him to get her out of the house. It makes it so much easier for her."

Marguerite noticed more than I would have expected. "Then why doesn't she sell the house?"

"That's an excellent question. She could find a nice condo for each of us and not have to bother with the upkeep. But then, what would happen to the children?"

"They're not children. Joel's older than I am, and I've been on my own for a while. He could take care of himself."

"But not his sister."

Maybe he just realizes she doesn't have anyone else who gives a damn about her.

But I was sure of one thing. Tamara was wrong about Marguerite's objection to Carl's marrying a "Jewish girl."

Nothing Marguerite had said to me indicated any prejudice of that kind. Clearly Tamara said a lot of things that might or might not be true, and she didn't have to be drunk to say them.

ⓔⓢⓔⓢ

The next night I was awakened by Marguerite's voice shouting a question. I couldn't be sure, but it sounded like, "Who's there?"

Her door was open. It had to be or I wouldn't have been able to hear her. Why was her door open? Who was in her room?

I flung the covers off and a chilly draft hit me. The door that led to the balcony stood open.

There was a dark form by my bed.

I opened my mouth to yell, but all I could do was

inhale before the shape snatched the extra pillow and crushed it onto my face.

Chapter 14

I fought like a rabid dog, but whoever held the pillow over my face had the advantage. Blankets wound around the pillow and lights flashed in front of my eyes. Oh, God, what a way to die! *Not now, not like this, please, Marguerite, Joel...*

The attacker let go. Footsteps scampered to the door and out.

I flailed my arms until the blankets and pillows gave way, took a deep gulp of air, and shrieked at the top of my lungs. I jumped out of bed and flung open my door just as Jenna emerged from behind hers. She looked at me as though I were running around naked in downtown Seattle. "What in God's name?"

"Someone tried to smother me with a pillow. They got in through that window." I pointed in the general direction of the balcony. Jenna stared at me and I could almost hear her thoughts. *Great, another crazy person in my house.*

"Louisa, are you all right?" Joel was there, his arms around me. His chest was bare and it didn't seem as though he had much on the bottom, either. I wore only my knee-length nightshirt and I sensed, rather than saw, Jenna's odd look.

I took another breath. I could feel my heart kicking

inside my chest. "Someone tried to kill me. Where's Tamara?" It came out sounding more accusatory than I might have liked.

Jenna gasped. "What are you saying?"

"How much clearer do I have to put it? Someone came in my room through the balcony door and tried to smother me."

"But you don't know who." Jenna sounded like a nursery school teacher with a hysterical three-year-old.

"Jenna, I wear contacts with a prescription stronger than Arnold Schwarzenegger to see during the day. How do you expect me to see someone in the dark, especially with a pillow over my head? You're pretty much a blur to me right now." I could make out her features and silky pajamas, but that was it.

"Relax. You're okay now." Joel stroked my hair.

Maybe I wasn't being as polite to Jenna as I should. "Uh, sorry, I don't mean to be rude. I'm just a little rattled."

"Joel, where's Tamara?" Jenna asked.

"I don't know."

I bet you do.

"I thought I saw you come out of her room," Jenna said.

"Why would I be in Tam's room in the middle of the night?"

Did Jenna notice he didn't answer her?

She didn't seem to. "Please look for her."

He went into his room.

"Joel?"

"Will you let me put on some pants, Mom? Or do you want me running around in front of all of you in my warm-ups?" He gestured to his drawstring nylon shorts.

"What's all the fuss?" said Tamara, and her head appeared over the top of the lower stairs.

"Where have you been?" Jenna asked her.

"In the kitchen getting a snack." Tamara flipped the switch to turn on the hall light and held up something that looked like a hunk of the devil's food cake we'd had for dessert. "Is there something wrong with that?"

"How long have you been down there?" I asked.

"None of your business," she retorted.

"I'd like to know, too," Jenna said.

Tamara glared at me. At least I thought she did. Trying to focus without my contacts made my head hurt, and I wished I hadn't taken them out. I'd gotten the new extended-wear disposables earlier that summer and liked the low maintenance of them, but leaving them in took some getting used to.

"About a half hour," she finally said. "I was drinking a Pepsi."

I snorted. "Yeah, right."

"Louisa, I'd appreciate it if you didn't speak to my daughter in that manner," Jenna said.

"Sorry—*Jenna*."

There was a noise from down the hall, and I turned to see Marguerite's door swing open. "What's going on?" she demanded.

"Nothing, Marguerite," Jenna said, so sweetly the words practically stuck to the wall.

Oh, God. I should have thought of Marguerite first and checked on her. At least she was all right.

Her door closed.

Jenna turned a patronizing smile to me. "You must have had a bad dream."

Was she really that clueless? "Oh? I guess you're going to tell me Marguerite did, too, and that's why her shouting woke me up?"

"What shouting?"

I wasn't going to get anything out of Jenna. I turned to Joel. "Didn't you hear her?"

He shook his head.

I turned to Tamara. "You had to have. Your room is right next to hers."

"Are you deaf? I told you I was in the kitchen."

Joel gave her a high sign. "Louisa, Grandmother has nightmares sometimes. She was probably talking in her sleep. You can see for yourself that she's fine."

What was this, Elm Street? As in, no one could tell the difference between a nightmare and real life?

Oh, hell. Even Joel was on their side. Well, why not? Why would I expect anything different? It was his mother and sister, after all, and I was—nobody.

Without another word I turned and slammed into my room. To hell with them all.

Except Marguerite. It wasn't her fault. She'd hired me to type her book, not to be her bodyguard. She'd had no idea I'd be shot at and nearly smothered.

But she knew her family wasn't right. And unfortunately, her family included Joel.

Well, she sure as hell hadn't brought me here to run after him with my tongue hanging out. It wasn't like I was Tamara's age, or younger, or a fool. There was no reason for me to perk up, light up, feel warmer and brighter, when some guy came around. Or smiled at me. Or acted like I mattered to him.

Or kissed me like nobody ever had.

But I wasn't sure I could believe anything he said.

I put my contacts back in—no more getting caught without them—and waited until the house was quiet again. I crept out of my room and down the hall to Marguerite's. I tried the door, and as I expected, it was locked. I went back to my room, out onto the balcony, and inched my way down to the door that led into Marguerite's room. Maybe I could get in that way.

The knob turned easily in my hand.

So the likely prowler, if he or she had caused Marguerite to shout, was Joel or Tamara. One of them had gone into Marguerite's room through the outside door then come down to my room and held a pillow over my face.

Why? Did they want to smother me?

I could hear my own breathing. Was someone trying to kill me? Or just scare me, maybe to stop me from going to Marguerite's aid?

What were they doing to Marguerite?

Tamara could have set everything up ahead of time for a plausible alibi. She was an athlete and she was fast. If she had the cake ready in the kitchen, or better yet, the dining room, it wouldn't have taken her long to leave Marguerite's room, which was the closest to the stairs, run down the steps two at a time, and into the dining room where her snack waited.

Or the kids had worked together. One went to Marguerite's room and the other to mine. The prowler had seemed tall and slim, in the brief glimpse I got. Either Joel or Tamara fit that description.

But so did Jenna.

The balcony did not extend around the front of the house to her bedroom, but she could have re-entered the house through Tamara's room, knowing Tamara was in the kitchen, and hurried back to her own room then back out to ask me what in God's name. It would explain how she'd been able to hear me over the headphones she wore to bed.

Maybe she didn't wear her music to sleep. Maybe the headphones and Walkman just happened to be on her pillow. Maybe I'd been loud enough to wake someone in a light sleep anyway. But the only way I would know would be to re-enact the scene, headphones, yelling and all.

Since someone would have to help me, it wouldn't happen. There was no one here I could trust.

Carol. But I couldn't involve her, not knowing what I now knew about her.

Marguerite. But I didn't know how I would explain it to her. She certainly didn't need the worry.

Oh, God, I hated this place. I longed for the boss who thought he was too good to dial the phone and the one who thought I was born on December twenty-fifth and all the others. Somehow they didn't seem so bad anymore. I wondered how I could have ever thought this was *intriguing,* was anything other than horrifying.

But I'd promised Marguerite I wouldn't leave her alone with them again.

I eased the door open and tiptoed into Marguerite's room. She stirred and muttered, "Who's there?"

"Louisa," I whispered. "I just wanted to make sure you were all right. I thought I heard you shouting at someone earlier."

She was silent for a few moments before replying. "I'm fine, dear. I thought someone was in here."

It would scare her, but she needed to be scared. "They were. Someone opened your door. Otherwise, I wouldn't have been able to hear you."

I could hear her inhaling, a long breath through her nose. "That's what I thought, but when I sat up and asked 'Who's there?' the door closed again."

Whoever was in her room escaped just as she awoke and called out. It wouldn't take much to move faster than Marguerite could, especially if she were awakening from a deep sleep.

If it was Joel, he could have ducked into Tamara's room next to Marguerite's, which would explain why Jenna saw him coming out of there.

It had to be the two of them, and they had to plan it all ahead of time.

Why? What did they want in Marguerite's room?

"It's all right now, Louisa. You can go back to bed."

"Why don't you let me bring some bedding in here and sleep on the floor? No one will try anything if I'm in here."

"Oh, Louisa, I can't let you do that. You'll be miserable on that hard floor."

Hers was the only bedroom I'd seen that was uncarpeted. It made sense—the wheelchair would move much easier on the floor. "Don't be silly." I tried for a light tone, but it came out sharper than I'd intended. "My grandpa used to take me camping all the time. I've slept on the ground on an air mattress more times than I can tell you."

"They won't do anything else anyway. Not tonight. We've been alerted, and they'd never get away with it."

"What about the next time?"

I could hear her swallowing.

I tried again. "Just let me go grab a blanket and pillow. I'll be fine, and you'll be safe."

"I'll be safe." She reached over and grasped my hand. "Make sure my door is locked and the balcony is as well. You know that I often sit out there during the day. I'll just have to be sure to lock the doors behind me when I come in."

And I'll have to stay here indefinitely. Even having me here wasn't enough to stop whoever was after her. Or me.

Why? What had Marguerite done? Or what did she know that someone didn't want revealed?

I didn't want to, but I went back to bed—until I heard movement in the hall outside.

I put my head against the door and heard the door next to mine—Joel's room—open.

"Let's go downstairs," Jenna's voice commanded.

A pause.

"I'm not asking. I'm telling."

My lips pursed in a soundless whistle. So she could get tough when she wanted to. Maybe she hadn't believed the kids any more than I had.

There was no opening and closing of a second door. Which meant both Joel and Tamara had been in his room.

In a spy operation they would call that *debriefing*.

I crept out of my room and down the stairs. If they caught me, I was in trouble. I could always turn the tables and say I'd gone to the kitchen for cake or coffee, but it wouldn't fly any more than Tamara's BS had. Jenna would go to Marguerite and politely ask her to find another secretary. It would be a conversation I would pay to hear, but I didn't want to cause Marguerite that kind of hassle. I'd have to be stealthier than a cat.

A light shone from the living room. They'd left the French doors open, and if I flattened myself against the wall by the stairs I could hear them.

"What happened tonight?" Jenna asked.

Tamara tried to sound innocent. "I wanted some cake, so I came down here to get it. Grandmother must've had one of her nightmares."

"You know," Jenna said, "We've been talking about your grandmother's nightmares, but I don't think she's had one in years. Not since about a year after your father died."

I covered my mouth so they wouldn't hear my breathing.

"What woke her?" Jenna asked.

Joel said something I couldn't quite hear.

"No. But I heard Louisa scream. And Louisa says she was awakened by Marguerite's shouting. I don't know Louisa well, but she doesn't strike me as the sort who would imagine that, or make it up."

I gave myself a thumb's-up.

"So you're going to believe her instead of me?" Tamara said. "I guess next you'll believe I tried to suffocate her."

"Did you?"

"*Mom!*"

"Answer my question."

Joel rescued her. Of course. "Why would Tam want to hurt Louisa? They get along fine. Tam likes her."

You think.

"She does? Then why leave her behind at the movies?" Jenna said.

Silence.

"Why do any of the things Tamara does?" Jenna said. "Why move Marguerite's chair?"

Tamara's voice, high and agitated. "Stop talking about me like I'm not here. I didn't touch her chair!"

Joel spoke again. All I could make out was the upturn inflection that meant he'd asked a question.

"I don't know, Joel. To antagonize Marguerite? Because Louisa seems to be more of a paid companion than a secretary, and Marguerite now has someone to talk to all day? And you don't," to Tamara, I assumed.

"So?" Tamara retorted.

"I'm losing my patience, Tamara."

"At what? I'm just sitting here."

"I asked you a question. Don't think I didn't notice you haven't answered."

Finally someone was holding her accountable. If Jenna

were like this all the time, Tamara would act a lot less loony.

"I told you, I came down to the kitchen for some cake, and I heard all this commotion, and when I came back upstairs Louisa was yelling at me. Why do you let her treat me like crap? Are you scared to tell her to act like the other servants? You wouldn't let Carol accuse me of stupid stuff."

I wondered if Carol would have the nerve to tell Jenna if Tamara did anything to her.

"Louisa does not treat you like crap," Jenna said. "She seems to go out of her way to be friendly, despite your rudeness. And if Carol did accuse you of anything, it would hardly surprise me. Your behavior is not only rude, it's—"

"Crazy?" Tamara interrupted. "Is that what you're going to tell me? I'm crazy? Mom, I'm not the crazy one. Louisa's not safe here."

I had to muffle laughter. *You would know.*

"Safe from what?" Jenna snapped.

"I think Grandmother is poisoning her mind."

Silence. I leaned closer, checking the floor and wall to make sure I wasn't casting a shadow.

Joel said something and all I heard was "Tell Mom…"

Fortunately Tamara didn't have the volume control he did. "I think Grandmother's convincing Louisa there's something wrong with us. That it's our idea she's holed up in her room, like we chain her in there or something."

Marguerite didn't have to do a thing.

"Does it bother you that your grandmother doesn't come downstairs anymore?" Was it my imagination, or was Jenna smiling? Just a little?

"No," Tamara said. "But I didn't put pliers in the elevator."

Silence. I held my breath.

I didn't tell them there were pliers in the elevator.

"Who did that, Mom? I didn't do it, because I was in the hospital. And Joel says he didn't, and I believe him. That leaves you."

"Don't be silly."

My heart pounded and an itchy spot on my leg made me twitch. I couldn't scratch it. They'd hear me. Or I wouldn't hear them, and I had to.

Jenna? Jamming the elevator? The last one I would suspect?

Jenna had too much class to do something so malicious. Tamara was lying again. She had to be.

Had I ever really caught Tamara in a lie?

Yes. The piano.

Jenna hadn't answered, or if she had I couldn't hear her. Tamara spoke again. "It's my turn. I'm asking a question, and you haven't answered me."

"Don't talk back to me."

"Mom," Joel interjected. I strained but couldn't make out his words. *Crap.*

Then his voice rose, just enough for me to hear, "But for the love of Moses, if you hate Grandmother so much, please put her out."

"You know I can't do that." Jenna sounded as though she were about to cry.

"But you..." One of the others shushed him and his voice dropped so I missed the rest of what he said.

"About what?" Jenna said.

"To accuse us of elder abuse."

I'd never been so still in my life.

"Did you make her sign something? Saying she wouldn't tell our business?" Tamara asked.

Ahh. They were worried I was going to narc on them for the way they treated Marguerite. Well, they should be.

"She doesn't work for me. She works for Marguerite.

Joel, I don't think she's going to do that. What happened tonight is easy to explain."

"I'm not taking the blame for the elevator," Tamara said.

Joel muttered something.

"You most certainly will not," Jenna retorted.

Joel laughed. "Solomon and the baby."

What?

Jenna: "Not quite. But I get the point."

Joel: "So do I. The point is that you can't stand to have Grandmother around, either, but you won't kick her out."

"You both know why I can't. I promised your father I would take care of her. I have to honor my promise."

"Why?" Joel said. "Dad asked you to take care of her because he knew you would do it and you wouldn't go back on your word. It was manipulative and you know it. He knew you and Grandmother hated each other. Why did he do that to you? When she would be just as well off in a nursing home?"

I knew it. I knew they were trying to get rid of her.

Jenna finally spoke. "She doesn't belong in a nursing home. Her mind is still sharp."

"As a rusty razor blade," Joel said. "And just as deadly. Tam's right. I don't know what she's up to with Louisa, but she's up to something. I think Louisa trusts her completely, which scares me."

And why wouldn't I? I wanted to say. *She's not the one trying to smother me. Or jamming the elevator to trap herself upstairs.*

"You know she took me in when I had nowhere to go." Jenna's voice sounded like she'd been up for three days straight. "How can I put her out?"

Joel said something I couldn't hear.

A whack. Jenna had slapped a table. "I'm not discussing that with you. It's ridiculous."

"You're right. It's off the subject, which is, when will you kick Grandmother out of here? Or..." His voice dropped again.

Son of a gun. I *really* wanted to hear this.

"Then I'll hire somebody." A rustling like Jenna stood up. I backed up and started up the stairs. "Since you're an adult, you're free to move out any time you wish."

The discussion was over, or close to it. I scurried away as fast as I could and barely shut my door before I heard footsteps coming up the stairs.

I got back in bed, but sleep wasn't going to happen. I lay awake trying to make sense of the night's events.

Who jammed the elevator? No one was admitting it. Tamara vehemently denied it. Of course, that didn't mean she hadn't paid—or blackmailed—one of the servants into doing it for her.

Maybe Joel had offered to take the blame and his mother refused to let him.

Did that mean Jenna had done it?

By herself, or did she get someone to do it for her?

Please, no. I'd thought better of her—sort of. Of course, there was always the chance I'd misunderstood something in the conversation. She'd never actually admitted to doing it. Nor had either of her children pressed her to do so.

None of them really wanted to know which of the others was guilty.

Whoever was in Marguerite's room tonight must have been looking for something. There was no other reason to go in there, unless they planned to hurt her, which they didn't need to do. As Joel pointed out, if they wanted to be rid of her, it would be easy enough to send her to a nursing home.

Except Jenna refused to do so.

That let her off the hook with the elevator, since she had more control over the situation than the kids did.

Or maybe not. Jenna made a promise to Carl, and she wouldn't break it because she never broke her word.

Jenna couldn't bring herself to kick Marguerite out, but if she could scare her, or make living here horrible for her, Marguerite might decide she was better off in the kind of facility that could care for her physical needs.

And then Jenna's word was safe.

Oh, hell, none of it made sense. All I knew was that I couldn't really believe anything anyone said. I'd caught everyone in a lie, or an omission, or doing something bizarre. Everyone.

Including Marguerite, who hadn't told me how much her family hated her. Or the lengths they would go to get rid of her.

Chapter 15

Maybe the next time Dad came for Sharon, he would stay out of it. The crack he'd gotten Tuesday left a bruise that even Mom noticed. "Gage, did you get in another fight at school?" she'd asked.

"Yeah. It's no big deal," he'd mumbled.

Did he have the stupidest mother in the world? If he fought that much at school, he'd be expelled. Of course, ~~telling~~ her what really happened wasn't a good choice, either. If he started ~~telling~~ people the truth, he'd have to ~~tell~~ Mom he got run over by the school bus.

"Telling" too many times. If he started saying the truth—speaking the truth—Mom would think he'd been run over by the school bus--?????

৩৩৩

"Can we talk about something?" I said to Marguerite

the next day, interrupting her musings on Chapter Five. Other than being a little subdued, she was rosy-cheeked and seemed none the worse for the previous night's escapades.

"We talk all the time." But she set the newly-typed pages on her lap to give me her full attention.

I licked my lips. "I think it's time to go to the police."

"And just what would we tell them?"

Were they all clueless? Or did she not want to admit it? "Someone was in your room last night. I think someone else, or maybe the same person, came into my room to stop me from going to you when you called out."

"You keep saying *someone*. The police aren't going to listen to that, Louisa."

I raised my hands in frustration and the pencil in my right hand fell to the floor. I ignored it. "I don't know who it was. It's not like anyone's going to admit it."

She closed her eyes.

"The problem last night was Jenna's denial. If she'd pressed the issue, maybe she could have figured out which of the kids was in your room and why."

Marguerite's eyes fluttered open. "Really? She could?"

I thought for a moment. Marguerite had a point. Jenna didn't seem to be in charge of her children—or anything else, except Airtech. "Then there's the elevator being jammed, and the trip wire, and the gunshot I think I heard that night in the pool."

Marguerite glanced at her closed door. "If we call the police, all three of them could deny everything. There's no proof. They could say you and I planned the theft of my chair to compromise them."

"That's nuts!"

"Is it? When it's their word against ours? We'd be

making accusations with no proof, and we'll look like a silly old woman and her sillier sidekick."

I tried not to laugh at the description. She was right. Jenna would change her mind about whether Marguerite belonged in a nursing home. Or an institution.

I wondered if the subject had ever come up.

"You must have some idea what happened to your chair. Did anyone wake you up that night? Maybe last night was supposed to be a repeat of that."

She shook her head. "No. I never awoke that night."

I twisted the ends of my hair in frustration. "I wish I could remember whether it was there or not, but all I remember is not noticing it either way."

She didn't answer.

"Jenna thinks Tamara did it. Or pretended she thought that." A cold finger prodded my spine. I'd believed the chair incident might be a conspiracy among the three of them.

But none of them knew I was listening last night, when Jenna asked Tamara why she did it, and Tamara said she hadn't.

Someone was lying. Maybe several of them. Maybe all of them. But I didn't know who, or about what.

Marguerite gazed at the pages in her lap and prodded them with her pen.

"What else?" I asked as gently as I could.

She looked up, her lips mashed tightly together the way a child does when she's trying not to cry. "This is my family, Louisa."

"All the more reason to find out who's doing this stuff."

"What about the others?" Her voice was thick. "What about whoever is the guilty party? I have to think of the repercussions."

I must have looked at her oddly.

"What if it's Tamara? Why would I want a troubled girl to suffer more? What if it's Jenna? What happens to Airtech? To my son's legacy?"

I hadn't really thought about that.

"What if it's Joel?" Her voice softened and I tried not to jump. Did she know how I felt? "What would happen to Tamara? He's the only one who cares for her. You know that."

She'd given this a lot more thought than I realized. "I'm more concerned about you. You can't let your fear of hurting Tamara's feelings put you in danger. Or me."

She let her pen fall to the papers and clasped my hand. Hers felt cool and papery. "You aren't in danger, Louisa."

"Someone put a pillow over my face last night!"

She jerked back in her chair. "They did what?"

I told her about the intruder and my suspicions that one person was after something in Marguerite's room and the other was assigned to stop me from going to her. "What could any of them want in here?"

"I don't know. Whatever it was, I doubt they got it."

It couldn't be the book. I kept it in my room. "It might be time for me to ask Jenna for a key to my room." *Or get out.*

But I couldn't. I'd made a promise, and I would keep it.

"I don't think anyone in my family is going to hurt you. In fact, I don't even think they want to hurt me. No, Louisa, these occurrences are more like the string tied across my closet the first day you were here—mischief whose purpose is to make me unhappy or uncomfortable."

Downplaying the danger to us could get us both killed. I drew a deep breath. "You think they're only trying to get you to leave?"

She shrugged. "Perhaps. I've told you Jenna wants to move. If she didn't have to worry about me, she could put the house up for sale."

That wasn't a good enough reason to do the things *someone* was doing. "Okay, then…"

She smiled for the first time. "Then what?"

"You could always move out. Then you wouldn't have to worry about any of this."

"Where would I go?"

"Anywhere you want. You're rich."

"I'm also old and infirm. I would either have to go to a nursing home or hire a live-in companion. I will not do either."

"Oh yeah?" I said before I thought. "What am I?"

Marguerite looked as though she were trying not to laugh. "A handful, as you've said." She touched my hand. "It's not as bad as all that. What would I do in an apartment or condominium all by myself? How could I write anything without the stimulation of other people around me? I would be as bored as Tamara is."

"If your family is so stimulating to you, spend some time with them."

"I don't need to. I can hear everything that goes on without even trying." She chuckled.

That was probably true. God knew I'd heard enough arguments between Jenna and Tamara to write a book of my own.

But I didn't think that was her real reason for staying. The house, and her family—whether they liked her or not—were reminders of her son. If she moved out, she would lose the small part of him she had left.

It made me ache. To think of being so lonely you would tolerate people who at best weren't interested in you, at worst hated you, because without them, you had nothing. She had money, of course, but I was fast learning that didn't count for as much as people thought.

At least my earlier question had been answered—why Marguerite would advertise for help when she could get Jenna to hire a professional for her. Of course she wanted to hire her own secretary/companion if she knew she couldn't trust Jenna.

And why she hadn't told me her situation up front. No one in her right mind would tell a stranger such personal details, not until she had some assurance I wouldn't go straight to the papers with the story. I wondered whether she was protecting the family or herself.

✧✧✧

Joel got in the habit of coming by my room in the evening to spend time with me. He'd ask me about my day, talk about what went on at work, put on headphones to listen to some of my music, and admire any drawings I'd done. As much as I enjoyed Marguerite's company, my heart didn't flutter like a middle-schooler's when I saw her like it did when I saw Joel. His warm smile was like being caressed, and when he sat next to me, even my skin felt more alive. I'd smell his fresh scent and think about things I hadn't thought of in a long time.

It took all of two days before his visits were the high point of my day.

Saturday night he asked me if I wanted to go out to dinner on Sunday. "I have a better idea," I told him. "I'm not really big on fancy restaurants. Why don't we go to Olympic Park early in the morning and take a picnic lunch? We could take that drive along North Beach."

His face lit up. "Yes. And to hell with Mrs. Wharton. We'll pack our own lunch. It'll mean bologna sandwiches instead of roast turkey, but who cares?"

"Bologna sandwiches with you will taste like filet mignon."

He grinned. "Shameless flattery."

"But of course."

He pulled me into a hug. "Keep it coming."

Sunday morning we put together a huge lunch, not bologna sandwiches, but leftover roast beef, apples, oatmeal-raisin cookies and a cooler of homemade blackberry cider. We took Joel's Mustang so we could take advantage of the weather and put the top down. Joel alternately shifted gears, drank coffee from a travel cup and rested his arm on my shoulders. His black hair ruffled in the wind and his dark eyes, when they looked at me, were warm and admiring. "Do you want to take the drive first?"

"Yes. We can hike when we get to the park, and by then we'll be hungry. That's a long drive."

North Beach is the longest driving beach in the world, and we had a perfect day to enjoy it. The sand was white, the sky was blue and the water was clean, and we reveled in the cool breeze that whipped my braid around my face.

"Do me a favor when we get to a stopping point," Joel shouted over the wind.

"What?"

"Let your hair down."

I grinned. I loved to wear it loose, but not on a day like this. "Okay. But I'll have to braid it again for the drive back. Then again, I could just sit on it."

"Why are you squinting? Does the wind bother your eyes?"

"Not really. It's drying out my contacts a little."

"How can you stick plastic in your eyes?"

"Because I look like a cartoon character in glasses. Or a kid from one of those comedy sci-fi afterschool specials, who builds a lab in the basement to blow up the world, and his parents are completely oblivious."

He either didn't get the reference or didn't think it was funny, from his expression. I wondered if he knew that kind of kid and didn't like my poking fun at him/her.

Maybe he just didn't like references to oblivious parents.

I looked away from him then out the window. I grabbed his arm. "Joel, look! An otter."

He glanced at it then smiled. "They're all over the coast in California. We saw plenty of them on our vacation the spring I was seventeen. That was the only trip we ever took as a family."

I didn't need to ask why. "I guess your father was too busy working."

Joel nodded. "He was like that song, 'Cat's in the Cradle.' That was my favorite song in high school. And I *won't* be like him. My family will be the kind I always wanted."

"I guess he tried." I couldn't look at Joel. The whole family made me sad. "I mean, once he knew how little time he had left."

Joel snorted. "That's not why we took the trip. Mom was about to leave him."

I swung around so fast my neck popped.

He put one finger to his lips. "No one else knows that. I only know because, well, I overheard things I wasn't supposed to hear."

I knew better than to ask what he'd heard.

"He wanted another chance, and she agreed to give it to him. The next day he called us all together—well, not Grandmother, just Mom, Tam, and me—and showed us a pile of maps and travel brochures for Colorado and California. We were supposed to pick one, but it was a tie vote, so we did both."

"What did you vote for?"

"Colorado. So did Mom. Our father and Tam wanted California. That's the leg of the trip that got cut short. His kidneys started failing while we were there."

"I'm sorry."

I could see a twitch in his cheek out of the corner of my eye. "Someday I'd like to take Tam back there. She loved it. We celebrated her thirteenth birthday with cake on the beach. But I don't know if it was California she loved or the fact that it was the first time we were a real family. And the last."

I turned to the window while I thought about what he'd told me. I didn't know why Jenna wanted to leave, but maybe it didn't matter. I wondered if she would have taken the kids, who would have been seventeen and twelve, with her, or left them with their father and grandmother.

If she were leaving him for another man, I bet she would have left alone.

If so, what happened to the other man?

Maybe there wasn't one. Maybe Jenna was just tired of Carl, who might have been a better husband to his work than to her. For a moment a wave of empathy drenched me and, in my mind, I was Jenna. I'd given up my family, my college scholarship, and my dreams of being a musician to sit in a house all day with two children who didn't need me and a mother-in-law whom I didn't like.

Maybe that was why Jenna wanted to leave—not to escape Carl, but his mother.

Did she really agree to give Carl another chance? Or had he manipulated, tricked, threatened her into staying?

I hadn't known Carl, and it felt wrong to assume he was a bad guy. But there was just too much wrong with his family.

Joel broke into my thoughts. "I didn't come out here today to talk about Tam or my father or Mom. I just want to enjoy you." He snapped a disc into the player and started singing along with a song about "Your Wildest Dreams."

"Did you let a dying goat into the car?" I teased him.

"Are you making fun of my singing?"

"No. I'm just telling you that you couldn't hold a tune with a lasso and a tube of Weldbond."

He laughed. "I know. Tam got all Mom's musical talent—I mean, she has a nice singing voice."

I wondered if he knew she could play the piano even though she had told me she couldn't. "How come I never hear her?"

"The same reason Mom doesn't listen to music anymore. Grandmother doesn't like rock and roll." He tipped his head toward the stereo. "This is pretty tame for me. In high school all I listened to was drug music—songs to get fried by. Jefferson Airplane and all the psychedelic stuff."

"I'm surprised neither of you likes modern music. I mean, I would expect Tamara to listen to Madonna or Public Enemy."

He pointed to the CD player. "This is modern. It's just not modern crap. That stuff you mentioned doesn't speak to me. I'm more into art rock—Pink Floyd, the Dead."

"The who?"

"Yeah, they're pretty good, too. *Tommy* was great."

"What?"

He looked over at me. "I guess that's not really your type of music."

"I don't even know what you're talking about." I wanted to, however, and not what a Pink Floyd was. "What do you mean, music to get fried by? Did you?"

"Constantly. I sat through half my classes either stoned or drunk."

I tried to picture that. "Did you ever get caught?"

"Of course. Once I almost got expelled. They called my parents but I swore there was nothing wrong with me and my father backed me up. He told them to quit hassling his kid." He made a wry face. "They did."

"Do you still do it?"

"No. I quit getting high after he died. But I guess it was too late, because Tamara was watching, and now she does whatever she wants. I know I'm responsible for that because she's always looked up to me. If I try to tell her to straighten up, I get, 'Who are you to talk?' And she's right." His voice dropped and I had to strain to hear over the car noise. "I taught my little sister how to smoke weed. Do you think I'm proud of that?"

I didn't bother reminding him that Tamara was old enough to make her own decisions. "She's going to get sick if she's on medication and drinking, too."

"Like she did at the movies? Don't worry. Most of the time I keep a pretty close eye on her. In a way, I think getting mono was the best thing that could have happened to her. She's pretty much under house arrest now, so she can't go out and do stupid things when I'm at work and don't know what she's up to."

"That must have been a hell of a case of mono if she's still medicated."

"There were a lot of complications. She's anemic, too, and she passed out a couple of times. She got down to about ninety-five pounds and we had to put her in the hospital so she could be fed with an IV. She also caught pneumonia."

"I'll bet she did. That's less than I weigh, and I'm about seven inches shorter than she is."

"It was my fault," Joel said, almost more to himself than to me. "I was the one who took care of her, and I didn't notice the symptoms as soon as I should have. The ER gave me hell for not bringing her in sooner. She could have died."

"Why was it your job to take her to the hospital? Where was your mom? What did she do?"

He shrugged. "The same thing she always does. Hides at work and pretends nothing else is important."

"What about Marguerite?"

"What about her?"

Okay, it was a dumb question. Marguerite couldn't drive.

I squeezed his hand. "Hardly anyone our age dies from pneumonia anymore. And they definitely don't die from mono. From what I've heard, they just wish they would." He was still trying to make up for teaching her to smoke weed. How long would it take before he wouldn't blame himself for everything she did? "How long was she in the hospital?"

"Two weeks."

"If that were my child," I said slowly, "I think I would have been with her a lot more and at work a lot less. Airtech will make the same money whether Jenna goes there every day or not."

"It's not all Mom's fault." Oh, I knew he would defend her. "What do you do when your child doesn't like you?"

"I wouldn't let it get to that point. I'd make sure I never lost her in the first place. No baby is born hating her mother. That's something Tamara has learned to do."

"She might as well have been. I mean, born, not hating Mom, but indifferent to her. She never had much to do with anyone other than our father and me. And now, well, you've seen how she treats Mom. It's too late for it to be any other way. Tam would have to decide she needs Mom, and it's not going to happen as long as I'm here."

"Jenna could do a lot toward making that relationship at least tolerable. I mean, for God's sake, Joel. Tamara almost died and Jenna worries about what kind of music she listens to?"

"Mom's been hurt a lot and she's built walls to protect herself. She doesn't think about how Tam feels about her, or she tells herself she doesn't care."

"Did she tell you that?"

"No. I can just tell by watching her expression." His was wistful, directed at the trees. "She wasn't always like that. When I was a kid she was a real mother to us. She remembered some of her mother's Polish recipes, and she'd cook the best food you ever ate. Our birthday cake was a lemon layer cake with a powdered sugar coating on the bottom. She hasn't made it in years. I asked her to when Tam came home from the hospital, and she pretended she didn't remember how."

"You know she was pretending? Maybe she really forgot." I doubted Jenna had cooked anything in years. There was no need for her to.

"That's not the kind of thing you forget." He was still gazing at the pines. "Sometimes when I look at the trees and mountains, I feel as though I could fly. Other times I just wish I could."

I switched the subject back to Carl. I hardly ever heard Joel mention his father. "Wasn't your father pretty close to Tamara? Marguerite told me how proud he was of her for being the swim team captain and about the honors science class she was taking. She said Tamara had a tough time when he died."

Joel didn't answer for a moment, and when I turned to look at him his lips were pressed tightly together. He glanced back at me before replying. "Yeah."

Was he jealous? Maybe there were real advantages to being an only child, like no silly competition for your parents' affection. But Joel seemed to be closer to his mother, so it balanced.

Except Tamara had no one anymore.

"Joel?"

He didn't answer.

I went on anyway. "It makes me kind of sad to see how no one in your family—I mean, except for you and Tamara, you don't *love* each other. One another." I tried to laugh. "I get along with my parents about as well as Jenna and Tamara do, but when I was growing up I always had my grandfather. He took me to powwows and taught me about my heritage and built me up and made me believe I was a big deal. I was, to him."

I had to take a breath. I hated how much I still missed him, how big the hole was. "He's not here anymore, but what he gave me will always be a part of me. If it weren't for him, I wouldn't even think about being part Yakima, any more than Tamara seems to think about being Jewish. And it would bother me a lot more that I'm not pretty by this society's standards, if he hadn't taught me that beauty is inner and what's on the outside doesn't matter."

"There's nothing wrong with your looks," Joel said softly.

"Except they're not what most white people go for. But when I hung out with Grandpa and his friends, I never felt I was anything other than what I should be."

"You're not."

"I know that because of them. Because of their influence. Being with them taught me to respect elders." I stopped myself from saying *I hate that you don't.* "I love old people—the stories they tell, the things they've seen, the lives they've lived, and what they remember. Once they're gone, it's all gone with them. Why doesn't that matter to any of you?"

Joel shook his head. "Your grandfather sounds like a great man, and I'm sorry I won't get the chance to meet him. But no one in my family is like that. You can't make us be what you were, or have what you had with him."

"Why don't you—you plural, all of you—try to love one another while you're still here? While you still can?"

He sighed. "What did I say before about wanting to spend this day with you, and I didn't mean talking about Shithead—uh, Tamara."

"I've heard you call her *metuka*. Is that what it means?"

His laughter was deep and genuine. I wasn't sure if I'd ever heard him laugh like that. "No, it's an endearment, like for a child."

"How does she feel about that?"

"She knows what it means. She knows I love her."

Well, she could hardly not know.

The morning fog had lifted by the time we got to the corner of the park we'd picked out, near the Hoh Rain Forest. The sky blazed cobalt behind the firs and with the help of Joel's binoculars, we could see snow dribbling down the peaks of the mountains like a giant melting ice cream cone. Joel bent to pick one of a batch of piper bellflowers. "The only thing that would make you more beautiful is a chain of these flowers in your hair. Purple is your favorite color, isn't it?"

"Yes. How did you know?" I put out a hand to stop him. "Please don't. The park should be left the way it is. These flowers belong here, not on me."

He smiled up at me. "You're an Indian, all right. You have a respect for the Earth that I guess we white people need to learn."

"You will."

He had plenty of opportunities, for we saw an eagle, several tree frogs, black-tailed deer, and a Roosevelt elk—though I cautioned Joel to keep clear of the elk. The end of the summer was their mating season and they were not especially sociable at that time. Joel thought that was pretty funny. "Sociable toward whom, their intended or us humans?" he asked.

"Intendeds."

He winked. "Oh, it's your turn to correct my grammar."

"No, your knowledge of biology. Elks select a harem. They don't mate with one partner like wolves do."

"You missed your calling, all right. You could have been a biologist."

"Don't bet on it." I looked away. "Most of what I know I learned from my grandfather. He brought me here when I was a kid, and he knew all kinds of stuff about the plants and animals. I don't remember even half of what he taught me."

"You sell yourself short."

"Is that a pun?"

"No. It's a shame." He pulled a penknife from his jacket pocket and cut a red leaf from one of the bigleaf maples. "You'll let me give you this, won't you?"

"Quit changing the subject. What do you mean, I sell myself short?"

"I mean, you could do a lot better than being a typist."

I shook my head. "I don't think that was ever Marguerite's intent. I think she wanted a companion. She needs someone to talk to a lot more than she needs someone to type for her. I'm sure typing is hard for her, and painful, but she told me she's always done it before."

"She has. Even though Mom's offered several times to hire a secretary for her."

"Marguerite's not going to let Jenna do anything for her. She's way too independent. I bet she's a lot like Tamara. I'm surprised they don't get along better."

I could see his throat moving as he swallowed. "Grandmother, she, doesn't like any of us. She liked my father and that was it. I've been in her way since the day I was born. You know they—my grandparents—had to support my parents when they were first married."

"I'm sure she's over it by now." When she talked about it, I hadn't sensed any emotion other than mild exasperation for Carl and Jenna's lack of foresight.

"Maybe. But there's no money in the bank. Meaning, no one ever built a foundation, a sense of family."

I weighed my words before I spoke. "It's one thing not to be close. It's another to do—stuff like I've seen. Did Tamara ditch me at the movies so I would leave? Or did she want me gone so she could hide Marguerite's chair and sneak into her room at night?"

"No."

"How do you know?"

"I know my sister. Louisa, you either believe and trust me, or you don't."

If only it were that simple. I could hardly ask him if he thought anyone murdered his father. Even if he did, I doubted he would share his suspicions with me.

It could be that whatever was going on in the Roberts' house had nothing to do with Carl or his death. But if Joel wasn't ready to tell me why they hated Marguerite, asking him wouldn't do any good.

Grandpa had often said that the head can misinterpret information and make mistakes, but the heart is harder to fool, and I should trust my heart. My heart believed in Joel, even though my head was saying *But what about*...

I had to make a leap of faith. I only hoped I wouldn't crash at the bottom and break into slivers.

Joel pulled me to him with one hand and kissed my forehead. A rush went through me. "Now, for the last time, can we forget everything else and just enjoy this day?"

Amazingly, we were almost alone practically everywhere we hiked. We'd seen only one other couple, two people in maybe their late twenties, and the husband had a baby in one of those knapsack-like carriers. I mentioned my surprise at the solitude.

"It's the shoulder season," Joel explained. "It's too early for the fall foliage tours, and the backpackers and campers that clog up this place all summer went home after Labor Day. The other Seattleites are probably out on the Sound with their boats. There might be some folks down at Rialto Beach, but we don't need to go down there, do we?"

No.

We snuggled in each other's arms, sharing cider and kisses, and the feeling I had went beyond simple happiness. It was more like a supreme contentment, as though if nothing good ever happened to me again, this would be enough. It was a sunrise bright enough for every night I'd ever see. But I prayed there would be more sunrises, because if anyone could love someone she had known only three weeks, I loved Joel.

We went to the rain forest, put on our ponchos, and trudged through the moist green haze of the Hall of Mosses, inhaling the rich, earthy dampness. Joel clowned around on the trees, pretending to be Tarzan, and got nothing for his efforts but a handful of green bits. We climbed on the stilt trees and fished playfully in the streams with our hands. By then it was getting late, so we went to the Hoh River and watched the sunset through the firs. Joel got a blanket from his car and we wrapped

ourselves in it to ward off the evening chill. And then we
made love.

Chapter 16

It was much later when Joel whispered to me. "We'd better leave."

"Already?" I didn't want to move. I wanted to stay in his arms, my head on his chest, as long as I lived.

He kissed my hair, my cheek, my lips. "It's after eleven."

I turned my face to smile up at him. "Wouldn't it be too bad if we had to spend the night here?"

"Well, you might be out of a job in the morning."

"So what?" It sounded cavalier and wasn't really true. I loved Marguerite and didn't want to leave her.

But I loved Joel more.

He held my underwear up, peering at the design. "What's Garfield saying?"

"'Morning is my second favorite time of day, after all the rest of it.'" I eased his arm down. "Not yet. I don't want to get dressed yet."

He put the underwear down and tucked the blanket over me. "Are you warm enough?"

"Yes. You're here."

He pulled me closer, if that was possible, kissed my hair and lips, and caressed my cheek. "One more time. Then we'll leave."

❧❧❧

It was past midnight when we did. I was heady with the feeling of being loved, of the memory of the look in Joel's eyes as we made love. It was like drinking the best elixir ever. Neither of us spoke until we got on the road and Joel played "Your Wildest Dreams" again. He turned to me with a smile so sweet I thought I would melt and reached over to stroke my face. "Tonight the universe was ours."

"It is ours," I told him. It'll still be ours tomorrow." It was a sad song. I wondered if he knew that.

I was starting to nod off. I wadded up my hair and used it as a pillow, dozing on and off for the rest of the drive. Once I awoke to melancholy guitar strains and a harmony of soporific English voices.

"And you think Bill Monroe is depressing?" I mumbled.

"Shh," Joel said. "Don't blaspheme the gods of art rock."

"Who's this?"

"Pink Floyd."

"What a name."

"They named themselves after a couple of blues singers. Shh. Go back to sleep. We're still a long way from home."

I smiled. "Not me. You're here."

He whispered something I couldn't hear, and I was too tired to ask him to repeat it.

When we finally got back to the house, it was nearly three o'clock and everyone else was asleep. Joel walked me to my door; held me tightly; and gave me a long, tender goodnight kiss. "I love you, Louisa."

"Oh, Joel, I love you too." He tried to break off the

embrace, but I held him tighter. "Please stay with me tonight."

"You know I can't do that."

"I would think you're too old to worry about what your mother's going to think."

"It's not Mom I'm worried about."

I just looked at him.

He sighed. "I'll stay with you until you fall asleep."

As I lay in his arms, I thought about his reluctance to sleep with me. *'It's not Mom I'm worried about.'* Who, then?

"Joel?"

He kissed me. "Yes, *ahuva*."

"Why are you afraid of an old woman in a wheelchair?"

Silence. Then, "Go to sleep."

Maybe it wasn't Marguerite. Maybe he was afraid of his sister, who was definitely odd, if not certifiable. She'd had him to herself for nineteen years. She might want it to stay that way. She might see me as an interloper, a threat.

But at the moment it didn't matter. Nothing did except Joel. Falling asleep was easy, with his arms around me and my cheek resting on his chest.

Chapter 17

I awoke the next morning to the smell of fresh coffee and Joel sitting by the side of my bed. I remembered the night before and smiled sleepily at him. "I thought you weren't going to stay all night."

He smiled back. "I didn't. I just wanted to be here when you woke up." He held a steaming cup out to me. "I brought you some coffee."

I took the coffee and sipped. It was perfect—hazelnut, rich, and flavorful. "Did you make this yourself?" Regular coffee was always served at the family meals.

He nodded.

"What time is it?"

"Seven-fifteen."

"Why are you up so early?"

"We have a meeting at work."

I was starving. I got up and dressed, which took a while because Joel wasn't exactly helping. At last I buttoned my blouse and we went down the hall. I pretended not to notice Joel's surreptitious glance at Marguerite's closed door. But once we were downstairs, he didn't seem to care who saw what, taking me into his arms for a goodbye kiss that didn't leave much to Tamara's imagination. "Excuse *me*," she said, eyes wide, as she scooted past us into the dining room.

She eyed me throughout breakfast, and it was hard to pretend there was nothing for her to notice. Apparently the in-love glow I felt inside was shining on my face, because Marguerite saw it too.

"You've seemed very happy lately, dear," she said as we worked on Chapter Eleven.

I smiled, hoping I didn't look too besotted. "Yeah."

"You've been spending a lot of time with Joel."

Uh-oh. "I hope that's not a problem."

"Not for me." Her tone was light and almost teasing. "You might have to watch out for Tamara, however."

"What do you mean?"

"Well, she may not be very happy about sharing Joel's attention."

I'd had the same thought, but didn't really want to hear it from Marguerite. "Tamara and I get along all right."

Marguerite's head tipped to one side, an amused, challenging expression on her face. "Is that so?"

I couldn't quite look at her. "You don't hear her yelling at me, do you?"

She settled back in her chair. "Well, you'll be good for Joel. You'll appreciate his sense of fun without letting it get out of hand."

I shouldn't have, but I asked, "Get out of hand how?"

"Oh, there have been times when he didn't know a practical joke wasn't funny. You'll have to have a limited tolerance for nonsense or Joel will run amok."

"Run amok? Are you kidding me? He's the only responsible person in this house. He's the one who takes care of Tamara. He fixed the hose in my car my first week here, when it would have been a lot easier to call a mechanic. He might not have the best job he ever thought he'd get, but he's at work every day, making an honest living."

Marguerite laughed, a thin, tinkly little laugh. "My, he certainly has you charmed, doesn't he?"

Something wasn't right. "Why does that bother you? He's your grandson. I would think you'd find him charming too."

"Well, I might have, until the day about three years ago when he called me from outside the house and imitated his father's voice on the telephone."

She couldn't be serious.

The tinkly laugh again. "I wasn't fooled for more than a second. Carl, of course, had been dead for three years. But it took me by surprise because I thought Joel was in Tamara's room. I could hear her talking to what turned out to be a tape recording of his voice."

Three years ago. The kids had been twenty-one and sixteen. Old enough to put together such an elaborate prank, but way too old for it to be funny. To be anything but gruesome and cruel.

"Why?" I asked finally.

"I beg your pardon?"

"Why?" I repeated. "That's not an ordinary practical joke. It's—awful. It had to be inspired by fury. Rage. Why was Joel angry at you? Why was Tamara?"

"How would I know?"

"You have to know! Did you do something to make them hate you?"

She lifted her shoulders in a helpless shrug. "I'm alive and their father isn't? I'm not close to their mother? I'm a burden because I'm in a wheelchair? It could be any of those things."

Or none of them.

'I'm alive and their father isn't...' And how did that happen? Why would they be angry at her unless they suspected there was a reason beyond the accepted explanation of Carl's death?

Fortunately she couldn't read my thoughts. "As you can see, there's almost no interaction among us. I don't have the opportunity to do anything to make them angry."

"Did you tell Jenna about the phone call?"

"Of course not. They would have denied it, said I'm a crazy old woman, and she would have taken their side." The helpless shrug again. "Besides, why break her heart?"

"Then why did you tell me?" I was overstepping and I knew it, but I didn't care. She owed me an answer.

"Because Jenna can't change them. You can't either, but you can assess Joel's character, decide if he's a man you want to give your heart to."

"I already have," was out of my mouth before I could think.

"So I see." She touched my hand. "I'm sorry, Louisa. Let's not think about that right now. I'm sure Joel has matured a lot since then. You're a bright girl, and if you're this enthralled with him, I'm certain he deserves your high regard."

The whole conversation had me feeling like I'd rolled in poison ivy. It was hard to hide my unease, but I had to. I didn't want Marguerite to feel she couldn't talk to me. She was the only one who could answer most of the questions I had.

If she would.

Who have I fallen in love with?

We went back to work on the book, and I was late to lunch. Embarrassing, because Jenna had taken the afternoon off and come home early.

"Sorry," I said as I slid into my chair. A fruit salad waited for me, as colorful as confetti, loaded with blackberries and topped with a sugary glaze. "Marguerite and I were working and I lost track of time."

"How is the book coming along?" Jenna asked.

"Well. We finished Chapter Eleven this morning. Marguerite thinks the first draft will be done by the end of this week or early next." I took a bite of the fruit salad. *Uhmm.* "This glaze is heavenly. What's it made out of?"

"Ask Joel," Tamara said without looking up from her stew. "That's his secret recipe."

I polished off what I had and got more, then ate two bowls of stew. Jenna looked at me with amazement and Tamara with amusement. I just smiled and kept eating.

And planning.

I'd been wondering about Joel's high-school girlfriend, Valerie, since we'd seen her at Northgate and Joel had been so dismissive of her. She'd worn a name badge, leading me to believe she worked in the mall. As soon as I had a chance, I would go back, find her, and see if she could tell me anything.

It was a long shot, but if she went with Joel for two years, maybe she could confirm or deny what Marguerite had implied—that Joel was much different from what I'd seen and fallen in love with.

I was glad the book was almost finished. It was time for me to leave. If Marguerite was right, and Joel had a cruel streak, I needed to get away from him while I still could.

If she'd—lied? Would she *lie* to me?

If she had, I had an even bigger problem.

Whichever it was, the morning's events had left me feeling off. Or maybe it was the fact that I'd eaten so much. We'd gotten back late and I hadn't slept more than a few hours, but I couldn't remember the last time I'd been this beat. Moving my body up the stairs would be as impossible as hauling a bag of wet cement to the second floor.

I decided to take a nap. I dragged myself to the living room and flopped across the sofa, landing face down with my right leg hanging over the side, and too damned tired to lift it.

જાજી

I couldn't figure out where I was when I woke up.

I remembered—sort of—collapsing on the sofa for a nap. But I wasn't on the sofa. In the first moments of semi-consciousness, I couldn't orient myself until I saw Joel's arm wrapped around my chest. A blue and brown quilt covered me. *That's right. This is my bed, here, at the Roberts' house.*

Oh, God, was I foggy. My head hurt, the way it often did if I overslept. "What's going on? What time is it?"

"It's almost six."

"Holy crap." I nudged his arm aside and sat up. "I fell asleep right after lunch and I just woke up at six? That's five hours."

He played with my hair. "You must have been exhausted."

"How did I get up here?"

"I carried you. I just got home from work about a half-hour ago."

Fear chilled me. "Did somebody drug me?"

Joel stared.

"Answer my question. Oh, hell, never mind. You wouldn't."

"Take it easy, *ahuva*." He pulled me back down onto his chest. "No one drugged you. You're fine. You were worn out."

"How do you know I wasn't drugged?"

He leaned over my face and peered down into my eyes. He held one eyelid open with his thumb as he gazed into it. "Your pupils look normal. How do you feel?"

"Groggy."

"That's normal after a long afternoon nap."

"I have a headache."

"How bad?"

I shrugged and pressed my temples. "One-aspirin."

"You're fine." Joel lay back down. "To be honest, when I got home and heard you'd slept all afternoon, I had the same thought. I asked Tam, and she swore she hadn't done anything."

"Oh, like she'd admit it."

"She would to me." Joel's tone didn't leave any room for argument. "Besides, how could someone slip you anything? Didn't you eat the same food everyone else did at lunch?"

"Yes. Except for the fruit salad." I jerked away as I remembered. "Which you made. Along with my coffee this morning." My mouth was so dry I could hardly form the words.

"Louisa." His hands were strong on my shoulders. "I drank the same coffee. I wasn't even there to put anything in your fruit salad, which I wouldn't have anyway. No one drugged you. Tamara didn't touch any of your food. Mom doesn't go around drugging people. Grandmother can't walk to get downstairs and put anything in your food. *No one did it.*"

What he said sounded reasonable enough—for anyplace other than this. "Can you blame me for thinking someone drugged me? All the stuff that's happened since I came here?"

He disregarded that. "You were tired. This is a stressful household. You've been working hard, we had a long day, and you got about four hours of sleep last night. Then you ate a big meal at lunch. I'm not surprised you crashed."

I jumped on that. "You're not kidding it's a stressful household. All the stuff that's happened since I've been here." I enunciated as though I were teaching English to a foreigner. "Like, gunshots being fired, and someone trying to smother me, and whatever all of you are trying to do to Marguerite."

"No one is doing anything to her."

"Joel, that's crap. What about the wheelchair disappearing and turning up in a closet somewhere?"

"I didn't move it." His hands rubbed my shoulders. "I never touched it. Neither did Tam. She was too drunk that night to do anything but collapse in bed. She wouldn't have been able to get the chair out without waking up Grandmother."

"So that means you think your mother did it."

"I would never accuse Mom of anything like that. She's not…sadistic."

Someone was, and he knew it. "No one is doing anything to Marguerite, huh? What about the elevator?"

"A repairman's coming Friday."

I hooted. "I could fix it for him, but Marguerite wouldn't let me." She didn't want me to get hurt if something went wrong with the cable when the pliers were pulled off.

Joel turned away.

I wanted to ask him how Tamara knew what was wrong with the elevator if she hadn't done it. But I'd have to admit I'd been listening to them Wednesday night. I didn't know how he would feel about that, and I didn't want to find out now, while my head felt like the Mariners had used it for batting practice. "None of you even *talk* to Marguerite."

"I don't want to get into that now." He sounded as though he were the one who needed a five-hour nap. "But I can tell you, no one has done anything to try to hurt her. Ever."

"What about the trip wire?"

He didn't answer, nor ask *what trip wire?*

"Joel, talk to me. Why do all of you hate her so much?"

"Is that what she says?"

"It's obvious." It was way past time to ask myself some hard questions—beginning with, why hadn't Marguerite ever answered me when I asked why her family hated her? She'd pretended not to know. The hell she didn't. She'd have to.

But I couldn't ask the most important question of all. *What* really *happened to Carl?* If there was a murderer in the house, I couldn't let them know I suspected the truth. Someone had gotten away with it for six years, and they would want to keep getting away with it.

I rubbed my forehead with my fingertips. "I just keep thinking, who benefits if she dies? The answer is, all of you."

His head jerked back and forth. "Not true. She's left her shares of Airtech to Mom. She knows Tam and I don't want it."

"Okay, so you don't benefit financially. Do you benefit personally? Like you don't have someone you hate in your house all the time? If she were mobile you could hope to have some peace from her. But since she can't go anywhere, she's always here, like a stain you can't wash off the wall."

There was a light tap at the door and Tamara stuck her head in. "I heard voices." She flicked on the light. "Louisa! You're awake!"

"Don't you know how to knock?" But Joel didn't sound angry at her at all. Relieved, maybe, that she'd come in before he had to answer my question.

"I did." She came to the side of the bed. "I'm glad you're okay. I was worried about you. You fell asleep right after lunch, and it's already past dinner. Do you want me to have a tray sent up to you?"

"No, thanks." I wasn't hungry.

Another knock. I figured it was either Jenna or Carol, coming to see if I needed anything. But when I said, "Come in," and the door opened, Marguerite wheeled herself in.

Tamara quickly scooted out of her grandmother's way and moved to stand by the bed—behind Joel, who had jumped up as soon as the door began to open.

What about Marguerite made them so uneasy?

Or was Tamara just being polite, getting out of the way of the chair?

Right.

Marguerite ignored both of them and focused on me. "I'm glad to see you awake, Louisa. I got anxious when you didn't come back to work after lunch, so I asked Jenna where you were."

Whoops. I wondered what Jenna said. Or how much she even knew. "Sorry. I fell asleep after lunch and just now woke up."

"I understand you had somewhat of a late night." Her tone was unconcerned and not at all accusatory. Even so I could feel Joel tense and his touch on my shoulder tighten. But Marguerite's facial expression was as unruffled as her voice. "You looked a little sleepy this morning. It's no bother, dear. I got a lot done, and we'll get back to work tomorrow morning."

I nodded. "Okay, thanks."

I was relieved when she wheeled out without another word. For some reason, I felt awkward with Joel being so close to my bed, as though we'd been caught playing doctor.

Tamara came out from behind the bed and headed for the door. "I guess I'll leave you lovebirds alone."

"Good idea, Tam," Joel said.

The door closed.

I turned to Joel. "Why did your mom take off early today? She never takes half days off in the middle of the week. Why today?"

"I don't know. I wasn't here."

"That's pretty unusual for her, isn't it?"

"Yes." He studied the bedspread.

"Does she have sleeping pills?"

"She didn't do anything."

"How do you know? Does she take sleeping pills or not?"

He didn't answer, which was an answer in itself. "So she does. She was home unexpectedly today. And she's put off having the elevator fixed." *And she jammed it in the first place, and you and I both know it.* "I know she and Marguerite don't like each other. You don't have to say anything, Joel. I've already figured that out."

"What else have you figured out?"

"That your sister's mental."

"Please don't say that," Joel said sharply. "She's unhappy. That doesn't mean she's psychotic."

"If you're going to defend her at my expense you might as well go."

He held me closely, despite my efforts to pull away. "I'm not leaving until you're better. And I'm not defending Tam at your expense. I just don't want you to call her 'mental.'"

I was too worn out to argue. "If one of you is trying to scare me off, so you can hurt Marguerite or for some reason I don't know, you might as well give up. I'm not going anywhere. Not until the book is done. I've spent my whole life walking away from things before they're done, and I'm not doing it this time."

"I hear you." Joel sounded as weary as if he'd run all the way from the Space Needle.

He might be right. I probably hadn't been drugged. Tamara wouldn't risk angering her brother, her one ally in the house. Jenna had better things to think about, and Marguerite couldn't have gotten to my food.

But I could tell Joel knew more than he was telling me, and my heart hurt worse than my head and stomach.

Chapter 18

The next morning I was up early and felt fine. I took a long shower, using plenty of the expensive perfumed soap, and wrapped myself in one of the half-inch thick towels. There were advantages to having money. At home, I used whatever soap was on sale at Pay 'n Save, and I could read the funnies through my towels.

As often happens in the morning, my fears of the previous night seemed exaggerated. But even knowing I'd only been tired, and my body got the rest it demanded, didn't stop my nerves from standing on end like they'd been shocked. Just even the fact that I'd thought I was drugged, that someone in the family would do such a thing, said it all.

The fact that Joel thought the same thing, enough to ask his sister if she had drugged me, said even more.

This would be a great time to get out of this nuthouse. But I couldn't. I would be leaving Marguerite alone with a family that not only hated her, but deliberately imprisoned her and tried to drive away her paid companion. Being ditched at the drive-in would have sent most people packing, and not for just one night.

But I couldn't do it, not again. I thought of my grandfather, and all the elders at the powwows. The ones who'd led the round dances, offered blessings, and passed down stories and recipes. They'd been revered, as elders should be, and it made me angry that an old woman could be treated like this.

Confused, too, because the rest of the family hardly seemed like monsters. Except maybe Tamara at her worst.

I remembered the look in Joel's eyes as we made love. He'd looked at me, treated me, with gentleness, tenderness, with love. How could that same person torment his elderly grandmother?

I couldn't believe it. I'd seen Marguerite's occasional lapse into snappishness, Jenna's cool distraction. I'd watched Tamara go from almost normal, to silly, to just plain unhinged for no apparent reason.

Joel hadn't done any of that. He was the most stable member of the family and the one who usually tried to mend things between his mother and sister. If anyone was off, it wasn't him.

What had Marguerite done to be hated so much?

I'd planned to go to Northgate and talk to Valerie. As soon as Marguerite and I were done working for the day, I would.

e∽e∽

It was a long shot, I realized as I walked into the far end of Northgate by Penney's. All I remembered was that Valerie had been wearing a name badge of some kind. Maybe she didn't even work at the mall. Maybe she worked somewhere else and had come to Northgate to do some lunchtime shopping.

No matter. If I had to walk into every store, I would.

Then I remembered. The badge had some kind of distinctive artwork—zeros made to look like camera lenses and heavily made-up eyes. *1000 Words*, that was it. A photography shop at the other end past Nordstrom's.

Bingo. I walked in and there was Valerie, going over proofs with a young mother with two boys in tow.

"Hi. Did you have an appointment?" another woman chirped.

I shook my head. "No, thanks. I'm here to see Valerie."

At the sound of her name she glanced at me, a slightly bemused expression on her face, but turned her attention back to her customers. I entertained myself by examining the sample portraits on the walls. Typical studio stuff. Kids, couples, and a few dogs against backgrounds of rich color and fake seasonal settings. Technically, they were all pretty good, as much as I could tell, but not very interesting.

Grandpa had taken me once to a Native American art exhibit that included a photographer who worked all in black and white, like Ansel Adams or Georgia O'Keefe. She'd done a series of photographs from one of the reservations, capturing the desolation and hopelessness better than anything Grandpa could have said to me. It was a good way to deliver a warning lecture.

I wondered what Grandpa would think about where I was now.

Valerie finished with her customers and came over to me. "Are you here to look at proofs?"

I turned away from a portrait of two black puppies with soulful brown eyes sitting in the lap of a bright red and white Santa Claus. "No. I'm here to see you." I put out my hand and she took it hesitantly. "I'm Louisa Berry. You saw me here early last week with Joel and Tamara Roberts."

She nodded. "I remember. What can I do for you?" Her tone was guarded.

I didn't blame her. Unfortunately, there wasn't any way to ease into what I wanted to say. "I work for their grandmother, and there's a lot of strange stuff happening. I was wondering if you could sit down with me for about ten minutes and tell me some of what you remember about the family so I can figure out if I need to run like hell and not look back."

When she didn't answer I said, "I'll buy your lunch at the seafood bar." Maybe I could write it off as a business expense.

"Yes," Valerie said. "Run and don't look back." She grinned. She was a pretty girl—woman, she had to be Joel's age—hair the color of a just-ripened apricot and enough freckles to have an appealing, fun look. It was easy to picture her and Joel as a couple, and a cute one. "I don't do seafood. I'm a vegetarian. Can we eat at the Greek place instead? Or I'll have Greek and you have seafood."

"Greek's fine. When do you go to lunch?"

She glanced at a pink UW Huskies watch. "Two o'clock. I'm lucky, I get an hour lunch today. I'll meet you in the food court."

She was punctual and polite as we ordered our food and found the most isolated spot we could, "isolation" being a relative concept in the food court. Valerie carefully lined her Greek salad with dressing and mixed it before speaking to me. "I can't figure out why you want to talk to me about Joel's family. We broke up six years ago, and I've seen him maybe twice since high school. After he ripped up the sympathy card I sent him when his dad died, I don't care if I never see him again."

I paused with my forkful of *dalmas* halfway to my mouth. "He did what?"

She shook her head and waited until she'd swallowed her mouthful of salad to answer. "I sent him a sympathy card, and he tore it up and mailed the pieces back to me. That's sort of typical of Joel."

"You mean typical of him six years ago."

"I mean typical of him period. He's still holding a grudge against me for breaking up with him. It wasn't like I stepped out on him, or embarrassed him publicly, or did anything he should be mad about now."

"There's something Marguerite—their grandmother— told me that's been bothering me." Briefly I related the phone prank story.

Disgust crossed her face, but didn't stay long. "It's plausible enough. It sounds like something Joel might think up to entertain Tamara on a rainy day."

"So they've always been close?"

"Close?" Valerie dabbed a morsel of feta cheese from the corner of her mouth. "That's an understatement. They're like Siamese twins—or they were when we were going together."

"What do you mean?"

She made a face. "When we went out, Joel almost always brought Tamara along. How would you like to have an eleven-year-old chaperone everywhere you went?"

"Why? I mean, why did he do that?"

She shrugged. "She was really dependent on him, and he encouraged it. Joel likes to take care of people. Especially her. All she had to do was say, 'Joel, I want those earrings' and five minutes later they'd be in her hand. Then he'd be down to his last two dollars and we couldn't afford dinner, but he could get Tamara a hamburger and a pop."

Not much had changed. Tamara was still running the circus. "Is that why you broke up with him?"

"Not really. I mean, I got tired of it, but it wasn't Tamara's fault. I liked her, even. I felt sorry for her. She was pretty close to her dad and her grandma, but she didn't have much to do with her mom."

"She still doesn't."

Valerie nodded. "It wasn't Tamara's fault we broke up. Joel just...maybe you haven't known him long enough to know this, but he can be so moody it scares you. Once he gets mad, it takes him a long time to get over it, if he ever does."

"Mad at whom?"

"Everyone who didn't give him his own way. He'd try to cover it up with that weird sense of humor he has. That story Mrs. Roberts told you doesn't surprise me as much as it probably should. I bet she did something he didn't like and that was his way of getting back at her."

"If that's how he handles being angry, he needs professional help."

"No. He just needs to grow up. I mean, he was my first love..." She paused. "You know you never forget your first. But Joel's a little boy. A sweet little boy, but still."

"What did you think of the rest of his family?"

She shrugged. "Not much. I didn't really see a lot of them."

"But in two years you must have formed some kind of opinion."

"What'd Mrs. Roberts hire you for?"

"I'm typing her novels. At least that's what she said. I think I'm more of a companion. No one in the family ever talks to her, that I can tell."

"I don't remember her. Joel's mom was really sweet, though."

I pounced on that. "But she didn't get along with Tamara?"

"I'm not sure. The couple of times I had dinner over there were the only times I really saw them together. His dad used to come to Tamara's swim meets, but their mom did only once. Neither of them came to Joel's tennis matches."

Huh. I wondered if Joel resented the favoritism.

"We went to a lot of Tamara's swim meets. And so did Mr. Roberts, but Joel wouldn't even sit with him. The one their mom came to, Tamara won a trophy about the size of that chair." She gestured to the table next to us.

I nodded. "It's in their father's study. But one of Joel's tennis trophies is with it, so I guess their dad can't be accused of favoring Tamara, can he?"

She didn't answer me. "I liked him pretty much. Mr. Roberts, I mean. But talk about intimidating! Whenever he was home, he was always cursing and yelling at someone on the phone. But he was nice to me. One time he had to drive me home because Joel fell asleep in front of the TV, and he asked me about my photography and talked about politics and stuff, like I was another adult."

"You were into photography back then?"

"Oh, yeah. I have been since I was a little kid. Real photography, not this." She made a rueful face and swatted at her name badge. "I mean, it's an okay job, but I'm still at U-Dub, working on an MFA, and when I'm done, I don't want to take pictures of screaming kids, or try to get dogs to smile."

"What do you want to do?"

"If life were perfect, I'd be working for *National Geographic*. But I'll settle for a local travel magazine."

I ate in silence for a moment while I thought about everything she'd said. One thing stuck out in my mind as significant, and probably not in a good way. "Valerie, I want you to think about something. Why would Joel want Tamara out of the house so much he'd risk losing his girlfriend to drag her with him everywhere?"

She looked uneasy. "I don't get it."

"Most girls wouldn't put up with their boyfriend's sister for two years. Most guys would know better than to try it. But Joel didn't care. Something made him want to get Tamara out of the house. To make sure she wasn't at home without him. The only way that makes any sense at all is if he thought she was in some kind of danger at home."

Valerie poked at her salad. "I never knew of anything like that."

"Maybe he didn't think he could tell you. But this is what it looks like to me." I paused to take a long drink of my iced tea. "A lot of things have changed in that house since then. Joel goes to work five days a week, sometimes six, and leaves Tamara at home all the time. What threat is gone?

"Carl's dead. Jenna works now and is rarely at home, even in the evening. From what I've heard, it's only been in the last year or so, since she got her MBA, she even gets home in time for dinner. Their grandmother can't walk. The maid who's there now wasn't working for them then. Tamara is older and can take care of herself."

Valerie's blue-gray eyes were wide. "What do you think it is?"

"That's why I wanted to talk to you. I didn't know them then."

"How long have you worked for Mrs. Roberts?"

"Almost a month."

"That's long enough to have some ideas." She tore open two packs of Sweet 'n Low and dumped them into her own iced tea.

"I think it must center around Marguerite. If it had anything to do with Carl or some servant who's no longer around, weird stuff wouldn't be happening, because there wouldn't be any need for it." *Unless Carl's death wasn't what everyone thought*, I started to say, but stopped. It would be a volcano of an accusation.

But I couldn't stop the nudging at the back of my mind. I had begun to suspect what Marguerite had done to make her family hate her, but accusing her of Carl's murder would get the white-coats called on me.

Valerie stirred her tea in silence, waiting for me to continue.

"Tamara doesn't like her mother, but she's not doing anything really vicious to her, just playing silly tricks like switching cars when Jenna has a business meeting. But it's more than that with Marguerite. Someone immobilized the elevator so she can't come downstairs."

"How?"

"They fastened a pair of pliers to the cable so the sensor doesn't work." I didn't really want to tell her Joel had accused his mother and she hadn't denied it. I still wondered if maybe she was protecting one of the kids.

Solomon and the baby.

I pushed my tray aside. I wasn't hungry anymore. "Then someone stole her wheelchair in the middle of the night and hid it in a closet so she panicked when she woke up and couldn't find it."

Valerie stared.

"It's like the Addams Family moved into the House of Usher. They'd be funny if they weren't so creepy."

Valerie arranged her trash on her tray. "I can't help you. I never saw anything that weird when I knew them. I guess I got away from them just in time."

Maybe I could learn something from her.

I thanked Valerie for talking to me, and she went back to work. I didn't leave right away, but lingered in the food court and scribbled notes on the napkins we hadn't used.

I couldn't assume Marguerite was the Bad Guy without thinking it through. Who had a reason to kill Carl? Who benefitted from his death?

Everyone.

Jenna inherited half of Airtech. For the first time in her life, she had power and money of her own. Maybe she wanted Airtech, or at least a role in it, and Carl hadn't allowed it. Maybe she had also counted on being free—to do what? Have the guy she'd been seeing on the sly, if there was a guy? Put Marguerite out?

But Carl stopped her from getting rid of Marguerite. If I could believe what I'd overheard last Tuesday night, he'd made Jenna promise to take care of her.

'She doesn't break her word...'

Of course the kids would gain from their father's death, as well. Someday they would inherit Airtech, and once they did, they would never have to work another day in their lives. Jenna had chosen to be a CEO. Joel and Tamara would likely hire someone and sit back counting their gold.

But they hadn't inherited a thing. Carl left Airtech to Jenna and Marguerite. Jenna could, and likely would, work another thirty years.

Well, no problem, from the kids' standpoint. Marguerite was in her seventies and had a degenerative disease. All they had to do was wait.

Maybe they were tired of waiting. Maybe they were trying to get rid of Marguerite as well. Maybe they didn't even care if Marguerite left Airtech to Jenna. Just being rid of their grandmother would be enough.

I couldn't believe it. I couldn't accept the idea of either one killing their father for money, money they hadn't even gotten.

Money was only one motive. What about hatred? What if someone hated Carl? What if he'd done something they wanted revenge for?

If Jenna wanted to be with another man, she'd changed her mind. Both Joel and Tamara had made it clear she didn't even date, and the only man she seemed to spend any time with was her late husband's best friend—who was married.

Well, it wouldn't be the first time.

I scribbled *Bill* on the napkin.

But clearly if there had been anything between Jenna and Bill, it was either over or hidden so cleverly no one noticed a thing. Hard enough to do for a short time, and probably close to impossible over a six-year period.

I shook my head and drew an X through Bill's name on the napkin. That just didn't feel right.

Where did Marguerite fit in?

She'd been diagnosed with MS when Joel and Tamara were…I did the math. Nine and four, maybe. The way I understood it, people with MS didn't get better, and Marguerite had every reason to know she would someday be in a wheelchair.

What if she was afraid Carl would put her in a nursing home? Her husband was gone by then, and her son was too busy with Airtech to take care of her. Carl had built his family a house that, if you took out the elevator—or jammed it—wasn't a great place for someone who couldn't walk. Maybe Marguerite and Carl argued. Maybe she tried to guilt-trip her son, reminding him that she'd taken Jenna in and supported Carl's young family. Carl might have responded that what his parents did in 1962 didn't matter anymore, and Marguerite needed a place to live where someone else could care for her.

Maybe that was what Carl and Jenna fought over when Jenna threatened to leave.

Carl had played right into his mother's hands when he made his wife promise to take care of her. Marguerite had a place to live as long as she wanted. But would she kill her own son to ensure a comfortable future for herself?

If Marguerite were a murderer, it would be a good idea to trap her upstairs.

And if she didn't kill him, I would bet the whole house and everything in it she knew who did.

My whole body shivered and I tossed my iced tea into the nearest trash bin.

Chapter 19

*S*haron hunched into ~~her~~ the chair, folding herself over until her chin nearly touched her knees. The latch slid into place as the door locked.

Passive voice, no good

~~was so loud she~~ covered her ears

work on this. Get across the idea of how it feels to hear the door being locked behind them

⁀⊱⊰⁀

Marguerite was frowning, pen to her notepad, when I returned. "Here's Chapter Twelve," she greeted me. "I won't give it to you just yet. I'm not sure I like the tone of it." The pages were heavily marked up, with whole lines crossed out and notes in the margins.

"The tone's been perfect," I assured her. "It's dark and heavy and mysterious, which I think is exactly what you're aiming for."

"It is. This chapter isn't quite measuring up."

"Don't expect it to be easy. It's a lot different from what you've done before. The best part of it is how you imply more than you show on the paper. That keeps the reader wondering."

She smiled. "Suspense. Alfred Hitchcock was the master. If you watch his movies, you'll see how little actual violence is ever shown. He leaves it up to your imagination."

I nodded. "He was known for using the camera angle to show clues. You had to pay attention."

She tapped the pages with her pen. "I'm trying for a literary camera angle. To show just enough to unnerve the reader."

"It's working."

She set the pages down on the nightstand and closed her eyes. "I hope so. Maybe I just need to take a short break from it. I'm finding that I tire more easily than I used to."

"Is there anything I can do?"

She didn't open her eyes, but her face softened. "Yes. Sit here for a while and let's talk about something else."

It wouldn't be easy, because I was still mulling over what Valerie told me. But I settled in the wingback chair, my hair draped over the side as I always did, and we talked. Marguerite told me more about her early life with her husband. She'd enjoyed gardening at their old house and did a lot of canning and baking. Her lips narrowed in a wistful smile as she talked of the difficulty of keeping Carl, who read at a sixth-grade level by second grade, challenged and out of trouble.

Like father, like son? I wanted to say, but it didn't seem like a comment she would welcome.

"Did you ever have pets?" I asked when she paused long enough for it not to be an interruption.

"No. We were always too busy to give an animal the attention it would need."

"My grandpa had a dog when I was younger," I told her. "A black Labrador Retriever, Koko." The name meant *Night*. "Koko would go with us whenever a festival allowed animals. When Grandpa got older, I think he felt he didn't have enough energy to exercise a big dog."

"What happened to Koko?"

"She died when I was in high school." Sixteen. Not long after I'd been grounded from the festivals.

"I'm sorry," Marguerite said. "That was a tough time for you, wasn't it?"

I shrugged. No point in hashing it over.

"That was a rough age for Tamara as well. Not that this one appears to be any better." She grimaced. "She has interesting ideas about what she'd like to do with her life, but doesn't seem to be able to get the kite off the ground, if you understand my meaning."

I did, more than she realized. "Do you think she'd be better off going away to school?"

"Maybe. But she won't. She's too attached to Joel."

૯૭૯

Dinner was steak marinated in some kind of black pepper sauce, baked potatoes the size of a boxer's fist, and fresh green beans. Tamara barely touched her potato, but she emptied the bowl of green beans onto her plate once everyone else had taken a serving. Jenna's eyebrows raised and I tensed, waiting for her to say something. Her mouth opened, then she glanced at Joel.

He shook his head ever so slightly, and Jenna's mouth closed. Joel smiled. *"Toda,"* he murmured.

"Huh?" Tamara said. "Thanks for what?"

"No one's talking to you." His tone was much softer and more teasing than the words themselves. "Eat up. Want more steak?"

"What, am I too skinny?"

"A little."

"Yeah, yeah," she muttered. "I'll eat an extra dessert." She addressed Carol, who had come in to clear the empty bowl off the table. "What's for dessert?"

"Baked Alaska."

Wow. If Marguerite didn't finish the book soon, I was going to have to go back to doing gymnastics.

Tamara made a face. "Is there any more of that chocolate cake?"

"No, Miss Tamara. You ate all that was left."

Her face fell like a little kid's. "I don't like meringue."

Here it comes.

Jenna paused with her water glass halfway to her mouth. "Tamara, please don't whine like a child."

Tamara just looked at her. Then she threw down her fork and left the table.

Jenna glared at her plate then carefully put on a neutral expression and looked up at me. "Please excuse Tamara's manners, Louisa."

"She's not bothering me," I said honestly. "Mrs. Wharton's worked for your family long enough to know Tamara doesn't like meringue, right? What would have been the big deal about making a second dessert she would enjoy?"

Silence.

Uh-oh.

Then I caught a glimpse of a smile on Carol's face as she shut the kitchen door behind her, and I grinned in response. "I'll take her share, and if you turn me loose in the kitchen, maybe I can make something she'd like. I used to cook all the time when I lived with my parents and had a big kitchen."

The adoring look on Joel's face made me weak. "Maybe I can help you."

"Yeah," was all I dared to say.

Joel excused himself not long after that, as did Jenna. True to my offer, I ate two hunks of Baked Alaska. It wasn't a dish that could be served at room temperature, or stored, and I didn't want it to go to waste.

When I left the table, I could hear piano music. I went to the music room with some vague idea of confronting Tamara with her ability to play. But it was Jenna who turned in the middle of "Will You Love Me Tomorrow."

I had to say something. "I, uh, didn't mean to sound disrespectful just now."

She gave me an amused look. "I'm sure you didn't. You're very outspoken. No wonder Joel's so taken with you."

It was one of those times when the best thing to say was as little as possible. "Right."

"I'm glad you're feeling better. We missed you at dinner last night."

"I wasn't sick. Just really tired."

She didn't seem to have heard me. "We're used to illness in this house. Tamara has been sickly since she was an adolescent. She never had measles, mumps, or chicken pox as a child, but she got them all as a teenager."

"I guess that's why you worry about her swimming."

Jenna nodded and switched to another song that I thought might be a Ricky Nelson number. "It's too cool in the morning and evening, and she would get chilled. I don't want her to end up in the hospital again."

"Why does she dye her hair?" I blurted before I knew I would. "I'll bet she's beautiful—I mean, even more so—

with her natural color. She'd look a lot like Marguerite must have when she was younger."

Jenna started. Her hands froze for an instant then continued, but with a slightly different melody, as though she'd gone from "Traveling Man" to "Young World."

"Yes, she does. Maybe that's why she colors it—so she can look like herself. She's very independent, as you've noticed."

I sat silently, hoping she would say more.

"She and Marguerite were closer when Tamara was a child. Once Carl died, it was as though Tamara didn't want anything to do with anyone except Joel." A noncommittal shrug, as though trying to convince me it didn't matter to her.

"She's a teenager. That's pretty normal." I tracked the glittering crystal lights of the chandelier with my forefinger. "Its lights are like prisms."

"We had it installed when we built the house. I love it."

"I'd be afraid it would fall on the piano."

Jenna laughed. "That's not likely. It's strong enough to hold our combined weights. I wish there were a way to take it with me when I move."

Of course I couldn't ask her when she planned to move. Or who would go with her.

I excused myself, leaving her playing something else I didn't recognize, and went to the kitchen to make the dessert I'd promised. I rummaged through the stocked cabinets and found the ingredients for loaded brownies and enough shiny pans for several batches.

Joel came in while I was mixing cocoa and sugar. "Can I help?"

"Probably not. But you can stay."

He did. We made two pans of brownies and clowned around the kitchen like little kids, feeding each other dabs of batter. At one point Mrs. Wharton came in to get something out of the freezer and gave us a dirty look. We tried not to laugh until she left the room, but it was futile, and I'm sure we didn't endear ourselves to her.

In novels, the servants were usually up to something creepy. I thought I could trust Carol explicitly, but I'd never been comfortable with Mrs. Wharton. I wondered how long she'd been with the family and how much she noticed or knew beyond what she'd told Carol.

When the first pan was done I pulled it out of the oven and put it on a rack to cool. "I hope Tamara's hungry at…" I looked at my watch. "…nine o'clock when these will be cooled. We can't cut them until then."

"Forget about cutting them," Joel said, sticking a soup spoon in the middle. "Let's just take this up to her and let her eat it out of the pan."

We went upstairs and knocked on Tamara's door. "Who is it?" she called.

"Me," Joel said.

"Yeah, come in."

Joel opened the door and I carried the pan in. "Here's your dessert."

Tamara eyed it warily as though she didn't quite know what to make of it. "Uhm, thanks." She took the spoon, scooped up a hunk of warm chocolate and savored it. "Hmmm."

"You're welcome," I said.

Tamara stared at the surface of the brownies as though she were counting the number of cracks. I couldn't quite read her expression. Humbled? Guilty?

She had every reason to wonder what I was up to. She hadn't exactly made me feel welcome, and the drive-in incident still rankled. But I wasn't really angry at her. Something was going on here that was beyond her coping ability.

Of course, if she was doing anything to hurt or frighten Marguerite, that was another story.

"Yeah." She twirled the spoon in the pan and the chocolate burbled. "Uhm, I mean, thanks."

Joel's eyes moved in my direction. Tamara paused with the spoon in her hand. "I, uhm, I'm sorry about the drive-in. I guess I thought it'd be funny."

No, she didn't. She wanted me gone so she could pull more pranks on Marguerite—or help whoever had stolen Marguerite's chair. Or maybe her plan for me was the same as the family's plan for Marguerite—to make life here so unpleasant I would leave.

But it was the wrong time to bring it up. We'd forged at least a temporary truce, and I didn't want to ruin it.

Chapter 20

I was just about to go downstairs for breakfast the next morning when there was a tap on my door. "Louisa?" I looked up and Carol was standing in the doorway. "A delivery came for you."

I frowned. "Of what?"

She smiled. "Maybe you'd better come down to the living room and see."

I checked my watch. I had about forty-five minutes before Marguerite would be ready. "Okay." I followed her out and down the stairs.

The world had turned purple.

There were purple flowers everywhere. Bouquet after bouquet, probably six or seven. Every kind of flower I could have imagined and some I couldn't even identify. They sat in purple baskets, festooned with purple bows, ribbons, and balloons. One bouquet rested in the fluffy paws of a lavender teddy bear. It was an explosion of purple. Immediately, I started imagining how I would paint them. The shades alone—there had to be ten distinct hues. Maybe I could use my charcoals to show the texture of the orchids.

I looked at Carol, who was still smiling. "I guess purple's your favorite color," she said.

"Who sent these?"

"If it was anyone other than Joel, I think you'll have two guys fighting over you," she said lightly. "Why don't you read the cards?"

Each bouquet had one, and on each one was neatly printed the same message.

Louisa,
I love you.
Joel.

What could I do?

I hoped the only thing he was guilty of was keeping rein—sort of—on his sister while trying not to narc on her. I remembered Sunday night and couldn't believe he had been able to fake the look in his eyes or the emotion in his voice when he told me he loved me.

But I needed a relationship based on trust, and I didn't think this was it.

☙❧☙

The day didn't get any better. By the time I was finished with Chapter Twelve, I had a nasty headache at my left temple. The book wasn't fun to read anymore, because Gage was getting too bizarre, just like the rest of this crazy house. It made me wonder if Marguerite's MS depressed her or made her moody to the point of irrationality at times. I had done a little research on the disease, and personality changes were a possible side effect of both the illness and the medications.

At least I knew she wasn't faking it.

Joel came home at four o'clock. I was ready to get away from the book and relax with my art supplies. I hadn't done any intense artwork in a while, and I missed it enough to persuade Joel and Tamara to pose for a pen and ink portrait. For someone whose medication supposedly made her drowsy, Tamara had enough energy to fidget like a monkey and put "rabbit ears" behind Joel's head that I did not include in my sketch. "I can't draw a blur," I finally told her. "This isn't an animated cartoon. Can you hold still for a minute?"

"Hey, this wasn't my idea."

"You're excused. I can finish with what I have."

She complied willingly. Joel gave me a concerned look. "Are you all right, Louisa?"

"Of course I am. How could I not be when the entire first floor is full of flowers for me?"

"Did you like them?"

"Yes. Thank you." I filled in his hair and added a couple of strokes to Tamara's sweater. "I'd like it better if I knew what's really going on around here. I'd rather know I can trust you than have all the flowers in the world."

"You can," he said softly. He glanced at my door, making sure it was closed, and pulled me into a hug. He tilted my face up to his and kissed me.

I set the pen down. "Then tell me what's wrong with everyone here."

His head leaned against mine, his chin resting on my hair, so I couldn't see his expression. "What do you mean?"

"I mean your sister shooting at me and trying to smother me—"

"Tamara did not shoot at you. Tam hasn't touched that gun in over a year."

"Why did she ever?" I wondered if he would tell me the same story Jenna had.

Joel hesitated. "Someone she met at the rape crisis center was staying with us to hide out from her abusive husband. He came out here looking for her. Tam shot at him and scared him away."

As best I could remember, that's what Jenna had told me. "What about Marguerite? Why is she so moody? Sometimes she acts weird, snapping at me or saying— stuff."

I hoped he wouldn't ask what *stuff*. If I had to tell him about the phone prank, he would either admit it—which would devastate me—or deny it, which would force me to wonder who was lying, him or Marguerite. Both possibilities stunk. "I wondered if she was angry at me for spending so much time with you, but she hasn't exactly discouraged that."

Joel didn't say anything.

I took a step back. "Sorry. I guess it's not my business. Can you let me finish this? I have a few more touches to add, and it's distracting to have someone watching."

He left, giving me a somber look.

The drawing was done by dinner time. Jenna, Joel, and I were served grilled salmon with a white sauce, but Tamara was eating pork chops with apple rings. I had my mouth open to ask her if she was allergic to salmon, but closed it when I heard a faint whirring noise that made everyone freeze. I didn't realize what it was until Marguerite's chair rolled into the dining room and took a place at the table next to me and across from the kids.

The elevator.

Had a repairman come? Or had someone simply removed the pliers?

My money was on the latter.

I wasn't too shocked to watch everyone's reaction. Joel's Adam's apple throbbed in his throat as he swallowed. Tamara's hand slipped from her water glass and landed on the table as though she'd dropped a glove. Jenna blinked rapidly and stared at her plate. Her expression wasn't surprised as much as resigned.

Well, I'll be damned. She'd removed the pliers. It had to be her, because she was the only one who wasn't surprised. She might as well have a screaming neon sign.

Marguerite, on the other hand, looked positively radiant. "How nice to be with my family again."

Silence.

Jenna finally spoke just as I was about to say something—*anything*—to break it.

"Thank you, Marguerite. We feel the same way." Her tone was controlled and professional, as though she were speaking to a NASA official.

Neither Joel nor Tamara had moved. Or breathed, from what I could see.

"The elevator's working again?" My voice sounded unnaturally bright and high and I wondered if they all noticed.

Marguerite beamed as Carol came in and put a plate of pork chops and apple rings, everything cut into bite-sized pieces, in front of her. "Yes. I don't recall a repairman coming, but on a whim, I tried it this afternoon, and it worked."

While I was drawing Joel and Tamara? It had to be. We hadn't heard anything because Tamara was so busy cutting up.

But why hadn't Marguerite told me of her intentions?

Joel's eyes moved in his mother's direction.

Jenna pretended not to notice. "I'll cancel the service appointment. May we get you anything else?" She gestured to Marguerite's place setting.

If so, it was my job to get it. Or Carol's. But Marguerite faced her granddaughter and the beaming smile hardened. "Tamara, dear, would you bring me a cup of coffee?"

Tamara shoved back her chair, knocking her knee into the table, and scrambled for the sideboard. Her hands shook so badly I could see the pot wobbling. She carried the cup back to the table, but just as she reached Marguerite's chair, she stumbled. The cup pitched forward onto the white tablecloth and drenched it, splashing my shirt and lap.

Tamara's mouth hung open and I could hear the breaths she took, short and huffy. "Uh—sorry. I—"

Carol appeared again. "It's all right, Miss Tamara," she said gently. "I'll get it." She put a cloth over the stain, poured Marguerite a fresh cup of coffee, and set it down on the table.

Tamara flopped back into her seat.

The tension could have been put on a platter and served as a dish.

"Are you all right?" Jenna asked Marguerite. "You didn't get burned, did you?"

"Nothing spilled on her," I said before realizing I'd butted in. "It all landed on the table or on me, and I'm fine." I'd have to stain-treat my shirt, but I didn't want Tamara getting any grief about it. Clearly she hadn't done it deliberately.

Marguerite eyed me from behind her china cup. "Those are lovely flowers, my dear."

I didn't dare look at Joel. "Thanks."

Jenna turned her attention to her daughter. She hadn't noticed the flowers, or didn't care, or she would have asked me about them. "Tamara, be more careful next time. You could have injured your grandmother."

Tamara's head bobbed in little short, sharp nods. "Okay."

"And please don't come to the table with those dirty jeans."

Why the hell don't you quit picking on her? I almost shouted, but Tamara's response stunned me into silence.

Calmly she removed her white cloth napkin from its brass ring and dunked it into her water glass. She scrubbed at her knees one at a time, dipping her napkin back into her glass whenever necessary. Then she turned a beatific smile to her mother. "They're okay now."

We gaped.

Seemingly oblivious to what she had done, Tamara served herself from a bowl of buttered peas and mushrooms then picked up her water glass, frowning at the bits of dust and mud floating in it. "What's wrong with this water?"

I didn't bother to excuse myself. I got out of there as fast as my little legs would carry me, almost stumbling over Marguerite's chair.

Chapter 21

I sat in my room, wondering what was happening to everyone in this lunatic family until there was a soft knock at the door. "Who is it?" I said.

"Carol."

I almost sighed out loud with relief. "Come in."

She did. "Mr. Joel sent me. He's concerned about you." Her eyes showed that she was, too.

I wasn't the one they needed to worry about. "Please tell him to come see me when he's done eating."

He showed up less than two minutes later. "What's wrong, *ahuva*?"

Beloved. Or, maybe that's what it meant. There was so much deception in this family I wasn't sure I could believe Jenna's translation. "Now tell me Jenna can't see that Tamara needs a shrink."

"Mom probably thinks Tam's tweaking Grandmother. Or her. She's done it enough times."

Aha. He admitted it. "Did she really not know what was wrong with her water?"

"I don't think she did."

I didn't even ask why the sight of her grandmother seemed to terrify her. He wouldn't give me a straight answer. "Joel, she scares me. She's nuts!"

He gestured helplessly. "She's my baby sister. I love her."

"Then get help for her. For God's sake!"

"It's not my decision."

"Like hell it's not. You're a responsible adult. Who else can do it? Marguerite? Tonight's the first time she's left her damn room since I've been here. Or Jenna, who hasn't left her planet? You're the only one who could help her."

"Not in the way you're talking about. You're talking about committing her. I don't even know if Mom has the legal authority to do that, since Tam's over eighteen."

"A judge could. And you know something, Joel? It's coming to that point. That's who she's going to be seeing before too long."

"I don't think so. She's not doing anything she could be put away for."

"Uh, trying to smother me?"

He looked away.

"She needs a psychiatrist. *Bad.* You know the most frightening thing about her? She's not always batty. Sometimes she's normal and likeable. But you never know which one of her you'll be getting."

He sat on the bed next to me and stroked my cheek. His eyes were dark and sad. "I know."

I took a deep breath. "Then do something about it, before…I don't know. Before Jenna has enough someday and blows up at her like Mt. St. Helens."

Joel drew my head onto his chest. His heartbeat was steady and rapid. *He knows it too. He's as worried about her as I am, more so, because he loves her.* "Is anything else bothering you?" His lips brushed my hair. "You were tense this afternoon too."

I snorted. "Where do you want me to start?"

He threaded my hair through his hands and kissed it. "Anywhere you like."

It was a perfect time to tell him what Valerie had said, and ask why she broke up with him, and why he tore up her sympathy card and never spoke to her again. But I wasn't sure I wanted to know. "I think Marguerite's book is upsetting me."

"How come?"

"The main character's cracking up. He's got all kinds of paranoid ideas about everything. He thinks everyone's out to get him, and he's always fantasizing about murder. He was supposed to be a sympathetic character, or I thought he was, and now I think he's repulsive." *Kind of like Marguerite herself,* I almost said but closed my trap just in time.

"Why let that upset you? It's just a story, right?"

"I guess."

"Maybe Grandmother's losing her touch."

"Like, maybe she had a few good books in her and she's written them all?"

Joel pulled back a little, a faint smile on his face. But his eyes were still sad. "Yeah, like that. MS can affect the mind, too, you know. We—the whole family—had to learn about it when she was diagnosed. Tam was just a little kid."

Poor Tamara, with so much serious illness in the family, and all at the same time. It would be overwhelming for an adult, much less an adolescent. "How did Tamara react to that? I mean, how'd she handle Marguerite being sick at the same time your father was?"

Joel shrugged. "She was never all that close to Grandmother."

That's not what Jenna said, I started to say, but thought better of it. Who knew Tamara better—Joel or Jenna?

But why would Jenna lie to me? Or be so deluded as to think her daughter had ever been close to a grandmother Tamara couldn't stand to be near?

But it wasn't just Jenna. Valerie had said it too.

Why was Joel pretending it wasn't true?

I couldn't wait to walk out of this house and never come back.

Joel pulled back to watch me carefully. "What's wrong? It bothers you that Tam doesn't like Grandmother? Surprise. None of us do."

"Why not?"

"That's something you should have asked Grandmother."

"I did. She won't give me a straight answer."

"No shit." Joel's mouth twisted in irony. "She can't. She'd have to admit she's never liked Mom. I think she believes Mom got pregnant with me on purpose to trap my father."

"But they were married before you came along."

"Uh-huh. She told you that, didn't she? That just shows how much thought she gave it. And yes, I'm *legitimate*." His tone put quotation marks around the word. "But without me, Mom could have gone home to her own family. With me she had to stay. Grandmother's never forgiven her for that. Probably not me, either. And God knows what she thinks about Tam."

My mouth was dry and I wanted water. "Maybe that's why she's writing this depressing story about this horrible kid."

Joel lowered me onto the bed and pulled me into his arms. "I hope you leave before you get to know Grandmother for who she really is. Not who she wants you to believe she is."

"I can't leave until the book is done."

"If the book is upsetting you, if Grandmother and Tamara are upsetting you, yes, you can."

"No." I turned to face him. "Along with all the other reasons I've already given you, I signed a contract."

A line creased his face between his eyebrows. "To do what?"

"To stay and work for her for the duration of this book. If I leave, Marguerite could refuse to pay me. I can't do that, Joel. I'm broke. My rent's paid through this month, but that's it, and I have to move by December or pay a fat rent increase. Good luck finding another affordable place. There's almost no food in my apartment, and I don't exactly have a lot of job prospects knocking on my door asking if this is where Louisa Berry lives."

He didn't answer.

I took that as a lack of concurrence. "You say having money's not a big deal, but believe me, *not* having it is a hell of a big deal."

"I know," he said into my hair. "We weren't always like this. I can remember our being regular people, when I was a kid and Tam was a baby."

"Were you happier?"

"I think Mom was."

"I meant you, singular, not you, the family."

"I was just a kid. What did I know?"

He would remember things like whether he played with his father, or what his grandmother was like when her husband was alive and she got up every morning and walked around the house. Whether Jenna packed lunches and hugged Tamara and told her she loved her and kissed her children goodbye as they left for school.

But I sensed it wasn't a good time to ask him all that. He was worried about Tamara, too, and I could hear something approaching despair in his tone.

"Let's talk about something else," Joel said abruptly. "Or do something else." He reached under my shirt with a lazy smile, his touch gentle but purposeful.

I pulled back. "I'm serious, Joel. I'm afraid for Marguerite. And myself."

"Don't worry about Grandmother." His hand made lazy circles on my back. "Don't let the wheelchair fool you. If anyone in this house can take care of herself, she can."

"What do you mean, don't let it fool me? Are you telling me she can walk?" The most chilling part of that thought was that it didn't shock or even surprise me.

"No, of course not. I'm just saying, Grandmother is…" He trailed off and I could hear his breathing. "Tougher and smarter than the rest of us."

"Can you elaborate?"

"No." He leaned forward and rested his cheek on mine.

He didn't want to talk about his family anymore. Neither did I.

He kissed my cheek, my ears, my neck. His mouth was soft and warm. "Would you marry me someday?"

"*Huh?*"

"I mean, this isn't a formal proposal. I just want you to know my feelings. My intentions."

"I've known you only a month."

One finger stroked my cheek. "We've talked about that before."

"We've talked about being in love," I reminded him. "Not about a lifetime together."

"I don't need to look any further."

I didn't either. The reckless part of me, the part that had never felt swept away like this, wanted to close my eyes and keep falling. But it was too much to think about, even if I wouldn't be marrying into the House of Usher.

"Not only is it too soon, but Tamara is your first concern. I understand why, but it means any talk about our being serious is a long way off."

"I can wait." The light tone was gone from his voice. "Can you? Would you?"

I'd have to, and who knew for how long. "I have to warn you about something."

"That you're as bullheaded as Tam? I figured that out already."

I smacked him with the pillow. "No, smart guy. You'll have to support my underwear habit."

"What?"

I pointed to the dresser. "Look in the top drawer."

He slid off the bed and went to the dresser. He had to jerk the drawer from side to side before it would open, and when it did, several stray pairs spurted out onto the floor. He said something softly in Hebrew as he poked through the mounds of cotton, taking a few out to examine them, holding up a lavender nylon that I loved and a Snoopy cartoon with the price tag still attached. "What do you do with all these?"

"Wear them, of course."

"How many times a day do you change?"

"I don't, unless I need to."

He pulled out a pair of black and gold tiger stripes and whistled. "I'd love to see you in these."

"Would you like me to put them on?"

He grinned wickedly and for the first time all evening his eyes didn't look sad. "Only if I get to take them off—with my teeth." He tossed them to me.

I caught them in my right hand. "It's a deal."

"But you have to be quieter than we were in the park. We can't have the whole household knowing what's going on."

I laughed. "Then it can't be as good as it was then."

He lay down and gently pulled my face to his. "We'll see about that," he said into my lips.

∾∾

Joel held me and stroked my cheek. "I love you so much," he murmured into my ear.

"I love you too." Whatever was going on wasn't about him. No one who looked at me or treated me with this much tenderness could ever hurt me.

But could he hurt someone else?

I wished I could quit thinking like that.

He reached around me and tossed the condom we'd used into the trash. "We should have thought of that Sunday. It's a little early to start a family."

I had thought of it Sunday, briefly, but hadn't cared. "The three or four kids we talked about?"

"We'll have plenty of time for that." The soft nightlight glow and the moonlight that came in through the balcony windows lit his pensive face. "I want my child to be welcome. Not like I was."

He knew he wasn't planned, of course. "Unplanned doesn't mean unwanted."

"No. Not always. But in my case it did." He rested his chin on my head. "You always talk about your grandfather and how much he meant to you. I barely remember mine, because he wasn't really into kids. I mean, he was a nice guy, but—you know, my parents were seventeen and eighteen when I was born. How could they have wanted me? When I'm the reason Mom never got to go to college, and she's had to live with a mother-in-law she doesn't like and doesn't like her? I'm not doing that to my child. I'm sorry, *ahuva*. I should have taken better care of you on Sunday."

"Joel, it's okay. It was just that once." I was glad we hadn't taken any more chances, but I didn't like his sudden change in mood. "Jenna went to college. She has an MBA."

He snorted laughter into my hair. "Do you think that was her dream? No. Mom's a musician. Or she was, until I came along. Now she plunks around on the piano about every month or so and sings maybe once a decade—when Grandmother's not around to hear her."

"I guess that's her choice. She could hire someone to run Airtech and do whatever she likes."

"I'm not sure. I don't know the company by-laws well enough to know if she's allowed to do that or not. Anyway, it wouldn't matter. She gave in to my father on everything, and she's letting him run her life from the grave just like he did when he was alive. Don't let me do that to you. If I get that imperious, put me in my place."

"You know I would."

"That's one of the things I love about you." He reached for the bedside lamp and flicked on the dimmer switch. A soft orange light glowed on the bed. He turned me to face him. "Would you consider converting?"

It wasn't a question I could answer in one evening, and he knew it. "I've been here a month and I haven't seen you go to, church? Synagogue. Don't you? Doesn't Jenna?"

He shook his head. "Mom hasn't been to temple in years. Not since Tam decided not to do her Bat Mitzvah."

"How come? I mean, why didn't Tamara want to do it?" I thought a Bar or Bat Mitzvah was sort of like a Catholic confirmation, only a bigger deal—for both the young person and his or her family.

Joel shrugged just as I realized Tamara's Bat Mitzvah would have occurred when she turned thirteen—right around the time of her father's death. I doubted she was in the mood for any kind of celebration.

But that didn't explain Jenna's abandonment of a lifelong faith. "If your mother were going to give up her religion, I would have expected her to do it as soon as she married your father." *As soon as her parents kicked her out.* "Why wait till you and Tamara were almost adults?"

Another shrug. "Too busy. Too hard to keep the rituals when no one else in the family except me was interested. But I'd like my children to be raised Jewish, even though by Jewish law they wouldn't be."

I assumed he meant *If I married you.* "Why not, if you are?"

"Because Judaism is matrilineal. They might have to formally convert, but maybe not. Reform Judaism is pretty liberal."

"I thought you were Conservative."

He gave me a funny look, head to one side, eyebrows scrunched. "Mom's family was. How did you know that?"

I didn't answer. Somehow Marguerite's and my talking about the family now seemed petty, like junior high girls standing around the locker room trading details of everyone else's business.

He went on. "I know your heritage is important to you, too. And I'm not saying we couldn't do both. I just think it's a closer, happier family when everyone shares prayer and worship time."

"How can I convert to a religion I don't know anything about? I don't even subscribe to the one I was more or less raised in."

"I can teach you. The basic values will be easy to learn, and they'll probably be ideals you can embrace." He winked. "Did you know it's my *duty* to keep you satisfied in bed?"

"Keep working at it." His hand rested just below my chin and I kissed the fingertips. "What else?"

"We believe in dignity in death as well as life. We don't do autopsies or go in for cremation, typically. And we believe that to save one life is to save all of humanity." Did I imagine a hitch in his voice? "We place a lot of emphasis on the acquiring of knowledge, of compassion for our fellow man, of justice, and of bringing ourselves spiritually closer to God."

"I'm not really monotheistic."

"How can you not be?"

"Because I come from a different cultural background. It's all what you're raised to believe in. My favorite song says, *I leave you with your white man. I curse their church that tells us that our fathers were wrong.*"

Joel drew back and stared at me. "What kind of song is that?"

"A song about my people." The composers were two white folk singers from Ontario, but we didn't need to get into that. "It's about a renegade who dies rather than give in to the white man's way of life."

Joel didn't answer.

I can't sing, but I did anyway. *"Our children cannot follow the old nor the new ways. And the poles of their fathers are rotting in the rain."*

"Let's talk about this later."

"You brought it up." Great. It was hard to look forward to a long and happy marriage if we couldn't talk about religion for ten minutes without arguing.

"I know. I'm not angry at you. I just don't want to be like my parents. They didn't have anything in common, and they were less husband and wife than roommates. Except that once my father got irritated at Mom and told her, 'Don't be stupid, Jenna.' Right in front of us. If I had a roommate treat me like that, I'd move out or kick him out."

She almost did. Now she had Airtech to herself, with no one telling her that her ideas were *stupid*. "Do you think she's the one trying to hurt Marguerite?"

Joel sat up and grasped my shoulders. "Have you seen anyone trying to harm Grandmother?"

"Well, not seen, but—"

"Then don't assume anyone is."

"I'm not assuming. What about that night I was almost smothered? Why did she call out? Who was in her room?"

He didn't answer.

"It was you, wasn't it? What were you doing?"

There were tears in his eyes "Louisa, I would never hurt you." His voice vibrated like a plucked string.

"Would you hurt Marguerite?"

"Not unless I had to."

"What the hell does that mean?"

"If she were trying to hurt you. Or Tam, or Mom."

My hands flew up, missing his face by an inch. "What can she do to any of us? We can walk away. She can't."

"It isn't that simple."

He wasn't making any sense. "Then let's talk about your sister. Let's talk about the piano."

He swiped at his eyes. "What about it?"

"Tamara told me she can't play the piano, and I've heard her playing it—well. As well as Jenna, if not better, and Marguerite told me Jenna was an accomplished musician. Why would Tamara lie about something like that?"

"She isn't lying."

"What?"

He lay back down, arms bracketing his head, resting on his folded hands. "She doesn't know she plays. I think she's sleepwalking. It's completely unconscious."

I lay there, stunned. "Is that even possible? Could her hands do that?"

Of course they could. One of the few college classes I'd loved was Abnormal Psych. What Joel was describing was dissociative behavior. The playing itself would depend on the muscle memory of her hands—pretty much the way any musician memorized a piece.

This was worse than I thought.

"But—why didn't Jenna tell me?" Just as quickly the answer came to me. "She doesn't know. Somehow Tamara learned to play without Jenna's finding out about it, and if Tamara plays only in her sleep, Jenna would never hear it. She goes to sleep with headphones playing sixties rock in her ears. She probably wouldn't hear Tamara playing the piano in the same room."

"What? Mom does what? How do you know?"

I didn't answer. "You were wrong when you said she'd given up her rock and roll because Marguerite doesn't like it. She hasn't given it up at all. She just makes sure no one can hear it but her."

"How did you know that?" he repeated, an edge to his voice.

I didn't want to tell him I'd gone through his mother's things. I'd felt kind of nasty at the time and even more so now.

"Answer me, please." The *please* almost, but not quite, took the edge off his tone.

"I saw the tapes and CDs in her room. With tape and disc players and spare headphones."

He didn't answer.

"It would explain why she didn't hear Marguerite calling out that night, but she did hear me, because I'm right across the hall. Then again, maybe she heard both of us and lied to me. Maybe she's not so far out of touch as we think."

Joel shook his head. "That's where you're wrong. Mom's a damn space cadet. There's a lot I think she chooses not to know. This family is crazy, Louisa, and it's only fair I tell you that before you consider marrying into it, but no one is trying to harm Grandmother—least of all Tamara."

"Tamara needs help and you know it. She's going to wind up down on First Avenue if she doesn't get it."

Joel snorted the worst imitation of a laugh in recorded history. "No. She's not going to be a prostitute, no matter how many times she plays the piano in her sleep."

"If she's not trying to get rid of Marguerite, then what's going on here? Who jammed the elevator?"

"You know Tam didn't do that. She was in the hospital when it happened."

"Then who? You?"

"No."

I threw my hands up again then got up and started dressing. It was almost impossible to have a serious discussion while naked. "That leaves Jenna. Are you asking me to believe your mother the CEO/MBA/BFD climbs around on ladders jamming elevator shafts with pliers?"

Well, why not? Didn't I believe it? And she'd removed the pliers because without them, even if I went to the police, or Marguerite did, Jenna had plausible deniability. *"What pliers?"*

Of course, that didn't mean she'd put them there in the first place—only that she might be protecting whoever had.

Joel reached over the side of the bed to hand me my blouse. "I'm not asking you to believe anything."

"Because you don't care if I do or not?"

Silence.

Joel filled it by pulling on his own shirt and rummaging at the foot of the bed for his pants. He swung his legs over the side of the bed and pulled his pants up to his knees. "Of course I care." He stood and tugged them the rest of the way on. He adjusted the lamp, then turned to me. "There are things I can't tell you. I don't know if you would believe me at this point."

"Try me."

"You wouldn't be in a position to do anything about it. Nothing is as simple as you think it is."

"Why don't you get away from this insanity?"

"I think you know the answer to that."

"Yeah. You can't afford to support your sister, and you don't want to leave her here alone, just like when you dragged her on your dates with Valerie."

He almost stumbled. "Who told you about that? Grandmother?"

"I guess I can keep secrets too, can't I?"

"What is she telling you about us?"

I didn't answer. It didn't seem like a good time to tell him about going to see Valerie—if there were ever going to be a good time for that.

He huffed out a sigh. "Listen to me. There are a lot of things you can't understand now. Like—whatever Grandmother's paying you to be in this family's business isn't enough."

"It isn't the money. My own parents think I'm a failure. And they're right. My last boyfriend dumped me for dropping out of college twice. All my life I've been criticized for not finishing anything I started. I'll finish this."

"Fine," he said softly, coming to pull me into his arms. "I want you to think about something. If Grandmother really thought one of us was trying to hurt her, why would she ask you to be her fall guy?"

"She didn't. She hired me to be a secretary—okay, a companion. Not a private eye or a bodyguard."

"But if she were who you think she is, just a nice old woman, and you were this afraid of her family, wouldn't she let you off the hook? Tell you that you don't need to be here anymore?"

"I haven't asked her to."

"Why not?"

"Because…" Why not, indeed? "Because, if Tamara, or anyone else, is trying to hurt her, I can defend myself, and she can't."

"I guess that's a good enough reason," Joel said. "At least to you, because your motives are a lot purer than hers."

"What are her motives?" Although I could guess. Had already guessed.

Joel wrapped his arms around me, maybe as much to avoid looking at me as anything. "She sensed something in you. You miss your grandfather so much, and maybe you feel bad about the time you lost with him." I stiffened and his arms tightened. "You think you've found someone like him and you can put your regrets to rest. But Grandmother is nothing like your grandfather. *Nothing*."

I tried to pull away.

He didn't release me. "Believe me, when the time is right for you to know everything, you'll know. And that time's coming, real soon."

Chapter 22

There wasn't anything else to say, so we didn't say it. Finally, Joel got tired of the silence and suggested we go downstairs, build a fire, and fix cheese popcorn.

Joel loaded logs into the fireplace and got the fire going. "Why don't you relax, and I'll go make the popcorn."

"I'll get it. How much cheese do you want on yours?"

"Put as much as you want on all of it." He poked at the fire even though it didn't need it.

When I returned to the living room with the popcorn bowl and two glasses of Dr. Pepper, Joel had arranged the sofa cushions in front of a large armchair by the fireplace. He motioned for me to sit next to him. I put the tray on the floor and sat down, next to one of the larger flower displays. They smelled earthy sweet and humid, like the Bromeliad House at the Volunteer Park Conservatory. It had always been my favorite of the greenhouses. I loved walking through the foliage and inhaling the aroma.

I hadn't been there in a long time. My old life seemed like someone else's. Like a movie I'd watched years ago.

Joel pulled me close to him and kissed me before putting a gluey handful of popcorn and melted cheese into my mouth. "I know you're angry and scared. But nothing's going to happen to you. I won't let it."

"Is that a promise?"

"It's a vow." He kissed me again. "Trust me. I won't let anyone hurt you."

We sat without speaking for a few moments. The only sounds were the crunching of the popcorn as we chewed and the willowing and crackling of the fire. Joel finally broke the silence. "Where are the Yakima people from?"

"Mostly south-central Washington."

"Tell me about them."

"What do you want to know?"

"Anything, since it's so important to you. What about folklore? Legends? Do you know any?"

I could feel one eyebrow lifting. "Do I know any folklore? When I was practically raised at the Yakima Nation festivals?" He grinned sheepishly. "Does the bay have water? Do trees have leaves?"

"Not in the deciduous forest in the winter."

I stuffed some popcorn in his mouth to shut him up. "What legend would you like to hear? I know a lot that my grandfather or one of the other elders told me."

"Any one."

"Most of them involve animals, whom we believe are as valuable to the Earth as humans, and who often represent human traits. Especially Wolf, Raven, and Coyote. And eagles are a big deal. The eagle is considered a brave's helper and protector, and his feathers and claws are sometimes worn in battle to provide strength. That's why Native American tribes can possess parts of a bird of prey, but it would be illegal for you to do it.

"Coyote is kind of a wise guy, a smart aleck. There's one tale about Coyote and Crow you've probably heard in some form. Coyote is traveling through the country, clearing the way for the People, and he is very hungry. He sees Crow on a ledge with a piece of deer fat in his beak."

"Uh-oh." Joel settled back on the cushions and pulled me onto his chest. "I think Crow is about to lose his dinner."

I sipped my pop. "Coyote is much cleverer than Crow. He calls out, 'Chief Crow, Chief Crow, please sing to me. I want to hear your beautiful voice.' So the flattered Crow opens his beak to sing, and the deer fat falls out and straight into Coyote's mouth. 'You are no Chief,' laughs Coyote. 'You are foolish and vain, and now you will go hungry.'"

Joel nodded in recognition. "That's an Aesop's fable, I think. But Coyote was a fox."

"Indians revere Coyote. He brought fire to the People when only the Skookums had it."

"The what?"

"Skookums. Evil spirits. Three old women who guarded the fire and took turns so none of the Animal People or Two-legged People could have any. But Coyote came up with a plan.

"He called all the animals together and had each take a place in a relay line. Then he climbed the mountain to the Skookums' lodge. He waited until the sisters were trading positions to guard the fire, then he raced in and seized a burning brand. He took off across the mountain with the three Skookums in pursuit. One grabbed his tail in her claw. He escaped, but her touch scorched his tail, and that is why Coyote has a black-tipped tail.

"Coyote passed the stick to Cougar, who ran through the rocks to Fox, who took the fire and ran till the brush became too thick. He then passed it to Squirrel, who jumped through the trees—but not before his neck and tail were burned. That's why squirrels have curly tails and a black spot on their necks.

"When there was nothing left of the brand but a coal, Frog leaped up and took it in his mouth. The youngest Skookum grabbed his tail just before he jumped into a river, and the tail came off in her claw. To this day Frog has no tail.

"Frog spat the coal into the Wood and Wood swallowed it. The Skookums gave up and went away, but since People did not know how to get the fire back from Wood, Coyote showed them how to rub sticks together to bring sparks, and to use dried leaves for kindling."

"That's a good one. What other Coyote stories are there?"

"A lot, but I don't know a lot of the ones that belong to other Nations. There's a couple about the Columbia River, and how Coyote made it change its course, but they're Sanpoil, I think." I thought for a moment. "'Chinook Wind' has Coyote in it. Do you want to hear that one?"

"Are you telling Indian ghost stories?" came Tamara's voice from the doorway, and her Jordaches swiveled in.

"No, just regular stories. Want to join us?" I held out the popcorn bowl in her direction.

She ignored me. "Joel, I have to talk to you. Alone."

"Can it wait?"

"No." Her voice trembled.

I started to get up and leave so they could be alone, but Joel put his hand firmly on my breastbone. "You told me you want trust and honesty. Part of that is that I can't have secrets from you." To Tamara, "Whatever you have to say, you can say in front of Louisa."

She looked at me, and her mouth opened, but nothing came out. "I…what's in there?" she finally said, pointing to the bowl.

I frowned. *Something's not right.* She sounded shaky, almost tearful. "Popcorn with cheese melted in it. Try some." I pulled my hair out of her way so she could sit with us.

She took one kernel, tentatively, making a face as she chewed it. "I'll take mine plain, thanks. Anyone want some mineral water?"

"No, thank you. We're drinking Dr. Pepper." Mineral water had become a big deal in the last couple of years, but I never figured out why. It tasted like sucking on a scissors blade.

Tamara picked a couple of cheeseless pieces of popcorn out of the bowl and washed them down with a sip from her brother's glass. "What were you saying about the wind and the coyotes?"

"Forget 'Chinook Wind.' I think I can find something Tamara would be more interested in."

"What's 'Chinook Wind' about?" Tamara asked.

"Coyote chopping off the heads of the wind brothers."

Joel hooted. "And Coyote was revered? For chopping off people's heads?"

"Not people—wind," I corrected. "The winds were making the people cold and miserable. Of course Coyote deserves to be honored. What would the people have done if he hadn't brought them fire?"

Joel's head tilted as he pondered this mystery. "Eat their salmon raw, I guess."

"*Raw?*" Tamara said. "Yuck. I can't stand the stuff cooked. I can't even think about it raw."

Joel threw a piece of popcorn at her. "Louisa, tell me how this girl can be Jewish and from Washington and not like salmon?"

"I'm only half Jewish, that's how."

"Don't be silly. You know as well as I do there's no such thing." He turned to me. "I love that you have such

close ties to your background. The High Holy Days—
Rosh Hashanah and Yom Kippur, the holiest days of the
Jewish calendar—are coming up, and Mom stopped
observing them years ago. We never have celebrated
Passover. I guess that's not all Mom's fault. It would be
pretty hard to get all the *chametz* out of the house if you
live with a family of Gentiles and they won't cooperate,
much less participate."

"The what?" I asked.

"*Chametz*. Leavening. Anything that causes baked
goods to rise. Bread, cookies, cakes, doughnuts, baking
powder, I think cream of tartar—"

"Beer," Tamara interjected. "That has yeast.
Remember how the Stooges all put the yeast in when they
were making their own beer?"

No, fortunately I didn't.

Joel nodded. "All of it has to be cleaned out of the
house and burned before Passover. That would be pretty
hard to do if you're the only practicing Jew in the
household. And then, no one else would honor the
Sabbath, so Mom quit doing that, too. She doesn't even
light *Shabbat* candles anymore. I'm the only one who
gives a damn about it, and I don't feel right doing it."

"Why not?" I asked.

"Lighting *Shabbat* candles is a woman's job. No, I
shouldn't say it that way. It's her privilege. It's symbolic
of bringing light into the world."

"So what does a man living by himself do?"

"A Jewish man who lives alone can light the candles.
But I don't live alone. I live with two Jewish women—"
He gave Tamara a significant look. "—and so it's not my
place, it's theirs."

"We've done plenty of stuff," Tamara said. "What
about *kever avot*? Aren't we doing it this year?"

Joel kind of shrugged. "I didn't think you wanted to. The last couple of years you've gotten pretty upset."

"Kay-what?" I butted in.

"*Kever avot* is a custom of visiting a, uh, deceased parent's grave before Yom Kippur," Joel explained.

"Interesting." I sipped my Dr. Pepper. "What does your mother do about her parents?"

Tamara stared, first at me, then at Joel.

Finally, Joel gave a sort of laugh. "Well, Tam, it's not like we thought she'd never find out." He turned back to me. "That's something you'd have to take up with Mom. She never talks about her family."

Oh, well. It was worth a try. "Are all your customs depressing? Where you have to clean out the whole house and fast and stuff?"

"Of course not. Purim is a blast. You get to put on costumes and drink wine and make noise."

"Remember that year I dressed up as Haman in Dad's bathrobe and a noose around my neck?" Tamara said. "That was more fun than Halloween. I think I still have my grogger."

"Mom doesn't pay any attention to that one anymore, either. Maybe if she would, she'd—" Joel broke off at a warning look from Tamara. I wasn't sure what he'd been about to say, but it was probably something Jenna wouldn't want me to hear. After all, in her eyes, I was still an outsider.

Maybe not just hers.

Joel changed the subject. "But, Louisa, you don't really believe those stories about Coyote, do you? I mean, I see them as sort of like parables—stories to make a point about how we should act."

"Why not believe them? They make as much sense as the Judeo-Christian beliefs."

"What religion are you?" Tamara asked me.

I laughed. "I'm a heathen, I guess, by Anglo standards. I follow my people's teachings. Our religion is the Earth and all that's on it."

"You worship the Earth?" Joel asked.

"Doesn't that make as much sense as worshipping a statue, or a god you can't see?"

"I don't worship statues. That's expressly forbidden in the Ten Commandments. And of course we can't see God. He said, 'No one may see my face and live.'"

I might tell him later I wasn't too jazzed about that *imperious* act.

"But don't you think you see God in a lot of things?" Tamara said "In the blackberries, or flowers in the spring, or how green it is after it rains? Or a rainbow, or the days when the mountain's out? In music. I hear God in music all the time."

"We believe in the Great Spirit," I told her. "But we don't really believe that the Great Spirit does it all alone, or that it's one being, especially not one male."

Tamara grinned. "I like that."

I thought she would. "We believe everything in creation is as important as we are, because you can't separate it. You think trees have no humanity? No soul? How would we breathe without them? How many animals depend on them for food, for shelter?" I looked from Joel to Tamara, seeing their skeptical expressions. "Just as this is hard for you to accept, your religion's teachings would be hard for me."

"How does your, tribe, or whatever, treat women?" Tamara asked. "That's one thing I hate about the Bible. All that misogyny. Women in Orthodox temples get stuck off to one side or in the back behind a curtain. Like men are so dumb they won't be able to concentrate on God if there's a woman there."

Joel laughed. "That's sort of the point, Tam. It's a

reflection on our weakness, not yours. Don't you know we believe women are on a spiritually higher plane?"

"You should be Cherokee," I told Tamara. "That's matriarchal. The grandmother is the decision-maker for the family." I paused to gauge her reaction. None. "Someone told me, all a woman has to do, if she's tired of her husband, is put his belongings out of the tipi, and he's history."

"How do you know all this stuff?" Tamara asked.

"My grandfather and the other elders taught me."

The elderly are special to me. Have you figured that out yet?

Tamara didn't take the bait. "Do you know anyone who did that?"

I shook my head. "It'd be kind of hard in this society. I mean, without getting a legal divorce. You could put your husband's things out, but legally he could come back and put yours out, too."

"Ha," Tamara said. "Nobody's going to put my records out. There's a difference between what's legal and what he'd actually get away with."

"Legal vs. ethical?" I said, even though I knew she didn't mean that.

"Hell no. Legal vs. does he value his life!"

We were laughing when Jenna stuck her head in the doorway. "What in the world are you talking about?"

"How to get rid of a husband," Tamara replied cheerfully.

"*What?*"

Tamara looked away. "Oh, never mind."

It was the best response. Explaining the context to Jenna would take all night, and I doubted she would find Indian lore interesting.

Joel hadn't moved a muscle, and I realized he hadn't laughed at his sister's comments. Jenna wasn't amused, either. She gave Tamara an odd look, somewhere between bemused and exasperated. "Please find a more appropriate topic of conversation."

The animation slid from Tamara's face like slush off a window pane. She got up and left the room, brushing past Jenna without a glance. Almost without thinking, I followed her and caught up with her halfway up the stairs, easing past her so she would have to shove me to get by. "What did you want to talk to Joel about that you didn't want me to hear?"

She didn't answer.

I forced a smile. "No point in shutting me out. I'm not going anywhere."

She licked her lips. "Because of Joel or because of Grandmother?"

"Both."

"This is a bad place for you to be, Louisa."

"What are you talking about?"

"Grandmother's mad."

"Mad? Like crazy? Or angry?"

"She's crazy," Tamara whispered. "But she's angry. She's ticked off about you and Joel."

I shrugged. "Well, that's funny. Because she told me you might be upset about having to share his attention with me."

"Not me. I'm not the one who hates you for wanting Joel."

I glanced behind me at Marguerite's closed door.

Tamara tried to move past me, but I blocked her way. "If that's how Marguerite felt, she would fire me."

"But Joel could still have you."

A shiver rippled through me. I glanced down into the hallway. Neither Jenna nor Joel was anywhere around, nor could I hear their voices.

"She doesn't want him happy." Tamara's lips

trembled. I felt a vibration and realized she was shaking all over.

"Are you okay?" I touched her quivering forearm. "Let me call your mom."

"No!" She elbowed me aside and scrambled up the steps to her room.

I went to my own room. I had to fumble with the latch on the doorknob several times before it clicked.

What if she's telling the truth?

How could I know? Ask Marguerite point-blank? What would she say?

I had yet to catch Marguerite in a lie. Tamara had been pranking me and doing wacky things since I'd arrived.

I slumped on my bed, took a deep breath, and closed my eyes.

Something about Marguerite was wrong, terribly wrong, for Tamara to be so petrified of her.

Or maybe it was Jenna she was afraid of.

Or both.

Marguerite was the only person—other than me—stuff was happening to. Did that mean anything? Had she done any of it herself, a diversionary tactic to make me think the family was crazy when in reality it was just her?

The cheese popcorn was an oily backtaste in my mouth.

Marguerite hadn't tied the trip wire. Her fingers wouldn't have the dexterity.

She hadn't jammed the elevator. She couldn't have gone to the third floor, much less climbed a ladder. She could get someone to do it for her, but that would be dangerous. To paraphrase the old saying, two people can keep a secret if one of them is dead.

I didn't even want to think she could hide her own chair, forcing herself to crawl back to her room, *just to lure me back to the house.*

So who had done what?

The trip wire was probably Tamara. Joel hadn't even reacted when I'd mentioned it, and it was too unsophisticated to be Jenna.

Jenna was the obvious suspect for the elevator. I could even understand why. I could almost hear her thoughts.

I promised Carl I would take care of Marguerite. If Carl were here, I could reason with him. He would see how afraid our daughter is. How terrible his mother is. But he's not here, so I have to honor my promise. My only way out is to drive Marguerite away.

Maybe Jenna's motive wasn't that insidious. Maybe she just wanted to be able to play the music she loved in peace. The kids had said she rarely played, but I'd seen her at the piano several times in the four weeks I'd been here.

Because Marguerite couldn't come downstairs and tell her to stop?

I had no idea.

If only I could ask Carol what she thought. She'd lived with the family a lot longer than I had and probably knew more than I did. But I didn't think it would help. If she was being paid to tie wires or jam elevators, she would hardly admit it to me.

Maybe it was time to go to Jenna. But I wasn't sure that would accomplish anything other than to make Jenna even more exasperated with Tamara. Tamara needed help, and not her mother's weird combination of useless carping and utter disregard. Or Joel's excusing her behavior.

Maybe Joel was right. Maybe it was time to tell Marguerite I was out of here, and if she chose not to pay me—

I was right back where I was a month ago.

But at least I would be out of this house. Tamara gave

me the chills, and getting away from her might be more important than all the work I'd ever do in my life.

❧❧❧

That night someone tried my door, ever so gently. Then left without making a sound on the carpeted floor. I wasn't surprised when the piano started up minutes later. It must have been Tamara at my door, and when she couldn't get in, she blanked out and sought the comfort of her music.

Or maybe she'd been blanked out all along.

I longed for the comforting warmth of Joel's body. His bedroom door had been locked since he came upstairs. The lavender teddy bear wasn't a very good substitute for him, and I wiped my eyes on its soft fur as I clutched it to my face.

But I didn't cry. In fact, once I recognized the song she was playing, I couldn't stop laughing.

> *Hush my darling,*
> *Don't fear, my darling,*
> *The lion sleeps tonight.*

Chapter 23

I was real popular the next morning. Joel wasn't at breakfast, but Tamara came in with a message that he wanted to see me when I finished eating. She looked like I'd always imagined a crack addict would look, thin and jittery. I knew the vanilla-maple French toast was a favorite of hers, but she didn't even glance at it. Nor did she make eye contact with me or Jenna as she took a cup of coffee—presumably, back upstairs.

Then Carol came in during the meal to tell me that Marguerite wanted me to come to her room as soon as possible. Jenna stopped chewing for a microsecond, and I could almost see her thinking the same thing I was—*Why is Marguerite up this early?*

I went to Joel first. It was the first time I had seen his room, since it was always locked and he always came to mine. I hadn't known quite what to expect, but I hadn't expected—nothing. It was as plain as though no one lived there. As though no one ever spent his childhood in there sorting baseball cards and reading comics, or his teenage years—smoking weed on the balcony? Other than a ceiling-high bookshelf stuffed to overflowing with books and CDs, the only thing that kept it from looking abandoned was something he was working with at his desk, which he hurriedly covered with the shirt he'd worn the day before.

He rose and came to hug me. Something dropped from his left hand onto the carpet, and I caught a thin flash of blue out of the corner of my eye. "Do you have any plans for today?" he asked.

"Marguerite was talking yesterday about sending me into town for supplies. I offered to let her use my drawing pencils, but she wants yellow highlighters. What about you? Aren't you working?"

He shook his head. "I called in sick. I have…things to do." His tone was abrupt, but the love in his eyes made up for it.

But I was concerned. "You look sick. You look awful." His face was droopy and wore a shroud of black beard stubble, his eyes were bagged and bloodshot, and his hair looked like a weed pile. I guessed he had not slept all night, for two carafes sat on the desk beside the shirt, and the room reeked of stale coffee.

"I'll be okay."

"Should I come see you when I get back?"

"No."

"Joel—"

"No, *ahuva*. Just do whatever typing my grandmother has for you." There was a strange twist to his lips and a sadness, no, beyond sadness, an agony in his eyes. "I love you more than anything in the world, Louisa."

He kissed me with lips that were dry and tasted of coffee then turned away.

I left. He might as well have shoved me out.

When I got to Marguerite's room, she was tapping an impatient rhythm on the arms of her chair. "Did it take you this long to eat breakfast?"

"I'm sorry, Marguerite. Joel wanted to see me."

Her fingers stopped. "Do you work for Joel or for me?"

It was a rhetorical question, so I didn't answer. Nor did she wait for me to do so. "Do you think I hired you to spend all your time with Joel?"

Where was this coming from? "You wanted me to be friends with them."

"*Friends*. I never suggested you sleep with my grandson."

The air went out of me in a *whoosh*.

"You seem to think you can make all the rules. No wonder you've had a difficult time keeping a job."

My head pounded. Was she really going to fire me when the book was almost finished?

Well, this would be the ideal time, wouldn't it? Even if she didn't like to type, she could probably handle the remaining two or three chapters herself. I didn't care, didn't need to know how the book ended, *really* didn't want to hang around this house of horrors any longer.

But I wasn't ready for another failure.

So for the first time I could remember I swallowed my pride. "You're right. Sorry. Uhm, did you still want me to go pick up highlighters?"

"You're changing the subject." The blue eyes were dark and cold as midnight. "You're in over your head with Joel."

"So what?" My mouth was sticky and I almost grabbed for the glass of water on her nightstand.

"You don't know him at all. You look at him and see his handsome face and you think what's on the inside is just as attractive."

All I could do was gawk.

"Joel never got along with Carl. Carl tried to be a good father, but Tamara was the only one who returned his affection. Carl wanted Joel to work at Airtech, and would have offered him a fine position, but Joel rebelled. He chose a field in which he had no talent or interest, solely to get a job away from Airtech."

"Joel's not the only kid who ever wanted to make his own way. You think fathers and sons never disagree on the son's choice of a career?"

She touched me with a hand that was icy and dry as cotton. "It went deeper than that. Joel was disrespectful and rude to Carl. He turned Tamara against her father."

She's lost control of me.

Whatever her game was, I wasn't playing anymore, and she knew it.

My voice returned from Pluto. "I don't believe you."

She withdrew her hand and I felt a hot flash of fear at the look on her face. "Is this another thing you do regularly? Talk back to people you work for? Call them *liars*?"

"You want to fire me, Marguerite? You go right ahead. Then you'll have no one. No one else gives a damn about you. If I have to choose between you and Joel, I'll choose Joel."

"I hired you."

"I love Joel."

She snickered. "You silly girl, you don't even know Joel. You're thinking with your panties."

I'd had enough. "I'm going to get the highlighters. Maybe when I get back we can settle down and finish the book like two adults."

"No, I don't think so." Marguerite's face was twisted with fury. "You don't believe me? Why don't you ask Tamara about her kidney?"

"Her what?"

"I told you she was the only one who matched as a donor for Carl. Other than me, and I couldn't give him one. Carl didn't want to take Tamara's kidney. He thought she was too young, and the operation carried too many risks for her."

"That sounds like a pretty loving father to me."

"Yes, he was." Her voice cut cold and clear as a skate blade on an ice rink. "He didn't even tell her. So I did."

My heart banged so hard I was sure she could see my shirt moving.

"She went along with it. She wanted to save her father. I had it all arranged. I would take her to have her kidney removed. Once the operation was done, Carl would hardly say no to such a loving gift from his daughter."

The French toast backflipped into my throat and I forced myself to swallow.

"But she wrecked it. Do you know what she did?" Her voice dropped and the next words came out in a deadly whisper. "The brat ran squalling to her mother."

I had to lick my teeth and lips before I could even speak. "Did Jenna tell her not to do it?"

She ignored me. "Jenna told Carl. And they were *angry* at me. Angry! For trying to save his life!"

No wonder Tamara's afraid of her.

"She had to tell Jenna." I hated myself for sounding so timid. "No thirteen-year-old can donate an organ without her parents' approval."

"*I* gave approval. I had it all set up. All Tamara had to do was keep her mouth shut."

But she didn't. And because she didn't, Marguerite, who'd already lost her husband and five babies, was betrayed by the only other member of her family she liked.

And her son died.

I leaned against the door so my quivering legs wouldn't crumple and send me pitching to the floor. "Joel had nothing to do with that."

"Oh?" Her face was hard and cold as prison bars. "Ask him what really happened to my son."

"What do you mean?"

"Joel poisoned him. He killed my son."

"You're insane."

"No, I'm not. And I'm not stupid. What happened to Carl wasn't normal. Millions of people take medication for high blood pressure and their kidneys don't fail."

"But Carl's did. That's what the news stories said. I looked them up and read them."

Her smile was cruelly triumphant. "You were suspicious, too?"

"Not anymore. How could Joel have…" I lowered my voice. I couldn't have anyone else hearing this ridiculous argument. "Poisoned him?"

"Antifreeze."

I just looked at her.

"Joel had antifreeze in the garage to use in the cars he worked on. One night Carl took him to task for making a mess with it. He told Joel how toxic antifreeze is and sent him away from the dinner table to go clean up the spill. That must have been what gave Joel the idea."

She'd gone completely around the bend. "So the whole family heard what Carl said. Why do you think Joel did it?"

"Because he admitted it."

I gagged.

Marguerite backed her chair up a few inches. "I told you that you didn't know him."

"Admitted it to who?"

"To me. When I brought the antifreeze to him and told him I knew what he'd done."

She had to be making this crap up. Maybe if I kept her talking I could catch her in a lie. "So how do Tamara and her kidney fit in?"

"Tamara could have saved Carl. If she'd given him her kidney, Joel's plan would have failed. He knew that. He probably told her to go to Jenna so Jenna could refuse to allow the donation."

"Why didn't you tell Jenna about this?"

"Jenna?" She spat the name. "She wouldn't have believed me. Or cared. She couldn't get my son in the ground fast enough. He died on Wednesday and she buried him Friday morning."

It did seem rushed, but maybe there was a prohibition against burying the dead on the Sabbath. Not that Carl was Jewish, but Jenna would have kept the requirements she'd been raised with and had followed for most of her life—even if she'd stopped observing the holidays. "Maybe there's a Jewish law about burial she had to follow."

"That's what she said. But why, since my son wasn't Jewish? What was her real reason?"

What, she thought Jenna and Joel colluded? How psycho could she get?

Damn this family and their damn secrets. "Jenna will tell me the truth."

Scorn twisted her mouth. "Jenna barely knows the truth. She barely knows anything. I wish Carl had married an intelligent girl instead of just a pretty face."

"Is that why you hate her? Because she wasn't good enough for your son?"

I had opened a faucet, and Marguerite's true feelings came flooding out like sewage. "No. I despise Jenna. She's stupid and weak."

"How can you say that?"

Her laughter sounded like Vincent Price on the late movie. "She doesn't have the guts to throw me out of her house, even though she hates me as much as I hate her."

"It's not guts she doesn't have. She doesn't have the heart. She can't throw you out after what you did for her, even if it was twenty-five years ago. Especially not when she promised to take care of you."

"She's doing that only because Carl told her to. She's never had a thought of her own in her life."

"Oh really? Like when she wouldn't let you take Joel away from her?"

"He would have been better off. We all would have."

My God. "There's nothing stupid about her. She had to take over Airtech, and she's grown the company beyond what Carl ever did." Why was I defending her when I didn't even like her?

"You think that's her doing? You have no idea how much help she's had. All of Carl's friends and advisors stayed on to work with her when they could have gotten better jobs elsewhere."

"That just proves my point. Why would they do that if they didn't believe in her? If they didn't have some loyalty to *her*, not just to Carl, who's been gone for six years? You just gave her the best tribute you could have and you didn't even know it."

She waved one hand in dismissal.

I had to get away from her before I exploded like a Molotov cocktail.

I banged through the door, charged down the steps, and slammed through the front door. Jenna was just pulling out of the garage and I ran for her car, waving my arms like a windmill. She screeched to a startled stop and I came to a halt by her window.

She rolled it down and gaped at me. "What in the world, Louisa?"

I didn't think before I spoke. "What's the story about Tamara and the kidney donation?"

"What are you talking about?"

"Marguerite says Joel turned Tamara against Carl and that's why she wouldn't donate her kidney to him."

She looked steadily at me for several long seconds, then shut off her car, got out and hoisted herself up to sit on the hood facing me. *My God, she* is *human.* "I wondered how long it would take her to try to destroy your love. God, how that bitch loves to stir up trouble."

Hearing *bitch* come out of Jenna's pretty mouth in her cultured voice was almost as much of a shock as Marguerite's words had been.

Her face softened. "However she told you that story, it's not true. Joel had nothing to do with it. He didn't even know."

"Then why would she say it?"

"Because she's a vicious, evil witch who enjoys hurting people."

"Whaaaaaat?"

"Do you not understand me? Do I need to clarify what I said? When Carl learned Tamara was a match, we agonized over it. For days. Kidney donations aren't guaranteed. Carl might have bought himself five more years. If the transplant took and his body didn't reject it. If his health improved. If medications advanced. If. If. If."

She sucked in a ragged breath. "Meanwhile, our barely thirteen-year-old child, who weighed about eighty pounds and hadn't even reached puberty, would have had a vital organ removed. What if there were complications with the operation? Tamara's been sickly all her life. What if she caught a staph infection? What if she needed her own kidneys someday? Carl made the decision that the risks to her outweighed the potential benefit to him. His exact words were, 'I'm her father. It's not her job to give me life; it was my job to give her life.'"

I couldn't speak.

Jenna's eyes hadn't left my face. "Tamara wasn't supposed to know anything about it. Marguerite must have eavesdropped and overheard Carl and me talking. She was as silent as a spider when she could walk. Thank goodness—thank *God* Tamara came to me. I almost fainted when she told me what Marguerite was planning."

I couldn't even move.

"You see, Louisa, you can always find a person with no morals who is willing to do anything for the right amount of money. Marguerite would have paid someone whatever they demanded to steal my baby's kidney."

This was worse than I imagined. "What did you say to Marguerite?"

Jenna made a *huh!* noise. "To use an expression someone your age understands, we ripped her a new one."

Not in front of Tamara. Please tell me she didn't hear that.

I must have said it aloud. Or maybe Jenna read my mind. "Carl gave Joel a wad of bills and told him to take Tamara to the movies and not come back until dinnertime. It was an ugly scene and the children didn't need to be anywhere near it."

"Carl was angry at his mother?"

"He was livid. He told Marguerite if she ever fucked with either of his kids again, not only would he throw her out, he would have her committed."

I'd stopped at *fucked.*

Jenna looked down at the ground, then up at me. "It's never been mentioned since. Marguerite came to her senses and realized it was completely Carl's decision, and he made it out of love for Tamara." She rubbed her arms in the early morning chill. "I can excuse anything that woman ever did to me, but I can't forgive what she would have done to my daughter. I've tried to be sympathetic.

She had five miscarriages and I had two healthy, beautiful children. She lost her husband, then two years later learned she had MS. All that made her bitter and hateful. I hoped her success with her writing would make her happy, but it seems she's as vindictive and dreadful as she ever was."

I was too stunned to answer.

Jenna reached out and touched my shoulder gently, briefly. "I'm sorry, Louisa. I hoped to stay out of this. But I've watched you fall in love with my son, and I have to caution you. Is Joel worth it?"

"Was Carl?"

She didn't answer.

She didn't have to. Carl hadn't been a bad person, maybe not the best husband, but at least a loving father to their daughter. But marrying him meant a life sentence of living with a mother-in-law who topped every horror movie ever filmed.

I didn't even know what was going to come out of my mouth until it did. "Carl had no business asking you to take care of Marguerite, knowing you hated each other, and also knowing you'd never say no."

"He felt sorry for her. He didn't want her to lose her entire family."

We were both bound to Marguerite by a promise we'd made. The difference was, at this point, I was pretty sure Grandpa would agree it was time for me to get out. But Jenna was afraid to betray Carl. "He should have felt sorry for you. How could you refuse your husband's dying request?"

"Indeed," she said, far more calmly than I would have expected, than I would have been if I were her. "How could I?"

"Who jammed the elevator?"

She didn't answer.

"Joel told me he didn't do it. It happened when Tamara was in the hospital. So that leaves you."

She looked down for a moment at the lap of her royal blue jacket dress, then back up at me with the barest trace of a smile. "Yes, it does."

I was struck dumb. It might have been the first straight answer—sort of—I'd gotten from any of them. She'd probably removed the pliers as soon as she realized I'd seen them. I hadn't checked, and neither had Marguerite—until last night.

"Don't worry," Jenna said. "If that were to come out, as in, if you go to the police, I won't let either of my children take the blame for it."

"You couldn't get away with blaming them anyway. You have more reason to hate her than both of them put together. They can leave. You can't."

What I didn't say was *why does stuff happen to me only when you're home?*

Nor did I tell her about Marguerite's accusation. If Jenna suspected Carl's death hadn't been natural, she wasn't saying a word. If she didn't suspect anything, I wasn't going to be the one to repeat something so unthinkable.

She eased herself off the hood. "I'm late for work."

I didn't want her to go. I wanted to ask her to stay, to take care of her family. But she'd already told me more than she'd ever planned to, and I knew it wasn't because she trusted me.

It was because Marguerite was twice as dangerous with someone on her side.

"Remember the gunshot?" I whispered as she got back into her car.

She stared up at me, the shoulder belt still in her hands.

"Marguerite said you're the only one who knows where Carl's gun is hidden. Did you check to make sure it was still there?"

"No." Only slightly hesitantly. "It's at the bottom of my hope chest under a pile of CDs and tapes. If someone went through them, I would know it."

No, you wouldn't. Because I'd gone through them and hadn't seen a gun.

I grabbed my keys from my pocket, jumped into my Subaru and screeched down the driveway. Thank God the gate was open or I probably would have smashed right into it.

Chapter 24

I bought the yellow highlighters, but didn't go back to the house right away. I stopped at Depot Park and walked over to Issaquah Creek. I hiked into the woods and snacked on the wild blackberries, which were soft and dripping juice. I thought best when I was surrounded by Mother Earth.

How could I make sense of everything that had happened in the last month? Hell, since last night?

The morning's events cast Carl's death in a whole new light.

Could Marguerite be telling the truth? Could Joel have gotten away with murder?

I'd learned in my college classes that autopsies were done only when the cause of death was unknown or there was reason to believe a homicide had been committed. The next of kin could request one, but there wasn't any point in this case. Carl's health had been failing for months and his death was completely expected.

Or was it?

How easy would it be to slip antifreeze into Carl's drinks and fool a doctor into thinking it was natural kidney failure?

Maybe Joel was innocent. Carl had spoken of the dangers of antifreeze at the dinner table. Presumably the whole family got a lesson in Poisoning 101.

Could I rule out Marguerite? What if she accused Joel as a smokescreen?

The whole story could be a lie. I'd already wondered if she'd made up the phone prank. But Marguerite wouldn't tell lies about Joel, knowing I could simply go to him and ask for the truth.

But I hadn't.

However, if Marguerite had killed her son, her fury at Tamara would make no sense. Similarly, Tamara was off the hook. She wanted to give her father her kidney—

According to Marguerite. What if Tamara didn't want to do it? What if she went to Jenna because she knew that would be the end of Marguerite's plans?

No. It would be too risky for her. There was always the chance Jenna would go along with the donation. If Tamara wanted her father dead, the easiest thing for her to do would be to tell Marguerite to go to hell, loudly enough to get everyone's attention. She hadn't done that, so the logical thing to believe was that she really had wanted to save her father.

That left Jenna and Joel.

Jenna didn't have to order an autopsy for her husband, and as his next of kin, she had the final say. She could claim religious grounds, but if she'd poisoned him, she would have another motive—like avoiding detection.

But I couldn't help thinking if she wanted out that bad, she would have just left.

What was more important than *who* was *why*. If I figured that out, the pieces would fall into place.

What had Joel overheard between his parents when Jenna was about to leave? Had Carl threatened her? Told her he would take all the money, take the kids, kill her?

No. Nothing I'd heard indicated Carl would do anything like that. Besides, if he had, once Jenna was free of him she would have dumped both Marguerite and Airtech.

Which left Joel.

My mind raced to find reasons he couldn't have done it. But all I could think of was how many times I'd asked him a question and he'd skirted around it. Like—who jammed the elevator? Who tied the trip wire? Who fired the gunshot? *'What gunshot?'*

No. I remembered his reaction when I'd asked if anyone else heard it. Whether he heard it or not, he knew I was telling the truth. Either he'd fired the gun or he knew who did.

He was convinced Tamara would tell him if she'd done it, and he swore she hadn't.

So if Joel could be believed, Tamara hadn't fired the gun.

I think I'd known that for a while. Tamara wasn't in the right position to shoot near the second-story landing. Neither was Jenna, who had just arrived home and was out in the garage for several minutes before coming into the house.

Joel could have done it then hurried back into his room and put on headphones to pretend he'd heard nothing. But if he'd shot at Marguerite, why wouldn't she tell me? Why try to make me think nothing had happened?

I'd wanted to believe Marguerite was what she pretended to be. But I couldn't be blind anymore. She could get to the gun if it was in Jenna's room on the same floor. She hadn't had a chance to return it, or I would have seen it in the hope chest. So if Marguerite still had it—

No. She didn't. The night someone put a pillow over my face, I'd suspected it was Tamara, and now I thought I knew why. She had to stop me from going to

Marguerite's room and finding Joel—where he'd gone to look for the gun.

There was nothing else in her room he would want, and there was only one explanation for the gun to be in her room.

I sank to the ground, crushing a stray berry under my jeans. Marguerite fired the gun out her window. She was the only person in the right place to do so. She hadn't shot anywhere near me, didn't plan to hurt me, but rather to unnerve me. To make me afraid of her family. She'd carefully picked a time no one would hear the shot and no one would believe me.

It worked. She now had someone on her side, who could accuse her family of trying to harm her. Jenna and the kids played right into her hands with the trip wire and the elevator. They would back one another up, but now they faced more than just one unbalanced old woman, and the odds had tipped in Marguerite's favor.

Except Joel believed me. He went looking for the gun. He knew Marguerite was up to no good.

She'd refused my offer to stay with her that night. Maybe by then she was afraid of her grandchildren—as she should be. But she was more afraid of what I might see or find if I moved into her room.

I hadn't asked Jenna if she'd hidden Marguerite's chair. I knew she hadn't. She'd accused Tamara of it, which she wouldn't do if she were guilty.

It wasn't Tamara, who'd been too drunk to remove and hide the chair without disturbing Marguerite and probably Joel and Jenna, as well. And I didn't think it was Joel, who would have been focused on taking care of his sister.

Tamara was afraid for me as long as I stayed in the house. She tried to dump me at the drive-in, figuring that would be the end of me. And it almost was. But she hadn't counted on Marguerite either overhearing the hubbub that night, or waking up and reading my note.

Or never being asleep in the first place.

Marguerite needed me there. Without me she was at the mercy of a family she'd been tormenting for years. She'd come up with a scheme to lure me back. One that required her to wait till everyone was asleep, go to the nearest unused room, get out of her chair, hide it, then make her way back to her room and her bed. She'd have to use her bedclothes for leverage, which would pull them nearly off—*as they had been*.

The signs had been there all along. Joel knew, but if he'd told me Marguerite hid her own chair to trick me into coming back, I'd have thought he'd gone mad.

He couldn't go to his mother because…I didn't know. Maybe he didn't think she would react the way he needed her to. But so many things now made sense. No matter what Marguerite did or said to her, Tamara would never tell Jenna. The last time Tamara confided in her mother, it had blown up in her face. I had no doubt Marguerite made her pay for *squalling to her mother*.

I could even hear her voice in my head, snapping like a slap in the face. *'You silly brat, if you'd kept your mouth shut we could have saved your father. Now he's going to die and it's your fault.'*

Please tell me Marguerite didn't say that to Tamara.

But of course she did. Oh God, that kid, that poor kid.

They'd been closer before then, both Jenna and Valerie had said so, but the relationship went to hell after that. Tamara lost two people she loved when her father died. Maybe even three, including Jenna.

I rubbed the heels of my hands into my eyes.

Could I be sure Marguerite hadn't killed Carl? She'd fooled me about everything else.

I still didn't know where Joel fit in. Why he couldn't sleep last night, what was on his mind.

But no, that wasn't right.

He'd been drinking coffee by the pot. He'd made a deliberate effort to stay awake.

He wasn't worrying. He was doing something. Something so important it needed to be finished before the morning.

Somehow, Joel knew everything was coming to a head. What had Tamara said to him last night?

Whatever he was doing, he'd hidden it under his shirt when I came in. I closed my eyes to remember the room. The desk, and Joel's shirt whisking onto *something*.

With his right hand. His left hand held…I couldn't remember. His right side faced me, so his left hand—

Held a pen. He'd let it fall to the carpeted floor just before he hugged me. An ordinary blue Paper Mate.

Like Marguerite's.

A whistle pierced my thoughts just before a fluffy retriever bounded up to me and gave me an enthusiastic bacon-flavored kiss. I wrapped my arms around him and hid my hot face in his fur. A woman's voice called, "Banjo!" and I pulled free to see a middle-aged jogger, leash dangling from her hand, come around the bend.

"Sorry!" Her ponytail bounced behind her as she jogged in place. "He's a little friendly."

"It's okay," I managed. "I like dogs."

She stopped and peered at me. "Are you all right?"

I tried to nod, but it made lights flash in front of my eyes. "Yeah. Thanks."

She was reluctant to leave, I could tell. Maybe she thought I was hurt or lost. I stood and gave Banjo a parting pat. "Enjoy your run."

I made my way back to my car. My thoughts picked

up where they'd been interrupted like the needle had been raised and dropped on a record.

I knew what Joel was working on.

And I knew no one had killed Carl.

Marguerite didn't believe that. She thought the kids had colluded, or at least, Tamara had sidestepped a chance to ruin Joel's scheme. If Marguerite was convinced Carl was murdered, nothing but an autopsy would satisfy her. And there'd been no autopsy.

She hadn't accused Joel publicly because she knew it would be hard to prove. But she would never just let it go. Without any legal recourse against her son's murderer, her only option was revenge.

It was the last place I wanted to be. But I had to go. I peeled out of the park and tore back to the house.

Chapter 25

When I stepped through the front door, the air was as still as though the entire building held its breath. My flowers still filled the living room and the moist sweet smell had settled over the entryway. It was as though I'd walked in on a funeral.

No. Not yet. Not if I could help it.

I leaped up the steps two at a time. Joel's door was closed, but I didn't bother to knock. I turned the knob and the door opened into an empty room.

Empty of people, that is. A stack of papers sat on the desk next to the discarded shirt. By then I was so familiar with the handwriting I could recognize the final chapters of the book even before I picked it up.

It had a title. *An Act of Love.*

I flipped to the end and read as much as I needed to.

Oh, my God, Joel.

I had to find him.

I ran down the hall, banging on each door in turn. "Joel! Joel, where are you? *Joel!*"

No answer. But I heard a rustling, something, behind Marguerite's door. I tried it, but it was locked. *Why didn't anyone ever give me a key to her room?*

I beat on the door until my knuckles hurt. "Marguerite!"

Silence. Then, "What is it?" Terse, almost gasped.

"Let me in. I have to talk to you."

Silence.

I pounded some more. *"Let me in, dammit!"*

"I don't have anything more to say to you." Bitter, dismissive.

Fine. To hell with her. I had to find Joel and tell him the truth.

I turned and rushed down the steps. "Joel!"

But it wasn't Joel who met me at the foot of the staircase. It was Tamara, and she had a crazed smile on her face and a butcher knife in her hand.

Sweat poured down my sides.

Her smile softened as she looked at me. "I'm sorry, Louisa. I didn't want to do it. But I have to. Grandmother doesn't want Joel to have you." She snatched at my hair with an arm that years of swimming had made muscular. Oh my God, she wasn't going to cut off my *hair?*

My senses returned. No, she was going to cut my *throat.*

I ducked the slicing blade barely in time to avoid having my necked chopped like a carrot stick. Searing pain in my shoulder made me look down to see an instant red stain on my shirt. A scream choked in my throat and I pulled away from her. I grabbed a glass floor lamp, grunting at the weight, and swung it at her.

She sidestepped the lamp, picked it out of my hand as easily as though it were a roll of wrapping paper, and flung it aside. It crashed to the floor. Glass shattered and the shade skittered across the waxed wood.

I ran.

In the wrong direction, but she was blocking the way to the front door and I knew I wouldn't be able to get past her. I dashed across the hall toward the music room. I could hear her following me, moving with a slow sureness that was more terrifying than a sprinted chase would have been.

I slammed the music room door and turned the latch, but like something out of a slasher film, the knob began to turn. *She had a key.*

I was trapped. It would take an act of God to break the windows, and there was no other way out.

Then I saw the chandelier, and I remembered Jenna's saying it would hold our combined weights. Probably an exaggeration, but it needed to hold only mine.

Tamara came in, pocketing a chain of keys, and made another grab for me. I climbed on the piano, bent my knees and swung my arms as I had done in gymnastics, and leaped. I caught the bottom of the chandelier and hoisted myself up to sit in the dish that held the light bulbs.

Tamara lunged at my dangling hair. I tried to yank it up, but my head jerked with the force of her grip, and through watering eyes I saw a strand fall to the floor. I scrabbled for the rest of it and pulled it out of her way.

The chandelier swayed and tinkled but didn't break. I was safe—for now.

A car backfired.

No. I knew that noise. I'd heard it before, the night in the swimming pool. Tamara knew it too, and she froze in place beneath me, clutching the knife.

"*Joooooel!*" I shrieked.

"Louisa! Louisa? Where are you? Tamara!" Joel yelled from upstairs.

Tamara started to climb on the piano.

Maybe I could stomp her fingers without losing my balance. "In the music room! Hurry!"

Footsteps thudded down the stairs, then down the hall, and he burst in. "Tam! Tam, what are you doing?" He gasped at the ten-inch hunk of my hair on the floor.

"Tam, what did you do to Louisa's hair?"

"I'm sorry, Joel. I have to do what Grandmother says. You know what'll happen if I don't. You know what Grandmother's going to do." Big hazel eyes stared at him in supplication.

"Tam, no. Give me the knife. Give it to me, Tamara." Joel wrapped his arms around his sister from behind and gently pried the knife from her fingers. He tossed it across the room.

She dissolved into tears, bending over double with the force of her sobs.

"Tam, honey, don't cry. Everything's going to be okay. You're going to be okay. She can't hurt you anymore." Joel looked up at me. He had shaved, combed his hair, washed his face and put on a clean green shirt. "Louisa, are you all right? You're bleeding. Here, come down."

"No," I whispered. "How could I be all right? All this time, I've been reading and typing the book, seeing what Gage was planning. Waiting for him to kill his father. We knew why—because his father was molesting his sister. But in the end Gage didn't kill his father."

"Who did?"

"Sharon—his sister." I was going to throw up. The French toast we'd had for breakfast would splatter all over the polished wood floor, and they'd never be able to get the stain out. "You know who killed him, because you wrote the book. Just like you wrote every book with Marguerite Roberts' name on it."

Joel's smile was that of a proud child. "I'm a damn good writer, aren't I?"

"Yes, you are."

"But no one knows it except you." The smile melted off his face. "Everything that should have been mine has gone to her. I'm the youngest winner of the Newbery

Medal, did you know that? I was nineteen when I wrote *I'll Take the One on Either End.* But no one knows it's mine, because she stole it from me."

Tamara looked like the Earth had disappeared in front of her.

I addressed her, hoping she was lucid enough to give me the answer I expected. "You didn't know. You would never let Marguerite blackmail Joel. How did she convince you to get rid of me? What's she holding over you? What was she going to tell everyone? The same thing she told me this morning?"

Joel looked up at me like I'd started speaking in tongues and pouring paint on the floor.

"It's not real," Tamara whispered. "I didn't believe her, Joel."

His eyebrows crimped. "Didn't believe what?"

"Then why come after me with a knife?" I asked her. "Because you would do anything to keep Marguerite from saying Joel killed your father. Why? Unless you're afraid he did?"

Tamara grabbed at Joel's arm. "She'll tell everyone. That's what she said. 'I'll tell what really happened to my son. Why he died.'"

Joel stroked her rumpled hair. "I know, *metuka*. You told me that last night."

I tried to swallow but there was no saliva in my mouth. "But it's not true, Tamara. Nothing happened to your father. Let her tell."

"I can't. It would be all over the newspapers. Mom would hate us if we made her look bad. She'd throw us out, like her parents did to her."

"It's going to be all right," Joel murmured. "It's still our secret."

"What is?" she said.

"You know," so softly I barely heard.

The book told the whole story—or what Joel thought was the story. If only I'd read it with open eyes. "No, she doesn't," I said. "She didn't kill your father, Joel."

"Who else could have done it? Grandmother, who's blackmailing me for it? *Mom?*"

"How about no one?"

Tamara jerked away from her brother. The crazed look was back and I glanced at the knife on the floor across the room. Maybe not far enough.

"No one killed him," I told them. "Use some logic. Don't you think his doctor would have figured it out if anything was done to him?"

"Antifreeze." Joel's voice was hollow and thin. "Ethylene glycol weakens the kidneys. It would be hard to trace."

"She told me," I said softly. "About Carl making you clean it up because it was toxic. She figures that's what gave you the idea."

"What idea? Grandmother brought some antifreeze to me she found in the garage, a few weeks after Dad died. That's when she could still walk. I was taking auto shop at the time and was replacing some guy's radiator, so I had a couple of gallons sitting around."

His intake of breath sounded like a drowning man's. "She told me how I'd killed him. I knew I hadn't, but I couldn't really tell her that, without implicating Tam." His eyes flickered to Tamara, but she didn't notice. She'd frozen as soon as Joel mentioned antifreeze.

"Grandmother was right." Tamara's voice was as cold and venomous as a cobra. "I asked her what she was talking about and she went, 'Heh heh, ask Joel. He knows.' I didn't believe her. But she was right. You killed my father."

"No, no, Tam, I—" Joel took a step back from her. "Tam, do you remember, after his funeral, when I went into your room, and you were sitting on your bed crying? Remember what you said to me?"

Tamara wiped tears off her cheeks.

Joel's throat moved as he swallowed. "You said, 'It's my fault. I killed him.'"

Tamara's face twitched. "I meant it was my fault because I could have given him a kidney and saved him and I didn't. I didn't mean I fed him poison!"

Joel's forehead scrunched. "What kidney? None of us matched as donors."

"Tamara did," I told him. "Your father wouldn't let her do it. Marguerite tried to force her to, and your parents put her in her place. She's hated Tamara ever since."

He barely glanced at me.

"Why would I kill him?" Tamara started sobbing again. "I loved him. I still miss him."

"Tam, I, what he did to you—"

"What are you talking about? What did he do?"

Oh, God. I was right.

"Tam, you don't have to hide it anymore. It wasn't your fault. We can get help for you."

"He thinks your father molested you," I interrupted.

Her head tilted up at me. "You're crazy!"

"Not me." I looked back at Joel. "I don't think Carl abused Tamara."

He didn't seem to have heard me. "What about all those times he took you in his study and locked the door? What was he doing to you?"

"Doing? What was he doing? Helping me with homework. Working while I did homework. Playing chess. Listening to Three Dog Night together." Tamara stopped crying and backed slowly away from her brother.

"Tam, he locked the door. Every time I tried the door it was locked. Why would he do that? What father locks his daughter in a room with him, night after night?"

"I locked the door, Joel. It was me. I wanted Dad to myself."

"You…" Joel's voice trailed off and he looked around as though searching for a soft place to fall.

Tamara's face was awash in tears. "If I wanted to kill someone, it sure as hell wouldn't have been Dad. It would have been Mom. Dad loved me. She doesn't. She got me in trouble. And then she let that horrible old…old dragon stay here!"

With a final outraged look at Joel, Tamara stalked from the room.

'*I wanted Dad to myself.*'

Carl might not have even noticed her locking the door. If he did, he probably considered his daughter's adoration a compliment. It would never have occurred to him how it could be misconstrued.

Such innocence, on both their parts.

I didn't know if it was safe to come down. Tamara might come back, and she could get to the knife before Joel or I could. But I had to do something about the horrified glaze in his eyes. I slid onto the top of the piano and Joel took my hand to help me to the floor. I winced as the knife wound throbbed hotly.

"Joel." All I could manage was a whisper. "If Tamara had killed your father, she wouldn't have responded to Marguerite's threats to expose you as the murderer."

"But no one else would have…" He blinked repeatedly. "How can you say she wasn't abused?"

"I'm not saying that. She was. But not by your father and not sexually."

His head jerked back and forth in dismissal. "The hell she wasn't. How many girls her age don't date? Don't talk to guys? Aren't even interested?"

"Jenna explained that to me. Tamara's work at the rape crisis center has made her cautious of men." Jenna wasn't as dense as I'd thought. As Joel thought. Sometimes she knew her family better than we expected.

"Mom's no psychologist."

"No. But at the very least, if your father did that to Tamara, she would have been afraid of him or not wanted to be with him. To the point that even Jenna would have noticed."

He tried to laugh. "You don't know Mom very well, do you? She doesn't notice anything. She doesn't have time. Dad's been dead for six years, and she spent five of them getting her BA and MBA. She'd go to work for ten hours and then to school for four. It's only been in the last year that she's even home at all before eleven o'clock at night, and it's too late for her to be a mother to her daughter."

I hoped not.

My legs were too rubbery to stand. I leaned against the piano, favoring my shoulder. "Both Jenna and Marguerite have told me how hard Tamara took Carl's death. If he were abusing her, it would have been a relief not to have to worry about him anymore."

"A thirteen-year-old kid?"

"Kids don't fake their feelings. Tamara wouldn't at any age. If she were glad to see Carl dead, you'd have all known it." As briefly as I could I told him what Jenna had said to me that morning. "Tamara feels guilty, because your father refused to take her kidney, and Marguerite heaped it on further by blaming her. That's what Tamara meant when she said she'd killed him. That's how Marguerite made her feel, and has been making her feel for six years."

"But Grandmother thinks I gave him antifreeze."

"In her eyes, Tamara could have donated her kidney and wrecked your plans. Marguerite thinks you talked Tamara out of it. But you didn't even know."

He didn't answer.

"Anyway, Tamara tells you everything. You've said it. Why wouldn't she have confided in you if something like that happened?"

"The same reason she never told me about her kidney? Guilt? Shame? Abuse victims don't tell. I did weeks of research before starting *An Act of Love,* and every article, every book, said the same thing. The victims blame themselves and they're ashamed. They're afraid they're not going to be believed."

"Maybe that's true. But why would you believe your father hurt Tamara? She just explained about the door being locked, and without that, you don't have any other evidence, do you?"

"She said 'I killed him.'"

"I know, Joel." My voice quavered. "But she just told you what she meant. And if Carl wasn't abusing her, she didn't have any reason to kill him."

His head was still making the jerking side-to-side movement. "She started acting out when he got sick, and I put everything together, and that's what I figured."

"Of course she was acting out. Her father was dying, her grandmother was blaming her, and her mother wasn't going to be any kind of ally, because when she trusted her mother with a secret, her world imploded." Not that Jenna hadn't done the right thing. It was a no-win lose-everything situation for Tamara the minute Marguerite got involved.

"I didn't know," Joel mumbled.

"Probably no one did, except Marguerite herself. What was Tamara supposed to say? A thirteen-year-old might not be able to identify emotional abuse as abuse. It would have been easier if she'd had bruises to show you. All she could say is, 'Grandmother said something mean to me.' What's the average person's response going to be? 'Well, get away from Grandmother. Go in your room and close the door. What did you do or say to make her angry?'"

"I wouldn't have said any of that."

"I don't think Jenna would have either. I think her reaction would have been strong and immediate if she'd known Tamara was being blamed for Carl's death. But Tamara was a grieving, scared kid and she made the wrong choice—to keep quiet. Bullies thrive on silence."

He stepped back, facing me. "You're speculating."

"What about the piano?"

He looked at it as though it could answer my question. "What about it?"

"Tamara's playing it in her sleep. How could that be connected to anyone but Marguerite?"

His shoulders moved and he reached behind him to tug at his shirttail. "I figured he must have done something to her while she was playing."

"No. That makes no sense. Why doesn't Jenna know her daughter can play the piano better than she herself can? Who taught Tamara?"

He just looked at me.

"If Jenna or a teacher had taught her, Jenna would know Tamara can play. You can't play piano, and neither could Carl. But Marguerite can. She's the only person who could have taught Tamara. Even Jenna told me Tamara used to be closer to Marguerite. I thought she was full of crap, but she was right."

"I don't remember Grandmother teaching Tam to play."

"I bet it was supposed to be a surprise for Jenna, for both your parents. That suddenly one day Tamara would sit down and play Tchaikovsky. Or the Chiffons. They probably spent hours every week, if not every day, making Tamara that good a musician. But Tamara's blocked it out to the point of sleepwalking and not knowing she's playing. What does that say about her relationship with Marguerite?"

Joel's shoulders slumped and he seemed to shrink. "Grandmother's never said anything about Tam's playing. As far as I know, only you and I know she does it."

"Marguerite's not going to tell. It's a symptom of an emotional problem that's connected to her. Of course she doesn't want to draw attention to it. What I can't believe is that she didn't go right to Jenna, or the police, to accuse you of poisoning Carl."

"I can explain that." He sidled up to the piano, still facing me, and leaned against it. Was he afraid to turn his back on me? "Tam had already told me she killed him. I thought it was to stop—to stop, his, the, abuse." He swallowed hard enough for me to hear it. "When Grandmother came to me with the antifreeze and accused me of poisoning our father, I figured that was how Tam did it. I mean, she sat at the table and heard his lecture about how toxic it was."

His voice rasped like dried leaves being rubbed together. "All I knew was that I hadn't done it. But I couldn't make Grandmother suspicious of Tam. So I said, 'What are you going to do about it?' And she said, 'Nothing…yet.'"

I shuddered. She'd sat on the information until she could blackmail Joel and wreck his life over it. Not only had she stolen his books and driven his sister around the bend, but she'd trashed his chance to have love.

No. I'd stand by him. Wouldn't I?

"What if you'd called her bluff? Since Carl's death

was already ruled as natural causes, if she accused you, everyone would have thought she was demented. She would be in an institution now, where she belongs."

"I couldn't take the chance. Tam might break down and admit it. I had to keep Grandmother's attention focused on me."

"Why would Marguerite think you would kill Carl? Did she think he was molesting Tamara, too?"

"We never got along."

"You and Carl?"

He nodded. His breath came hard enough for me to smell the stale coffee. "Never. And once I thought he was doing...that to Tam, I couldn't stand to look at him. Grandmother got suspicious when I didn't grieve when he died. *Grieve?* I was relieved. There was no one to tell my mother she was stupid or make my sister's life hell."

"Did you ever think about going to your mother with your suspicions?"

He rubbed at his eyes with his right hand. "I was afraid he'd just deny it and put me in a juvenile home or something. Then who would be here for Tam? And what could Mom do? It wasn't like she had a job or a home or anyplace to go at that time. She'd spent her whole life following him and doing everything he told her to do. Even six years after he died, she's still running the company he founded and living with his mother.

"There wasn't anyone I could go to. I was going to tell Valerie, my girlfriend, but she broke up with me before I could. 'You're too moody, Joel.' Gee, how come?"

"But, Joel, how could Carl have mistreated Tamara? I know you didn't know this at the time, but he died rather than put his child through an operation that could have harmed her, even if it might have saved his life. Does that sound like a child molester to you? To me it sounds like someone who put his daughter's welfare above his own life."

"I figured it was guilt."

"To *die?* Do you think molesters feel that much shame?"

"No, no. Not him. Tam. Her reaction to his death. She'd hang out with me until I had to tell her to go to her own room. She wouldn't have anything to do with Mom. Or she would sleep in Dad's desk chair in his study." His head rocked back and forth at the memory. "The first time she did that, I couldn't find her and I thought she'd run away. Mom was at class. I looked for Tam for three hours before I found her."

"She was trying to be close to Carl. Does that sound like an abused child? For God's sake, Joel, you've just said the most convincing thing of all. She knew she'd be safe with you. If her father, a man she loved more than anyone in the world, mistreated her, do you think she would trust another man so explicitly?"

"His funeral. When they played 'One,' she was tapping her foot in time to the music. Like she was enjoying it. I put my hand on her knee to stop her but you could still see her toes moving inside her shoes."

"She was communicating with him. It was all she had left. Music is her way of connecting, of making sense out of the world, like art is for me. Think about when she plays the piano. She does it when she's upset."

He just looked at me and moved slightly farther away.

"Just like Jenna, music is her voice. Why would she want to hear her father's favorite music if he'd done that to her?" I remembered the look of peace on her face when she said Three Dog Night's music felt like being hugged. I couldn't imagine her associating it with anything other than being loved—in a good way. "She'd have probably broken all those Three Dog Night records by now. She sure wouldn't risk Jenna's wrath by dancing on the coffee table to them."

I was still afraid of her. She might have killed me if Joel hadn't come in. My shoulder burned, and I couldn't even look at the pile of hair on the floor.

But I wanted to cry for her. Only two people had ever loved her, and one was dead, and the other thought she'd killed him.

Marguerite didn't count.

"Do you really believe your sister is a murderer? I think she was forced to do this." I pointed to my bloody shoulder. My shirt was ruined, but the bleeding seemed to have stopped. "She's scared and desperate. She knows something's wrong but she's not sure what, or what she can do. But if she were a murderer, she would have killed Marguerite. A long time ago."

His head dropped forward till his chin was level with his sternum.

I had finally made him believe me.

When he looked back up, his face had collapsed. "I don't think Tam wanted to hurt you. You haven't done anything to her. She likes you, in fact. Grandmother, on the other hand, would be happy to see us all dead, except without me she wouldn't be a famous author."

"She isn't."

"She's famous all right, but she isn't an author." He stroked my forearm. "How did you figure that out?"

"Little things started to add up. Your reaction the first morning when I said something about boys who can't type. The way you corrected my grammar that one time, over something most people never think about. But a writer would. The contract."

He frowned. "What contract?"

"The one Marguerite had me sign. The one she made you sign her name on, because of course she couldn't sign her own name. I would see the difference in handwriting. It would be impossible to duplicate your scrawling." It had taken me much too long to realize I'd never seen Marguerite write a word. Nor Joel.

"Then today, I knew. I put it all together when I saw you stayed awake last night. When I started thinking about why, what you could have been doing that was so urgent, I remembered you had a pen in your hand. I figured you had to be finishing the book."

He nodded again.

"That's why you never go out or have any kind of social life. It's not because of Tamara. It's because you're busy writing. It's why your door is always locked."

He examined his hands. For the first time I saw the callous on his left middle finger, the ink marks at the tip of his thumb.

The manuscript pages were always full of blots and smudges. Paper Mates wrote easily and well, but his leaked, and he must have washed his hands constantly to keep anyone from seeing the stains. "How did it start? I mean, did she just come to you and ask you to write books for her?"

"No. I started writing novels in college. One day I came home from classes and she was sitting in my room, reading *I'll Take the One on Either End*. She said, 'This is quite good, Joel. You're a natural storyteller.'" There was a hitch in his voice. "She took it from me. She typed it up and started researching publishers and the submission process. I think she even took a class at the college on manuscript preparation.

"Of course I couldn't have been like every other writer and take years and piles of rejections before getting published. I—she—sold *Either End* to the third house she sent it to. She's never even needed an agent."

"Couldn't you hide your stories?"

"Not once she caught me. If I stopped writing, or sent my stuff out under my own name, she would narc on me—or Tam. At least that's what I thought."

"She was so clever," I whispered. "She talked to me about how she plotted. How she created suspense."

"No. She talked about how *I* plot and create suspense."

I tried to think of painting pictures that would hang in a museum under someone else's name. But it was unimaginable. "How in God's name could you let her do that to you?"

"What choice did I have? Let her accuse me? Go to jail? Or rat out my sister and make her tell a courtroom full of strangers just *where Daddy touched her*?"

"But he didn't do it."

He covered his face with his hands, but when he took them away the anguish was still there. "What would you have done if you were me?"

"Told my mother. Jenna probably would have laughed, especially at the idea of either of you as a murderer. The problem is that Marguerite convinced *you*." I knew I was making him feel worse, but it didn't matter. It had to come out. "When I figured out that you're the author, not her, that's when I knew no one had killed your father."

His eyes narrowed. "Huh?"

"You'd never give up your books to save yourself. Especially once you won the Newbery Medal, you would have gone public. If Marguerite accused you, she would have to prove it. There were no witnesses, just a grieving old woman who found antifreeze in the garage—where you would expect to find antifreeze. If you denied everything, Jenna would back you up. The only reason you would let Marguerite steal your books is if you were protecting someone.

"It wasn't your mother. If Jenna wanted to be rid of Carl, she wouldn't have let him talk her out of leaving. That left Tamara—who didn't do it because she wanted to give Carl her kidney. And she didn't have any reason to kill him. Therefore, no one did."

Joel's expression was that of someone driving a car into a lake because there was no road anymore.

"I'm kind of surprised Marguerite let you write a book about abuse. Of course, it probably didn't register, since she never suspected the things you did about Carl."

He nodded. "I told her it was based on a story from New York, where the girl hired someone to kill the father. I even showed her the article. I had other ideas for it, maybe sticking closer to the original facts, but when you came I knew I had to end this. She'd dragged an innocent person in, and I didn't want you getting hurt."

It's too late, Joel.

"It was the best way to tell our story. Just like me, Gage fell asleep on the job, and Sharon had to protect herself."

Their mother played almost no role in the book. Now I knew why. "What will Jenna think when she reads *An Act of Love*?"

"I guess a lot of that depends on you, Louisa."

"Me? Why?"

"You'll know," he said softly. "Will you finish typing it?"

I didn't answer that. "When do you think she would have revealed everything?"

"Maybe never. Maybe she would have died with it, and there's no way I could prove myself as the actual author, especially not without giving away why she was blackmailing me. But then she couldn't type anymore, and I can't type, and she wasn't ready to give up just yet.

So she had to hire a typist, and that's where you came in."

That was the real reason Marguerite hadn't let Jenna hire a secretary for her. Someone older and wiser, whose emotional baggage didn't need a steamer trunk the size of Wyoming, might have figured out her game long ago.

My teeth gritted. I'd been such a dupe. "You were right. I fell for everything she said because I thought I'd found the perfect place for me."

If Grandpa were here he'd tell me to get rid of my guilt. He'd say it had already done too much damage.

Joel caressed a strand of my hair. "Maybe she just hired you because she wanted someone who likes old people and would side with her against us. But then you and I fell in love, and she knew she could use that against us."

"She told me she wanted both of you—especially Tamara—to have someone your age to hang out with."

"Maybe she wanted you to get information from us. Why do you think I've been so careful what I tell you? I didn't know if it would go right back to her."

I opened my mouth to deny I would have repeated anything, but closed it again. There was a time when I'd trusted Marguerite more than the other members of the family.

It seemed like a lifetime ago.

"I think when you slept all afternoon Monday, she figured out we'd been out most of the night Sunday, and made a pretty good guess why, and what we were doing." The words dragged. "She knew she had lost you. That's why she told Tam to get rid of you."

"That doesn't make any sense."

"Sure it does. In Grandmother's dreams, Tam would go to the nuthouse or to prison. You know what would happen to me. And Mom would be a wreck. I think Mom's about to find out she loves Tam more than she thinks she does."

I couldn't stand up anymore. I sank to a sitting position in front of the piano and leaned on one of the legs. "What's going to happen now?"

Joel sat down facing me and pulled my head onto his chest.

I didn't want to talk about Marguerite. I didn't want him to tell me what I already knew, what the backfiring noise had been. I took his hands in mine and held them tightly, remembering him twining my hair around his fingers, holding and caressing me.

Had those same hands just committed a murder?

Maybe they hadn't. Maybe I did need to know. "What happened to her? What did you do?"

He didn't answer.

"You have to tell me, Joel."

His head moved slowly back and forth against mine. "No."

But I knew. He'd planned it since last night, when Tamara went to him and told him Marguerite ordered her to kill me. That was why he had to finish the book before this morning.

"Why didn't she let me in when I came to the door?" I asked.

"She couldn't reach the door."

"Why didn't she call for help? I would have broken the balcony doors if I'd had to."

"Why?"

I didn't know.

"She wanted you dead. She didn't even have the guts to do it herself. She would destroy an innocent girl to kill you, just to hurt me." He took a jagged breath. "That's why she couldn't ask you to help her. I think she knew it was over."

I gasped, hearing the unspoken *when she saw the gun.*

He kissed the top of my head and held me close. I tried not to squirm away. "I have some very old-fashioned ideas. I believe God created Woman to give life, and Man to protect hers. I finally did it the only way I could."

My stomach lurched and I covered my mouth to suppress a gag. "Last night you told me you believe to save one life is to save all humanity. But what happens if you take one life?"

"Louisa, as long as she was alive, none of us could have a life. I can't anyway. I knew last night I could never have you. But Tamara has a chance. Tam was nothing as long as Grandmother was alive to torture her. I had to fight for what's left of my sister's life and sanity."

My hands shook in my lap. "But what about our life?"

Gently he pulled me to my feet. Tears dripped down his face. It was the first time I had ever seen a man cry. "Louisa, I love you so much. Eternally. Do you understand that? Do you believe me?"

"Yes." My legs wobbled so hard he had to ease me to the door.

"Then keep that and remember it, because it's yours forever, and no one will ever be able to take it away from you."

He opened the door and guided me out into the hallway with his right hand. His left hand reached behind his back and pulled something out of his waistband—*the gun?*

No.

I started back in, but I wasn't fast enough. Joel closed the door in my face and I heard the *click* of the lock.

Oh, God, no. No.

"Joel, please, let me in." I pounded on the door.

No answer.

"Joel, no, *no*." I slumped to the floor, my fingers in my ears. But I still heard the shot, like a small explosion.

Chapter 26

L ouisa? What's going on?"
Jenna's voice. I looked up into a royal blue blur. I opened my mouth, but all that came out was something between a grunt and a whine.

Then Tamara was there, looking almost normal, her face smooth and childlike as she held out her key ring. "I have the key."

"No." I struggled to my feet and grabbed at Jenna's dress. "You can't let her in there. Don't let her in."

But Tamara was already opening the door. "Where's Joel?"

"Don't let her in there!" I stumbled for the steps and charged up to Marguerite's room. If that monster wasn't dead, I'd finish the job personally.

She had fallen from her chair and lay on the floor, trying to stop the flow of blood from her chest with her coverlet. "Louisa—call—ambulance." The gasped words ended in wet coughing.

"No!" I shouted. "I'm going to stand here and watch you die, because you did worse than that to your family. Those kids never did a thing to you."

She looked up at me, eyes dark and glittering with hate. "Joel murdered my son."

I wanted to claw out her eyes. "No one killed Carl. He was sick. His kidneys gave out from his blood pressure medication. The doctors even said so."

"Then why did Joel admit it?" she demanded in a whisper.

I didn't owe her any explanation. I wasn't going to try to understand her. I didn't care how many tragedies she'd suffered or how many people she'd lost or how sick she was. Nothing gave her the right to destroy her son's family—*her* family.

"If there's a devil, you're it," I snapped, as close to her face as I could stand to get. "How long did you think you could get away with this? Now the whole thing has blown to hell, and you're going with it."

I could hear sirens approaching. I left her on the floor and crept downstairs.

I reached the bottom of the steps just as a couple of cops broke open the door to the music room. One of them took a step in and came quickly back out to pull Jenna away. "Don't go in there, Mrs. Roberts. There's nothing to see."

"Joel?" Jenna whispered.

"Your son's dead, ma'am. I'm sorry."

Jenna began to cry, little ladylike sobs, tears streaking her makeup down her cheeks.

Please tell me this didn't really happen. I sank to the floor at the foot of the steps, holding the railing like prison bars. "The old lady's been shot," I said to one pair of navy blue legs. "Second floor, first door on the right."

There was a keening noise. Was I making it? No, it was Tamara, her hands, shirt and lap soaked with blood, being sedated and strapped to a stretcher by three struggling paramedics.

One of the cops came to me and touched my shoulder. I gasped. The stab wound ached like someone was repeatedly punching me with a hot fist. "You'll probably need medical attention for that. How did it happen?"

"I don't need any medical attention." I was not riding in an ambulance with any of them.

Two other medics hustled past us and up the steps with another stretcher. The one who was talking to me helped me to my feet and moved me away from the foot of the stairs. "We'll need a statement from you. What happened here?"

Jenna watched, one hand on Tamara's forehead.

"It's her," I said, pointing in the general direction of Marguerite's room. "Marguerite did everything."

"Did she stab you?" the cop asked.

"No." I took a deep breath. I would have to tell it, and Jenna would have to hear it. "It's not Tamara's fault. Don't arrest her or anything."

Jenna quivered. Oh, God, if only one of them had told her, had trusted her enough to confide in her. She would have fixed everything for them.

If only, if only.

"Coming through!" The two medics from upstairs made their way down with Marguerite on the stretcher.

Jenna let go of Tamara to approach them. "What did you do to my children?" she demanded in a voice that shook with horror and fury.

Marguerite snarled up at her, her lip curling back to expose small teeth. "Nothing they didn't deserve."

I grabbed Jenna's arm and pulled her away. "Don't. Don't talk to her. I'll tell you everything."

The officer waited.

We had to move out of the way so the police and investigators could process the crime scenes. Sirens wailed as Marguerite was taken away. I answered the officer's questions, trying not to listen to Jenna as she wept and even swore a couple of times. Then they wanted to talk to her privately, so I went to the front windows and watched as two more ambulances pulled away, the first with siren and flashing lights, the second quietly and unobtrusively.

Except to me.

I once read a science fiction novel where convicted criminals were banished to other planets. I felt like one of them. The world belonged to everyone else, and the only part of it I cared about was gone. Anger had pushed my grief to the back long enough to get me past everyone, but I hurt too much to even be angry anymore. I just wanted to get away and forget I ever knew any of them.

Chapter 27

Marguerite lived for a few hours on life support then died. Jenna paid me for the work I'd done for her, but I wasn't finished. I used my remaining adrenaline to finish typing *An Act of Love*, then sent it off to Joel's publisher with a notarized affidavit explaining everything.

I didn't hear from them and didn't really expect to. It didn't matter. Once the book was in the mail, I crumpled like an empty dress. During the day I slumped in my apartment with the phone unplugged and the door locked and the shades pulled. At night I lay in bed with my bluegrass music playing, all the tragic songs like "You'll Find Her Name Written There" and "In the Pines," tears running into the hair above my ears and drying cold and itchy on my cheekbones.

တတတ

September turned to October and Jenna's check lay uncashed on my kitchen table. I finally talked to my parents, and they grabbed the first flight to Seattle. They stayed long enough to pay my rent through December and fill the refrigerator and pantry with groceries I couldn't even look at. I knew I had to start eating again, but I didn't care. One night I started to open a can of tomato sauce, but had to throw it away when it made me think of the blood on Tamara's clothes. Another day I spooned peanut butter out of the jar. One morning I tried to make coffee but couldn't figure out what to do with the grounds.

By November it was time to see the doctor.

❧❧❧

It was a typical chilly and overcast November morning when I stood on a sidewalk in downtown Seattle, staring up at the white sky and the Airtech building. I clutched a paper in my hand and shivered in a jacket that was too light for the day. Funny, I'd worn the same jacket last November and been fine.

Maybe it was because I was so thin. The doctor had told me the first order of business was to gain back the weight I'd lost since September.

Inside. Security. Elevator. Second floor. Third, Fifth, Seventh. *Ding.*

I trudged down the hallway to the executive offices and pressed a buzzer. The glass door opened and a middle-aged woman with a stylish blonde bob and a forest-green business suit looked up at me. "Hello, ma'am. Who are you here to see?"

"Jenna." I had to clear my throat. "Tell her Louisa Berry is here, please."

"Is she expecting you?"

Lady, she's not expecting a thing. "No. But she'll see me."

Or maybe she wouldn't.

"You can have a seat." Blonde Bob picked up the phone.

I did, but it was less than a minute before Jenna stepped through the doors behind the reception desk. "Louisa." She stopped in front of me, her expression concerned and puzzled. She was dressed more subtly, maybe even subdued, than I was used to, in a beige business suit and simple ivory blouse. I wanted to say something to her, *yes* or *hello* maybe, but I couldn't make my mouth work.

"Come back to my office." She turned to Blonde Bob. "Hold everything, please."

I followed her. She moved differently. The glide was gone and her steps were heavier, hesitant. She closed the door behind us and faced me. She looked like someone who'd had the flu, tired and pale except for the smudgy pouches under her eyes.

I wondered if she'd had a funeral for Joel. How Tamara was doing.

I wanted to ask her if she hated me, but I couldn't. Hell, how could she not hate me, when if it weren't for me, none of it would have happened.

Or maybe it would have. Everything, everyone, had reached a breaking point, and like a vase teetering off a shelf, it was too late to stop it.

Music played softly, some sixties number I didn't recognize. I remembered Joel saying his mother wouldn't sing in the house because Marguerite didn't like it. Now Jenna was free to do what she wanted.

I didn't know if she would ever sing again.

"How are you?" I managed.

Her mouth opened, but all that came out was a sigh. She shrugged. "How are you?"

I tried to laugh. Why, who knew, because nothing was funny. "Mentally, not so great. Physically, I guess I've never been better." I handed her the paper.

She looked at it, then at me, as though it were written in Sahaptin and she was waiting for me to translate.

So I did. "I'll give you three guesses who the father is."

She stared at me, her green eyes wide and damp. "I—I didn't know you and Joel were that close."

That time I did laugh. "Well, it's hard to argue with proof like this, Jenna."

She handed the paper back to me. "Please sit down." She motioned to a sofa and settled into a chair perpendicular to it, close enough to touch me. One hand moved toward my hair, then stopped. Tamara had left a jagged hunk stopping a few inches below my left collarbone. I hadn't been able to stand the thought of cutting all of it to match the sheared part, so I'd trimmed it, dressed it up with beads and let it hang.

I'd thought it would be the only permanent reminder.

Now that I was here, I didn't know what to say. I'd been too stunned to rehearse anything, and the one thing I'd imagined telling her, that I didn't want my baby to be part of her psycho family, suddenly seemed impossibly cruel.

"Uhm, how's Tamara?" I'd refused to file any charges against her, but I wasn't excited about the thought of her hanging around my child. Being my child's aunt.

"Still hospitalized. The doctors don't know when she can come home." Her lips twisted and I heard the unspoken *if*.

Okay, so much for telling her I didn't want her crazy daughter near my baby. "Did you ever hear from the publisher?"

She sat up straight, a slight surprised lift to her eyebrows. "Yes. You told them everything?"

I nodded.

"They came to the house. They brought an investigator who found Joel's original notes for all the books. She took handwriting samples and came to the conclusion that Joel was indeed the actual author. If Marguerite were alive, she would be facing not only attempted murder charges, but extortion and fraud, as well." She stood and gestured toward a mini-kitchen in the corner. "May I offer you a cup of tea or coffee?"

My stomach growled. For the first time since September I was actually hungry. Jenna heard it and almost smiled. "Or maybe something a little more?" She went to the kitchen area and fumbled around for a few minutes while I tried not to look around the office. I knew I would see pictures and I wasn't ready yet. I'd taken the sketch of Joel and Tamara with me when I left the house, but wrapped it in a towel and put it on the top shelf of my closet. Looking at it was out of the question until I was less fragile.

Jenna came back with a cup of fruity-smelling herbal tea and a plate with several English tea-style triangle sandwiches, a bunch of grapes and two chocolate truffles. "You're thin," she said as she handed it to me.

So was she, but there was no use pointing it out. "I know." I was already eating.

"Morning sickness?"

"I don't think so. Just not taking care of myself." I pointed to my test results with a handful of grapes. "I guess I'll have to start. What about the publisher?"

"They're going to re-issue all the books under Joel's name. And the Newbery Medal." This time she smiled for real. "They're predicting several award nominations for *An Act of Love*."

I swallowed and took a breath. "I, uhm, didn't come here to ask you for money. I won't. But, the books, especially that one, I'd like the money to go to a trust fund for the baby. Please."

"Yes." Jenna's tone made it clear she would never consider anything else. "But—maybe another time, when this isn't a shock for both of us, we can have a real discussion about the baby."

"I've already decided on names. A boy will be Joseph after my grandfather. A girl will be Annelies."

Jenna's head tipped to one side and her face softened. "Where did you hear that name?"

"Anne Frank. Joel told me he'd always wanted to name his daughter after her."

The smile warmed her face. "It's a lovely name. They both are."

"And, uhm, I want her, him, to have my last name."

Jenna nodded. "I would feel the same way if I were you."

Whew. "Uhm, Joel, he, it was important to him to pass on being Jewish. I mean, I'll raise our child to honor that part of its heritage." I heard her intake of breath. "But I'll need your help, since I don't know anything about it."

Our children cannot follow the old nor the new ways... but mine would, both the old and the new.

"I'll do anything I can."

This was going a lot better than it could have—than I'd honestly believed it would.

But I'm scared.

She must have heard it even though I didn't say it. She moved to sit next to me on the sofa. "This might be a little too much for you right now. But whether you ask me for anything or not doesn't matter. As soon as this child is born—right now, in fact—he or she is a one-fourth owner of Airtech."

I paused with a truffle between my teeth.

She nodded. "Marguerite left her shares to me. However, the by-laws forbid 100% ownership by anyone. I couldn't inherit her half, so it went to her survivors. Until ten minutes ago, Tamara was her only survivor."

The room was fuzzy.

"I…" I whispered. "I, uhm, Jenna, I'm not asking—"

She held up one hand. "You don't have to. Joel's and your son or daughter is entitled to one-fourth of this company." She touched my hand, the one not holding the truffle, gently. Tentatively. "You don't have to worry about your baby's future. Ever."

Holy crap.

Out of everything I could have imagined her saying to me, that wouldn't have even been number1,289 on the list.

I had to say something. "Thank you. But that's the baby's. I have to figure out how I'm going to take care of myself." I hadn't told my parents yet, and I didn't know what they would say or how they would feel. I wouldn't accept anything other than their devotion to the baby. It was time for me to take care of myself.

I tried to laugh. "I guess I have to go back to school again, and do it right this time. I just found this out at ten o'clock this morning. Maybe it's still sinking in."

"I went through that as well," Jenna said. "If I can make this easier for you than it was for me, I will. What do you think you'll study?"

"God knows." My mind was still spinning. "Jenna, I haven't even gotten out of bed for more than a few minutes at a time for two months." Maybe I could finish my criminal justice studies, even combine them with an art degree, and be an art investigator or a police artist.

Maybe. Someday.

"Start thinking, and let me know." I must have looked at her strangely. "I hope you're not going to let your pride stop you from accepting any help I can give you."

"I already told you I'm not asking you for anything."

"I'm offering it." Her hand closed over mine. "Louisa, I have millions of dollars in the bank I will never need. Please, let me use some of it to help you. For the baby's sake. For mine."

I knew it would be even crueler to say no than it would have been to refuse to let her be a part of Joseph/Annelies's life. "It might take me a while," I finally said. "To figure out what to do. For a living. I mean, I dropped out of college twice because I couldn't decide on anything."

She actually grinned. "Wait till the nesting instinct kicks in. You'll be more focused than you ever thought you could be. I want you to promise me something, though."

"What?"

"Pick a subject you love—like your art. It's important to support your child, but it's also important to do what you dream."

"Like, don't be an MBA when your heart is a musician?"

The smile vanished. "Exactly." She studied me for a few moments, and I realized that she'd begun to recover in the time I'd been there. Her color was back and the pouches had receded.

I'd given her hope.

"Thank you," she said softly.

"For what?"

"For not making the decision that might have been much easier." At my puzzled look she said, "To not have the baby."

I'd never even considered that. "Maybe it would have been easier. But it's not just about me. It's not just my baby." I wasn't explaining myself well at all. But our baby didn't belong only to me, or even only to Joel and me.

This was a chance to heal several broken people. There was no way I could walk away from it.

She nodded. "I understand."

"I, uhm." There wasn't any easy way to bring up the subject of Jenna's family. Or how I knew what they'd done. But Jenna wasn't stupid, far from it, and she'd known her mother-in-law better than I ever would. "I think you should try to find your family." As much as I never wanted to think about it, Marguerite was my child's great-grandmother. *I need to know what else you come from*, I silently told Joseph/Annelies.

When Jenna didn't say anything I rushed on. "If you won't, I will. I mean, that's my daughter or son's great-grandparents and great-aunt, and I want him, her, to know them."

"Aunts," Jenna said. "I had two sisters. Have."

Maybe switching to the present tense meant she'd at least think about it. "I'd like their contact information. Please. I want my child to have a family."

"I wanted mine to have one, too. A family that knows you never turn your back on your child, no matter what she—or he—does. Or how you feel about it."

"But they…" I trailed off. I hadn't really thought of it that way. Maybe Jenna hadn't been protecting just herself, after all.

But it was still wrong. And sad. Someday the chance would be gone, and I didn't want to see her make a mistake I knew she would regret.

She went on. "There's more to the story than you were told. Or could possibly know."

"I know. But I won't change my mind. They tried to make it right with you and didn't know how. Sometimes fixing what you broke isn't easy."

"Sometimes it's impossible."

I shook my head and the beads swished. "But this isn't. Call them. Write them. While you still have the chance, while they're still here. They're a part of your daughter. And your grandchild." Maybe I was manipulating her. But I didn't care. "I guess we're all students at the school of second chances, huh?"

She inhaled a long breath through her nose. "How about this. Give me some time. If I haven't reached out to them by…" I watched her do the math in her head. "May, a month before your baby's due, I'll pass their letter on to you."

I frowned. "You threw it away."

"Carl took it out of the trash and put it in safe deposit." Marguerite had told me the truth. "He thought our children might want it someday. He made me promise to keep it for them."

Another *if only*. Maybe the kids could have called their grandparents, their aunts, and said, *Come help us. We need you.*

No one would have said no.

I made the mistake of looking up, and straight into a photograph of Joel and Tamara that hung on the wall. Maybe it was a year or two old. They were on Bill's boat, Tamara's hair blowing in the breeze, Joel's arm resting protectively on her shoulders, smiling into the camera and the sun. As happy as they ever were.

A longing for something I could never have twisted my heart and I turned to Jenna. "I knew him only a month. How can I miss him so much?"

She didn't reply.

I took a deep, shaky breath. This was real. Our baby was real, and would get more so. My hand went to my belly before I knew it would, as though to caress the bean-sized life growing inside it. "I always did want children someday. But I didn't think it would be like this. I never thought I'd be doing it alone."

She leaned closer and rested her chin on my head, just the way Joel used to. "You won't be alone."

THE END

About the Author

Laura Stewart Schmidt is a lifelong avid reader and writer who was inspired by "Good Books for Bad Children" such as *Harriet the Spy*, *Emily of New Moon*, and *Otis Spofford*. She studied Political Science and Criminal Justice at the University of Missouri, St. Louis, and spent several years working as a community education coordinator, encouraging parents to read to their preschoolers and starting reading clubs for middle-school students. For two years she was a family court advocate for at-risk youth and parents suffering from substance addiction. She worked for several years at a non-profit agency offering one-on-one support for children and adults with developmental disabilities and their families.

Her mystery *Step Daughter* won third prize at the 2016 All Write Now! Flash Fiction contest. Her short suspense story, "With Friends Like These," appeared in *Heater Magazine*'s September 15, 2016 issue.

Like *Don't Fear, My Darling*'s Louisa, Schmidt spent several years as an active member of the American Indian Society and is a veteran of the powwow and festival circuit. Schmidt is a member of Sisters in Crime, the Society of Children's Book Writers and Illustrators, and the Pacific Northwest Writers' Association. She lives near St. Louis, Missouri, with her husband and two dogs.